The Nurse

Julie-Ann Corrigan was born in Mansfield, Nottinghamshire. She studied in London, completing a BA (Hons) Humanities degree, majoring in Modern History and English Literature. Travelling in Europe for several years, she taught in both Greece and Spain – countries and cultures she found fascinating. On return to the UK she gained a BSc (Physiotherapy), becoming a Chartered Physiotherapist. She lives in Berkshire with her family.

Also by J. A. Corrigan

Bad Sister

THE
NURSE

J. A. CORRIGAN

CANELO

First published in the United Kingdom in 2021 by

Canelo
Unit 9, 5th Floor
Cargo Works, 1-2 Hatfields
London, SE1 9PG
United Kingdom

A CIP catalogue record for this book is available from the British Library.

Print ISBN 978 1 80032 375 9
Ebook ISBN 978 1 80032 374 2

This book is a work of fiction. Names, characters, businesses, organizations, places and events are either the product of the author's imagination or are used fictitiously. Any resemblance to actual persons, living or dead, events or locales is entirely coincidental.

Look for more great books at www.canelo.co

Printed and bound in Great Britain by Clays Ltd, Elcograf S.p.A.

For Steve, with respect and love

Always

What's done cannot be undone.

Shakespeare, *Macbeth*

Prologue

This new space is too quiet. No music, no background chatter, nothing. The young man tries to move his lips to ask if someone can put the radio on, but the muscles in his face won't obey his command. He can breathe, obviously, and hear, but he can't move, or speak. Can't seem to open his eyes either. A male voice, he thinks his doctor, told him that he's been brought out of an induced coma and moved from intensive care. He's now in the hospital's high dependency unit. As well as silence, a dense humidity envelops him in this new room. He wishes a nurse would take off the sheet.

He attempts to remember something about his life, anything, but the fog inside his brain is making it difficult. He tries to move again, but his limbs are utterly unresponsive. Then a familiar aroma enters the unfamiliar room. It's the nurse, he thinks. She smells of cinnamon and she's the one who talks to him. He likes that. The other members of staff never talk; they perform their duties and leave.

She's moving around his bed, but she hasn't spoken. His mother smelt of cinnamon a long time ago, and it's as if his senses and subconscious are working to create another plane of time. A fragmented memory stabs. His mother has been here to see him – before, when he was in intensive care – and told him something she thought he couldn't hear. She didn't think he'd pull through.

He listens hard. He won't know for certain who's in the room until they speak.

1

What did his mother tell him? Her words are somewhere inside his mind. He will remember. Soon.

He gives up attempting to think and instead allows himself to give in to sleep, and to his relief, a curtain begins to close across his consciousness. It is only the smell of cinnamon that stops him from drawing the other in the matching pair. Then a voice speaks.

'I'm so sorry.'

He's uncertain of its timbre, unsure if it's a man or a woman, doubtful of the smell, and panic begins to press inside him. Something is very wrong.

All the moments of his existence come together in a kaleidoscope of images, and he sees his wife, her already burgeoning belly taut, the dark skin of her face translucent with happiness, and as his life ebbs away, he acknowledges that his efforts to find the truth have all been in vain.

The curtains close, with no gap remaining for the light to enter.

He has gone.

1

Rose

8 December 2015

My eyes sweep the courtroom and settle on my husband, and I accept my life is over. Despite his love, and perhaps because of it.

I look at the woman who will soon deliver my sentence. She is petite, pretty, and too young to be a judge, surely. A mixture of expressions have passed over her features during the course of my hearing: well-veiled disgust at what I've admitted to, frustration that I've given no reason for what I have done, and sadness when confronted with the victim's wife and baby. But today, for a moment, I see a sliver of compassion. She has no questions left to ask me. I have confessed to Abe Duncan's murder. And that is that.

A shaft of winter sun finds its way through the high-set windows, slicing across her left cheek. She leans forward, and a silver crucifix slips out from the collar of her white blouse, glinting in the laser light. And as I question whether she should be wearing this statement of her faith, she lifts her hand and pushes it back beneath the silky fabric. We all need to share the consequences of our decisions sometimes.

Again I look at my husband. I cannot bear to see his pain, which is not only mirroring my own but amplifying it also.

He's the one who's been here for me. Always.

The room is filled to capacity, and my gaze shifts to a man in the public gallery who is staring at me with intent and inquisitiveness. He has nut-brown skin and wears an unzipped North Face jacket; he must be so hot. I study him for a few more seconds, but then turn away and focus on the judge.

Her dark, intelligent eyes move over the faces packing the courtroom as she sums up my crime: its premeditation, its callousness, my admission of guilt. She ends her soliloquy with the heartache that I've caused Abe Duncan's wife and family, although his parents have been absent throughout my hearing. This is one thing for which I can be grateful.

I wait.

Twenty years.

I'm almost relieved.

19 March 2016

I've been in prison for three months, and the monotony, the routine, the ambiguously pleasing absence of freedom are turning out to be surprising comforts of life inside. There is, though, a lot of time to think and analyse, and my therapist encourages me to do both in our sessions, although our encounters are exhausting because I spend them avoiding answering his questions. I know this frustrates him. He senses something I'm not saying, as I suspect the judge did too. But the answer will stay within me. I'm in here and it's where I should be. Where I deserve to be. Where I want to be.

Restless, I stand, take the few steps towards the other side of my small cell.

Through the closed and locked door I hear the post being delivered to the rooms on my floor. Since being in here I've received a fair amount of correspondence from various members of the public keen on an epistolary relationship with a convicted killer.

I look up as my door is unlocked.

'Letter, Rose,' the custody officer says.

'Thanks.' I nod and take the thick envelope from him. My stomach drops a little, as it always does, when I hear the turn of his key as he locks the door again, despite the fact that a part of me – a big part – is relieved to be in prison.

Sitting on the narrow bed, I open the fat letter. I read the first line thinking I won't go further, but I do.

Dear Ms Marlowe,

My name is Theo Hazel. I'm a novelist and non-fiction writer. I followed your case with much interest and, to be honest, intrigue too.

I've written several non-fiction books about women who have been convicted and incarcerated for murder; your case stood out for me.

I am very keen to meet you, to hear what you have to say. I would, and I'll be blunt, very much like to write your story.

At the end of the letter, Theo Hazel lists his five published works. Three are non-fiction. An unaccustomed smile lifts the edges of my mouth at the title of one of them. I'm intrigued, and even though an instinct to like this man nudges at me, there is no way I'll be speaking to him. I cannot.

His letter is engaging and he is erudite. He includes lots of detail about his life; I know he's doing this to gain my trust. Tucked away in between the penultimate and last pages is a photo. Maybe he is another mad member of the public.

I study the image. Dark hair, quite long, skimming the collar of his cream shirt, a zipped-up black North Face jacket. I'd say around my age, maybe younger. I look again. Yes, a bit younger. I'm good at guessing ages, I think many medics are, from years of looking at birth dates and then at the face accompanying the paperwork. I nail him at forty-four, maybe forty-five. Three or four years younger than me.

Nut-brown skin. I recognise his face from somewhere, and I dig deep into my memory. The man sitting in the public gallery on the day of my sentencing.

It is him, I'm sure of it.

There is a church in the background, and in the left lower corner a gravestone. There's a digital number at the bottom of the photo. Time and date. It was taken last week. I read through the letter again, happy to be able to put an image to his name.

Recently I've begun teaching basic biology to a few inmates who've decided to broaden their educational CV. I love the teaching, but also the opportunity that being in the prison library gives me – access to a computer.

I will google Theo Hazel the next time I get a chance.

3

Sitting on the edge of my bed, I'm thinking about Theo Hazel's letter, but then my mind flits to the image of Abe's wife in the courtroom. And their baby. I know the child's name and try to un-know it. The inside of my head hammers.

I lean forward and stare at the blue of my cell floor. I'll never be able to live with what happened. What is the alternative, though? To not live with it? I'm not brave enough for that, despite what I know is happening inside my body.

I've no fear of death, but I can't instigate it.

A heavy and solid terrible guilt drags at me. It's always worse in the late afternoon, and that is when I want to sleep, when I don't want to be alive; though it's been the same for years, and not only since Abe Duncan's death.

Abe died at 9.50 in the evening. The timescale of that day is carved into my soul. I'd been working part-time on the unit for four years and my husband twice as long as a consultant anaesthetist when Abe was brought into intensive care. He was admitted on my day off, and when finally I was on the shift coinciding with one of his mother's rare visits to see her son, I don't know who was more taken aback, her or me.

I peer at the annoying red horizontal stripe painted midway up the cell's wall, which circumferences the entire room and mirrors the prison's themed decor.

Being here is my punishment for everything, and not only Abe.

Lying down, I pull the thin duvet over my legs, up to my chin, close my eyes and turn onto my side in the foetal position, Abe inside my mind. My hands are tucked between my thighs, nails digging into the softness, and eventually the sting of ruptured skins hits. And then the bite of salt on my cheeks.

The free association bell rings and I wait for the knock on my cell door, which has been opened in preparation for the part of the day that indicates a type of freedom. I don't particularly like freedom time, although I do like it when my friend Cathy appears, and thinking of her conjures her up. She loiters outside.

What do we have in common apart from being in here? My therapist thinks it's our lack of remorse. He couldn't be more wrong.

As a med student, and then a nurse, I was never lured by the alchemy of psychiatry, but since Abe, I've been obsessed with how the mind works, how it shuts off, how it can trick itself; mine and other people's.

How it can make a person who has always been one way become another.

'Hey, you.' Cathy takes a step inside my cell. 'Duvet day?'

I don't answer, but I know I won't get away with it for long.

There is no discernible expression on her features, although I've learnt this doesn't mean she isn't feeling *something*. It's just that her feelings are separate from her, hang outside of her. That small separate entity understands there is something very wrong with leaving your three kids home alone whilst you go on holiday, but most of her, the other, bigger part, doesn't comprehend this. It's as if there are two Cathys.

I've tried to understand why I get to see this separate part of her. At first I thought it was because she believed I was like her – camaraderie and all that – but I've found out that that's not the case.

I manage a smile.

'That's more like it,' she says, smiling herself, although Cathy's smiles are always veneer thin. 'Don will put you on the happy pills if you stay in bed.'

I sit up, my head still drumming. I laugh, but it hurts. 'It would make his life easier.' And I think it would. I sense that my therapist doesn't particularly like me, and I can see how perhaps a Rose numbed and dumbed with antidepressants might be a good scenario for him.

Cathy's smile is now long gone. She pushes me gently and I move over so she can lie next to me. This cosiness is alien to her, and I wonder again what it is about me that draws her. Most days I don't like the answer.

But despite what Cathy actually is – the bigger part of her – I like the part of her that she shows only to me, or the part only I can see.

It's ironic that I'm so discerning in prison.

'It's your husband you should be talking to,' she says, now under the cover. The bed's much too small for two.

The hammering inside my head has now turned into an undulating thrum.

My kind and dedicated husband. The man who both saved and condemned me.

–

An hour after Cathy returns to her own cell, the hatch in my door is opened. 'Rose. It's visiting time,' a custody officer says through the small hole.

I look at the calendar. It's not my husband's visit day, but then I remember. I agreed to a visit from my mother. Her request was a surprise; I have not seen her for more than twenty years.

'Did you hear me, Rose?' he's saying. 'Your mother. Marion Trahern.'

'Okay.' I get up as he unlocks the door and follow him through the newly painted corridor, keeping one step behind as he leads me to the visits hall, and to my mother.

There are around twenty tables in the huge room, and she's managed to sit at exactly the same one as my husband does on his visits. She's peering into a compact mirror and doesn't see me until I'm only a few metres away. When she looks up, I see the ravages of time, undoubtedly mirroring what she identifies in my features. Without wanting to do so, I acknowledge how physically alike we are. Why is she here? Maybe my husband has asked her to come. No, he wouldn't do that.

'Hello, Rose,' she says.

For a moment I think she's going to shake my hand, and this brings a wry smile. It's been that long. The fifth of July 1992. The date is hard-wired into my memory. I'd gone to visit her, a spontaneous decision, and encouraged to do so because I was planning to get married. Despite everything, I wanted to tell her myself. A stranger answered her front door, and it took a few phone calls to find out she'd moved. When I finally found her and my brother at their new address, I stood outside for at least ten minutes trying to work out how she could afford a house in a nice part of West Bridgford. The visit didn't go well; we argued, but about what exactly, I don't know now. I was still raw, and she was still adamant that everything was my fault. My impromptu visit had all the ingredients for the disaster it was.

My head thumps. I pull out a chair and sit down. 'This is a surprise.' Immediately I begin to pull at the skin around my thumbnail.

She tries not to watch my hands. 'Don't be like that, Rose.'

'You look well.'

She doesn't return the compliment. 'I'm sorry I haven't been before.'

'You didn't even come to my hearing.' I grip my hands together, attempting to calm myself.

She reaches towards me. I don't move, or respond.

'You shouldn't be in here,' she says.

I'm about to touch her, to try and make peace, because I cannot stand the constant conflict of everything. But then she says, 'You were always a bit unstable, Rose. You should have allowed your barrister to plead insanity.'

My hand reverts to its resting place on my knee, my quest for peace obliterated. 'Me unstable? That's a bit rich coming from you.'

Her eyes flick around the room. 'Always defensive. Always with a temper.'

'Of course I'm defensive. I haven't seen you for over twenty years.'

'And whose fault is that?' She says this with her eyes fixed on the visit room's back wall.

'You carried on working for him.'

'It was a job. I needed the job.'

'You could have found a cleaning job anywhere.' I study her coat, which she's hung on the side of the chair. Jaeger. When did my mother begin buying coats from there? Probably the same time she moved house.

'What is this, Rose? I feel as if I'm on trial. And I haven't done anything wrong.'

'Haven't you?'

She moves her chair back; her coat falls to the floor. She doesn't get up. 'It was you who cut ties with me, and your brother.'

'I haven't heard from him either since this happened… since before this happened.'

'Since you took the life of an innocent man, you mean?' Now she does stand. 'You were not sane when you did what you did.' She puts on her coat. 'I knew coming here wouldn't work. I'll come another day when you've calmed down.' She pauses. 'I'm sorry, Rose.'

'For what? For not helping me that night? For not being there for me when I needed you the most?'

'You blame everyone but yourself.' She takes a breath. 'You killed a man, and I don't understand why.'

I don't reply. There is no point. I watch her walk hurriedly towards the exit, then look down. My left thumbnail is streaming with blood.

4

24 March 2016

I'm sitting at my small desk, pushed up against the side wall of my cell, Bella Bliss's letter laid out in front of me. It's a wonderful name. She's an English literature student at Manchester University and I find some meaning in this as her letter came so soon after the writer Theo Hazel's. You do this in prison. Give connections to things that have absolutely no connection.

My yes to Bella Bliss's visit came from a place of loneliness, and was perhaps also a reaction to my mother recently dropping by. Bella's currently doing research for her dissertation, which is about works of fiction with a female protagonist who is a murderer. Her letter, like Theo's, didn't read as if it'd been written by a mad person, and so in a moment of my own madness, I agreed. The only visitor I get is my husband, and my mother's was the disaster I'd known it would be. My old housemates from university have been to see me once too. I appreciated their effort but told them not to come again. I can't bear their pity, or their horror.

The custody officer knocks on my cell door, unlocks it and enters.

'Change of plan,' he says. 'Bella Bliss is here, but there's also a detective waiting to speak to you.'

'A detective?'

'DI Alison Greenwood. She'll be seeing you in the room where you meet with Don.'

I want to ask if I have any say in who's allowed to interview me, but think better of it and don't even bother asking what this is about.

So instead of walking immediately to the visits hall to meet Bella Bliss, we take a detour to Don's therapy room.

A woman is standing by the small window. DI Alison Greenwood is tall; her hair is short and straight, strawberry blonde, a perfect bob that oozes efficiency. She gives me a wide smile, and despite the impromptu arrangement, I like her immediately. She has an honest face.

'Mrs Marlowe. Thank you for agreeing to see me. It's good to meet you.'

I don't mention that I had no choice in coming here; she'll know that anyway. 'It's nice to meet you too, DI Greenwood.'

She pulls a notebook from her pocket, takes off her coat, hangs it over a chair and sits down, indicating I should do the same.

'This is all pretty informal, Mrs Marlowe—'

'Call me Rose.'

She nods. 'I followed your case and hearing with interest.' She pauses. 'I'll be direct. It's come to my attention that you were in a relationship with Abe Duncan's father, Daniel Deane, during the early 1990s.' She finds my eyes. 'This did not come out at your hearing.'

My fingers find the edge of a thumbnail and I start picking and pulling. Alison Greenwood flinches as a bead of blood leaks from my cuticle.

'It was irrelevant.'

'I don't think it was.'

'Why are you here, DI Greenwood?'

'I'm here to try and understand more about the Mount Clinic, a private establishment in Nottingham that Daniel Deane was heavily involved with during the 1990s, at the same time as he was the manager of Bluefields private hospital. Any information you might have about the Mount Clinic and

14

Daniel Deane...' she pauses, and an expression of real distress appears on her face, 'during the period of your relationship would be very helpful.'

She sits back in her chair, more comfortable now she's got all that out. She tugs at her brown fitted skirt; she doesn't look like a woman who would wear a skirt. Perhaps it's her rebellion in the male-dominated world of the police.

'I've never heard of the Mount Clinic.' I study her well-structured features. 'I don't think there's anything I can tell you. I really don't.'

Alison Greenwood attempts to muffle an exasperated sigh. 'I've tried to locate the records and notes made during your admission to Bluefields Hospital in January 1992. It's something you should have shared with the judge at your hearing. At the very least with your barrister.' She takes a breath. 'It would perhaps have had an effect on the severity of your sentence.'

I dip my head. 'My records have gone, I'm guessing?'

'They have, though it appears many records have disappeared from that period, not just yours. You were a medical student at the time; did you ask to see them?'

'I did. They were in order.'

She clears her throat. 'Did you have any reservations about your experience at Bluefields, before, during or afterwards?'

'No. Of course I didn't.'

This isn't strictly true, because towards the end I did have concerns, although not about the hospital.

'There is nothing I can tell you, Detective,' I finish.

She closes her notebook and smooths a hand through her tidy hair. 'You took the life of a completely innocent man, Rose. Why?'

She's looking at me intently now, and I try to erect a mental barrier between us. I'm glad it wasn't Alison Greenwood who led my case, because the woman sitting in front of me has an intuition the detective who did lead it lacked. I think of the Deanes, and a cold sweat breaks out over my entire body. It's too hot in this room.

She carries on. 'You'd never seen Abe's mother – Daniel Deane's wife – before you met her at Queen's Hospital, where she was visiting her son. Is that right?'

Automatically my hand moves to my stomach. The hollow pain is still there.

'No, I hadn't met her before.'

She scrapes back her chair and stands.

'In the time you spent with Daniel Deane, did you meet any of his acquaintances, anyone we might contact in connection with our investigation?'

I think of the people I met more than twenty years ago, but I can't give their names to Alison Greenwood. It will open everything up again, within me and around me. I think of my husband. I say nothing.

After a beat of silence, I stand up myself. 'No, I don't remember anyone.' I watch her. She doesn't believe me.

She walks to the door and opens it, but then turns. 'Is there something you'd like to tell me, in confidence?'

'No, but thank you for being kind.'

She nods and leaves, closing the door behind her. I hear the guard outside locking it, and then the detective's heels click-clacking down the corridor. I slump back into my chair, listen to the digital clock on the wall and wait for the officer to rescue me and take me to meet Bella Bliss.

5

I'm disconcerted after DI Alison Greenwood's short interview and the mention of an establishment in Nottingham of which I've never heard. I use the half an hour it takes the officer to return to gather myself. By the time he opens the door to accompany me to the visits hall, I've calmed down.

He leads me to the table where Bella is sitting. She has her back to me. She has very sleek dark brown hair and is wearing a sweat top with her university logo on the back. I shouldn't have agreed to this. Cathy said so too.

As I approach, she turns. She recognises me, and a pink tinge appears on her sweetheart-shaped face. She has alabaster skin, and her eyes, a striking violet, sparkle with vivacity, although she's clearly very nervous. I decide I'm going to make it easy for her, although I don't know what she wants from me. I will wait to see. She has an A4 notepad in front of her on the table and a neat list of questions.

'Bella,' I say as I sit down. 'So sorry you've had to wait. Busy afternoon.' I grin. 'Which is a little ironic given my situation.' I want to break the ice. She really does look terrified.

'Thanks for agreeing to see me, Mrs Marlowe.' I can almost hear her exhale with relief. 'I didn't think you would.'

I give her what I hope is a proper smile. She's about the same age as I was when I met Daniel Deane. So young. I scrutinise her features. 'It's no problem, but I'm not sure how much help I'm going to be.'

The pink is now swallowing up her cheeks.

'It's okay,' I carry on. 'I will try to help.' She looks down at her list. 'Perhaps it would be better if you just ask what comes into your head to start? Make it less formal?'

She looks at me full on. 'Mrs Marlowe—'

'Call me Rose, please.'

'Rose... I'm not here for my dissertation.'

'Oh.' And oh. Maybe she is a nutcase. I glance upwards and catch a custody officer's eye, but he ignores me. 'What *are* you here for, Bella?'

She shuffles uncomfortably. 'Something else, but I didn't want to write it in a letter.' She appears to be in a horrible torment, and I feel for her, regardless of why she is here. She continues, 'It's about my brother. He's in a relationship with someone who I think you might have known when you were younger.'

Whatever I was expecting, it wasn't this. 'Who is your brother in a relationship with?'

'Ed Madden.'

My heart drops like a boulder, and I'm sure that if I look down I will see it beating on the electric-blue tiling of the visits hall's floor. It destabilises me still, the effect his name has, even this many years later. I don't answer. Can't answer.

'He told my brother... something. And it's killing him keeping it to himself. It's why he told me.' She stares at her notebook. 'I wish he hadn't.' Tears mist her honest eyes. 'But I wanted you to know.'

'What is it you want me to know?' A terrible anticipation is rolling through me.

Bella fidgets again. She drags her chair backwards.

'Don't go. Please,' I plead. Leaning over the table, I touch her notebook. 'I appreciate that you came. It must be important, what your brother has told you—'

'I shouldn't have come.'

'But I need to know... It will stay between us, I promise.'

Bella closes her notebook and puts it in her rucksack. But then she pulls her chair closer to the table and lays her arms where the notebook was sitting. Her voice is so low I can barely hear her. 'Your mum—' She stops abruptly and takes a breath. 'I'm so sorry, but I can't say any more.'

'Please,' I say.

She gets up, a mixture of resoluteness and anger crossing her features. 'What you did was terrible. But you should know... what was done...' She's turning around, leaving.

Coming here has cost her dear. I don't want her to get into trouble, and it will not be because of me if she does.

She continues, 'Tell who you want. I don't care any more. My brother and I will deal with it.'

'I won't say anything to anyone.' I pause, find her eyes. She's not going to tell me, but she's told me enough. 'My mother knows something?'

She pulls her bag onto her shoulders. 'I think so.'

The same feeling I had on the last day of Abe's life returns, and my stomach contracts as if it's wrapping around itself.

—

I've managed to get out of the meeting with my therapist, saying I have a migraine, which I do. Bella's visit, and Alison Greenwood's, has unsettled me.

Before seeing Bella, I'd replied to Theo Hazel saying I wouldn't be accepting his request to talk with me, but back in my cell, I write to him again.

I try to focus on how I will compose this second letter. Before becoming a writer, he was a journalist, and a good one from what I can glean, his journalistic tenacity evident in the non-fiction books he's written. Brilliantly researched and executed, according to the reviews. He's discovered things about long-ago characters from history, some guilty of their crimes, others who've turned out not to be. I'm worried I might have missed my chance with him, though, and I have to make sure he visits me, because I think he can help me. I stare at the wall, lean back in my chair and touch my right breast, and for the first time in years a trace of purpose twists through me.

It even crosses my mind to make an appointment to see the prison doctor.

How can I entice Theo Hazel? He wants a story. He wants to kick-start his career. This is all I know about him really.

I need to dangle my tale in front of him, let him know I'm willing to give him everything. Or nearly everything. Eventually I hope he will be able to help me discover if what Bella has told me is true.

I start to write the beginning of my story for him.

My first meeting with Daniel Deane, in a restaurant in Nottingham.

A day in the spring of 1991. The day I fell desperately in love.

6

Leaning against the serving station, I slugged back a double espresso. Christ, I hoped Noah couldn't see me. Absolutely nothing should pass my lips whilst on duty. Normally I'd have snuck down to the storeroom to drink it, but I didn't have time. Busy day. My section was packed. Good Friday, and the property tycoons of Nottingham were out in force ordering enchiladas and champagne. What a disgusting mixture, just like most of the men in there. Some came in with colleagues, some with girlfriends, some with mistresses. None of them ever seemed to bring a wife.

As I scanned the tables, my line of vision moved towards the floor-to-ceiling windows that overlooked the parking area, settling on a gleaming white car. Roof down. Deep crimson leather seats. One monthly payment on that car would equal my yearly medical grant. I sucked in my tummy, preparing to give them what they all wanted. A smile and the promise of a chance. The job was all about the huge tips. Times were good for the diners of Mussels, even if they weren't for the rest of the country. Sky-high interest rates had divided the nation into the quarter per cent and the rest. The rest didn't come here for the microscopic enchiladas and champagne, and to be honest, they were the sensible ones.

I was in a bad mood, which wasn't unusual. The fourth year of med school was killing me, and I was falling behind; even though I possessed a photographic memory, I was a long way from being a genius. I had to work hard, and to survive I spent too much time at Mussels. But as I sauntered over towards my section – *always look as if work isn't a problem*, Noah had advised on my very first shift – I admitted that that last thought wasn't strictly true. *I* could survive financially; my mum couldn't. A thirty-quid tip saw her through a week's grocery shopping.

From the corner of my eye I saw Miles lifting his arm to get my attention. He wasn't sitting in his normal place by the window at a table for two; today he'd taken a table for four. He must be expecting people to join him. I was intrigued as to who they might be. Miles was a quiet and distinguished-looking bloke, a doctor at the local private hospital and one of the nicer guys who frequented Mussels. He always wore a jacket and tie, his hair perfectly cut – short at the back but with length at the fringe, which he swept to the side in a very pleasing way – and he was the epitome of good manners. Sometimes I noticed an oddness about him; nothing creepy, only that on a couple of occasions he'd seemed a little out of it, his words not quite coordinating with his expression, as if he were drunk or something. But he wasn't a drinker – strictly an orange juice or water customer.

I made my way over. 'Hi, Miles. You expecting people today?'

He looked up and gave me a massive smile. He really wasn't a bad-looking bloke. Just not my type. And too old for me anyway. 'I am, Rose. My boss, actually. You don't mind me taking this table?'

'Course I don't. Want to order a drink while you're waiting?' Miles wasn't the most laid-back of men, but today he looked even more uptight than normal.

'Orange juice would be good, thank you.'

'What's your boss's poison?'

'Daniel'll have a tonic water.'

I went and placed the drinks order at the bar. Served a few more tables, then picked up the juice and tonic water to take to Miles. As I turned away after putting the two glasses on the table, I bumped into a man I assumed was his boss.

'I'm so sorry,' I said. The man gave a huge kind smile and my eyes lingered for a moment on his calm, and definitely not unpleasant features. He was a similar height to me, slim but not skinny. Dressed casually, but well thought out. A dark grey fitted shirt, no tie, chocolate-coloured trousers, tan leather shoes. Everything matched in that thrown-together-but-not-really way. Dark eyes, jet-black hair, greying at the right temple only, but no older than thirty-five. Against all my instincts, my stomach pulled.

He looked at me, really looked, and my gut inverted. Then he sat down at the table and picked up his drink. 'Thanks, Miles.'

'Cheers, Daniel.' They clinked glasses.

'You both ready to order food?' I asked, at the same time clearing away a half-drunk glass of wine from the next table.

'I'm okay,' Daniel said. 'You?' he asked Miles.

'Just a bowl of olives,' Miles replied.

'Great. Won't be long.' I turned quickly, wanting to get away. Miles's boss had unsettled me, although not in a bad way, I had to admit.

'Whoa, slow down!'

I'd collided with a customer, and the half-glass of wine was now all over his shirt. 'I'm so sorry,' I said again – I was so bloody clumsy today – and began brushing ineffectually at the spreading stain.

'Hey, I like that.' He grabbed hold of my bum, his fingers startlingly close to where my legs met my groin. I pushed him away. Bloody punters.

It was then I noticed the snake tattoos running down each of his fingers. What a creep. His face was a bright and alarming red, and he had *future heart attack* scribbled all over him; wouldn't last to his late fifties. I really hoped the statistics were right, although I hated myself for even thinking it. It was not the thought of a soon-to-be doctor.

'Keep your hands to yourself,' Miles's boss said sharply.

Tattoo Man nodded and winked. 'She should watch where's she's going,' he said before sauntering off.

'You shouldn't have to put up with that crap.' Daniel looked at me, his expression concerned.

'Goes with the job. Do you know him?'

'No, I don't. Thank God. My apologies for the male species. We're not all like that.'

'I know that.' I glanced at Miles. He was definitely one of the good ones.

'Maybe we can discuss this sometime?' Daniel said, his dark eyes shimmering.

'I don't go out with punters... I mean customers.'

'My name's Daniel Deane, by the way.'

'Rose,' I replied.

He pushed his chair backwards and sideways a little, away from the table, so he could face me without turning his head. 'When do you finish work, Rose?'

I'd been given that line so many times before, and my stock answer was always *I'm never sure*. It was the answer I'd given to Miles months before.

'Six.'

'I'll wait outside in the car park for you.'

'Okay.' I watched for his surprise at my yes. *I* was surprised at my yes. But not really. There was something about him.

I caught Miles smiling, sort of frigidly, and I felt bad.

'Excellent.' Daniel turned to him. 'Shall we go straight to the hospital? Talk there? Noisy in here today.'

Miles nodded. 'Of course.' He was already standing, and handed me a twenty-pound note.

'But I haven't even brought you the olives. And there's change.'

'It's okay, Rose, it's your tip,' he said, already walking towards the door.

At the end of my shift, I gave ten per cent of my day's haul to the kitchen and saw Noah smile at me. The rest would go to Mum.

It was exactly 6 p.m. when I left the restaurant. The sun was low and bright, and I squinted as I scanned the forecourt. Daniel Deane was nowhere to be seen. Disappointment flooded through me. I walked round to the back of the building, where there was extra parking. And that was where he was waiting. I caught my breath, unsure if it was in delight or anxiety. He was sitting inside a blue Mondeo. Company car, I guessed.

He opened the window and grinned at me. 'Glad you came. I didn't think you would.'

He wasn't exactly handsome – his nose a little too wide, his chin a little too small – although I didn't really do handsome. But he was charismatic, and different. A strong sexuality flowed from Daniel Deane. It was unmistakable.

He leaned over and opened the passenger door, and I got in.

His car smelt of aftershave and leather polish. In the centre compartment a mobile phone and a brown leather wallet sat in perfect symmetry. A tube of chewing gum lay in exact diagonal alignment across the wallet. A petrol-blue jacket hung on a chunky wooden hanger in the back. He watched me take everything in; he missed nothing, and I liked that, because I liked to think that neither did I. Nevertheless, I shuffled sideways and my hand moved to the door handle, thinking for a moment that somehow he'd locked me in. A mini movie played inside my head. A long drive to a deserted road, torture, rape. Unspeakable things.

But the door opened.

'You're free to leave whenever you want.' He grinned again. A hint of asymmetry in his features; maybe the reason he liked everything else uniform. His skin loved the sun, and the colour of his eyes, an intense brown, verified this. I guessed a touch of the Middle East in his genes.

Pulling the door closed, I said, 'I don't, as a rule, do this.'

'Glad to hear that.' He said it with an overly serious expression but amusement in his eyes. 'Where do you live, Rose?'

I thought twice about telling him, but then loosened up and gave him the address. I was inside his car, for God's sake. 'I haven't seen you in Mussels before,' I said.

'I spotted you weeks ago. It's taken me a while to pluck up the courage to sit in your section.' He'd pulled out of the car park. A motorbike zoomed by, overtaking us.

'So Miles works for you?'

'He's an anaesthetist at the private hospital I manage in the city, but I've known him for years.'

'Bluefields Hospital?'

'That's the one.'

I wondered if he was a doctor by training or just an administration guru. I glanced at him. 'Where're we going?'

'For dinner. Would you like that?' He took in my waitressing gear and suddenly I was aware that in the rush to get away from the restaurant, a rush instigated by the thought of Daniel waiting for me, I hadn't used deodorant. Heat rose in my face.

'I'd planned to swing by your house so you could get changed. That's why I wanted your address.'

'Dinner would be lovely, but will we get a table at such short notice on a bank holiday?'

'Of course we will. It's not a problem.'

He turned his attention back to the road, concentrating on the traffic. The med student in me noted that the joints in his neck were showing a reduced range of movement. Could be early arthritis, or just tension. Orthopaedics and the mechanics of bones was an area of medicine I had no interest in, but my mum believed there was more money in it than paediatrics. I had no idea how she knew any of this, but she probably had a point. I thought about the year I'd be adding to my training if I messed up my exams. I couldn't afford to fail. I peered through the window at the office blocks lining the road. Working in an office would kill me, but what was the alternative if I failed? Nursing?

That would kill me too.

'You still here, Rose?' Daniel lanced into my thoughts.

'Sorry, yes.'

'I'll sit in the car and wait for you to get ready.' We'd nearly reached my road.

'Should I make an effort?' I asked. I was already thinking about what I'd wear, which was unlike me.

'Only if you want to.'

He pulled up in front of the dilapidated terrace in the wrong part of Nottingham. Our landlord was useless. Nothing ever got done on the property's upkeep. I was glad Daniel didn't want to come in. It made it easier. That was another thing I liked about him: the way he seemed to know what to do. I supposed that might have been because he was older. He hadn't asked me if I had a boyfriend, and that was another reason I was glad he was staying in the car. My ex was one of my housemates. Tom and I were cool, but our break-up was relatively new and I didn't want to rub anything in his face.

'Take your time, no rush.' His expression broke into a smile, the dimple on his left cheek deepening. He really was gorgeous.

'Give me ten minutes.'

7

Theo

30 March 2016

Finding the prison in Peterborough is more difficult than Theo anticipated. He really does need to buy a new sat nav to replace the one that was nicked a month before, but then he thinks of his bank balance, or lack of balance, as well as the two maxed-out credit cards, with a third on its way. His ex-wife's offer of financial help is still stubbornly lurking inside his mind, but there's no way he'll take her up on her proposal, despite being grateful for the thought behind it. Their meeting a week before at the cemetery, when she'd made her offer, was bittersweet. As it always was.

Stuck at traffic lights after yet another wrong turn, he takes a gulp of the latte he picked up at the service station and thinks about his son. Tears threaten and he places the coffee on the passenger seat. He unzips his North Face jacket as heat overwhelms him. He always cries on Elliot's birthday, although as a rule he doesn't allow himself to weep for him at any other time. Sophie and he agreed they couldn't be sad for ever. It was one of the few things they did agree on, although since their split, they've been more united than they ever were during their fifteen-year marriage. He closes his eyes for a moment and recalibrates his emotions. Opens them and turns his brain away from his son and Sophie, back to his work and the task in hand.

He *will* make this book about Abe and Rose a success. He has to. And he can, because with what Rose Marlowe has already revealed, he has a small piece of dynamite. Throughout Rose's hearing, no one was aware that Abe Duncan's father had been her boyfriend in the early 1990s. Theo spoke with his editor yesterday and heard the enthusiasm in his voice, and he hasn't even mentioned this connection yet. He's keeping it to himself for now.

Eventually he pulls into the only available space in the prison car park and the decrepit Fiesta shudders to a stop. Unclipping his seat belt, he grabs Rose's file from the passenger seat and takes out her letter. It was certainly a turnaround. Her reply to his initial enquiry had been a very polite no, but her second letter arrived within a week of the first, and included pages of handwritten text describing her initial meeting with Daniel Deane. Theo could hardly believe his eyes, and is still questioning what has changed her mind – because his instinct tells him something has.

From the file he pulls out the notes he made on his meeting with Marion Trahern, Rose's mother. It was Rose who suggested he contact her. *If you're really serious about writing my story*, she said, *my mum will be able to give you information about my childhood.*

Returning everything to the file, he jerks the rear-view, checks his reflection, pushes the mirror back, and swings aching legs from the cramped space of the car. He opens the back passenger door and takes out the holdall. Rose asked him to bring her some clothes, specifying *Topshop, plain and boring. Size 10, 34inch-leg jeans.* He suggested it might be better if her mother did the clothes shopping, or Miles. *My mother doesn't visit me and my husband loathes shopping.* He was surprised that prisoners were allowed to wear their own clothes.

He can almost smell the conflict and missing information in Rose's story. This really is the most optimistic he's felt about his career for a long time. He's certainly been going through a barren period. Very barren. After four okay-selling books, he sank into oblivion with the fifth. Several gruesome years followed when nothing he sent to his editor was commercial enough. *Your work's lost its edge*, the grey-haired wolf said.

An investigative non-fiction book about Rose Marlowe and Abe Duncan is his big chance.

It's begun to rain, so he flings a coat over his head and, with the holdall slung on his shoulder, makes his way to the prison entrance, where he waits with at least ten other visitors, getting soaked, until the security officer unlocks the door.

Theo has never been inside a prison in his life and has no idea about the protocol. He's told to drop his phone, wallet and the entire contents of his pockets into a box. *Collection on the way out.* The holdall will be searched and taken directly to Rose.

Following a grumpy custody officer, he makes his way through newly painted corridors to the visits hall, which features a collection of cheap plastic black tables and even cheaper electric-blue chairs placed either side. Two windows sit up near the room's high ceiling, giving the space its only natural light.

There are around twenty prisoners dotted around, but Theo recognises Rose immediately. Dark blonde hair, corkscrew curls. Symmetrical features, wide-set eyes, a fine nose, as though it were sculpted from sandstone. Her hair, though, is spritzed with white, more so than when he'd seen her in court and her skin, normally the colour of pale honey, is almost grey, like a sunless English day. Her demeanour is guarded, sunken, but when she raises her head, her caramel eyes catch and hold him. At forty-eight, she remains astonishingly beautiful. She wears a pair of over-washed black jeans and a multicoloured blouse, its crash of shades the colours of an Antipodean coral reef, utterly out of place in this grim location.

She moves in her chair, comes to life. 'Theo. It's so good to finally meet you,' she says, her voice low but distinct.

A thread of excitement unrolls through him, and he's unsure if it's because of the story she's already begun to share, or the anticipation of discovering why she's changed her mind about seeing him.

She shakes his hand; hers is warm and soft. 'Were you at my hearing?' she asks. 'In the public gallery?'

'I was.' He smiles. 'I feel like a stalker or something.' He pauses. 'How did you know? I didn't mention it in my letter.'

'I remember seeing you.'

He's not sure if this is a good or a bad thing.

She carries on. 'And then the letter you sent me, and the enclosed photo – I remembered your face.' She stares at him. 'It was taken in a cemetery?'

'It was. My ex-wife took it.' It was the day he told Sophie about his idea of writing Rose Marlowe and Abe Duncan's real-life story. She was all for it, and this pleased him. Even now, he still needs her approval.

'I see,' Rose says, interrupting his thoughts, her voice laced with softness and compassion.

'I brought you some clothes,' he says. 'Hope you like them, and they fit.'

'Thank you. I shouldn't have asked you. I'm sorry. Are they plain and boring?' A hint of a smile. Theo's eyes settle on her blouse. 'I know... I'm not wearing a very good example, am I?' She yanks at the frayed skin around her nail, drawing blood. He winces. 'Take a seat,' she says quietly.

'It's so good to meet you in person, Mrs Marlowe.'

'Call me Rose. I'm glad you contacted me.'

'I'm glad I did too. I have my ex-wife to thank for that. She encouraged me to write to you.'

'It's good you're on amicable terms,' Rose says, dragging him away from his thoughts.

Contemplating how much information to give, he decides to be candid, because he'll be asking Rose to be frank with him. Quid quo pro. 'Sophie and I meet at the cemetery annually to commemorate our son's birthday.'

He watches her expression and slight guilt rumbles through him. He didn't need to tell her that. He never tells anyone, not unless he absolutely needs to. Rose's features have fallen and she hasn't answered.

He carries on. 'It's not sad. Soph and I try not to make it sad. It's a celebration of Elliot's life. It's our routine.' She's listening hard, taking in everything he says. Rose Marlowe is one of those people who listens as well as hears. Pays attention. 'Been doing it for four years… it's good to have a routine.'

'I'm so sorry.'

'Please don't be. I'm not normally a sharer. Maybe I overdid it?' he says, smiling.

And Rose smiles back. It's a beautiful expression, like indoor sunshine. 'No, you didn't.' She leans forward slightly, the sunshine gone, as if a heavy cloud has filled the sky of her face. She pulls again at her nail beds, with even more vigour. 'Have you managed to meet up with my mum yet?'

'I have. I met her a few days ago at a café in Nottingham. I did ask if she'd like me to bring her today, but she said she had something on.' He isn't being truthful. Marion said she didn't want to come. Theo agreed he'd go and see her at her home for their next meeting.

'I'm sure she has,' Rose replies.

'To be honest, I was a bit surprised when you suggested I get in touch with her. I mean, I'm glad you did, but…' In her letters, Rose gave him the distinct impression that she and her mother were not close, and after talking to Marion, peering in between the lines of their conversation, this was verified. Rose hinted at her mother's mental health problems – something that had profoundly affected her in her early years. It would seem that, back then, she had looked after her mother, as well as her younger brother.

'I thought she could enlighten you on my childhood,' she says. 'Background, you know, from another viewpoint.'

'Yes, and it was an excellent idea.'

She leans forward in her chair. 'What did you think of her?'

In truth, he isn't sure what he thinks about Marion. 'I'm meeting her again in a couple of days.' He catches her eyes. 'I think she wants the best for you.'

'It's a fair way for you to come from Manchester. Maybe you can visit me again on the same day you go and see her. Kill two birds with one stone?'

'I'd like that. Like to see you again.'

'Good.' She smiles properly now. 'You look exactly like I thought you'd look. Like a writer.'

He laughs at that. 'What does a writer look like?'

'What does a murderess look like?'

'Touché.' He's unsure whether to laugh or cringe.

'The prison director told me he's asked you to run some writing classes,' she says.

'He has. I'm looking forward to it.' He isn't, but he surmises that getting the director onside wasn't a bad idea, and they're paying him too.

'Apart from Mum, who else have you been in contact with? Anyone?'

Heat consumes his face. 'Abe Duncan's wife, Natasha.' He's spoken to Abe's widow via Skype. She's already given him a lot of background on Abe's early life, which confirms Theo's suspicion that there is indeed much more to this case than first appeared. Natasha Duncan agreed to meet him on her next visit to London for work. She's flown in from San Francisco today.

'I see,' Rose says.

'Say if you're uncomfortable. Please.'

She slides back in her chair and rubs at her eyes. 'Tell me about her.'

'She seemed glad to have someone to talk to. Her family distanced themselves when she married a white man… Abe.' Theo stops and studies her expression: intent, concentrating and sad. She inclines her head for him to carry on. 'My first Skype call to her was awkward.' He grins. 'Bit like now, really.'

'What made you decide to write about me… and Abe?'

'I had the idea on a walking holiday in the Peaks. I'd booked into the same B&B Abe was staying in when he was rushed into hospital… your hospital. Got talking to the guy who runs

33

the place – as you know from my letter.' He unfastens another button on his shirt. 'Are you sure you want to hear this?'

'I do. I'm sorry about my first refusal.'

He should ask why she initially declined his request, but holds back.

She carries on, although her tone is subdued. 'What did the B&B owner say about Abe?'

'Pleasant, well-mannered, but a quiet guy. Kept himself to himself. He checked in and spent the following day walking, then the next morning he got togged up and went off in the car. He returned upset and agitated. That night he became very ill. Lost consciousness at dinner. The owner called an ambulance. Soon after admission into hospital, he had to be put into an induced coma—'

'He had pneumonia,' Rose interrupts, her voice a whisper. 'It was imperative he was intubated. None of us who'd been caring for him thought he'd pull through.'

'Yes,' Theo says. It's as if they're talking about someone else, and not about Abe, the man Rose is in prison for killing. The man who was her patient. 'I was determined to follow it up. I contacted Natasha, and then you. And then at your suggestion, I got in touch with your mum.'

'You'll be telling Abe's story too?'

'That's my plan. Do you object?'

She shakes her head and crosses one long thigh over the other, her movements quick and anxious.

'Your mum's helping me on your childhood, but anything you can give me would be great.'

'Let her tell you. It'll be interesting to get her perspective.' She clasps her hands together and her knuckles shine bone white.

'Maybe she just doesn't know how to handle all of this?' he says.

Rose unwinds her hands and pushes the tips of her fingers into the pockets of her jeans. 'Maybe.'

'She does seem worked up about visiting you again.'

'Any theories on why?' she asks, scrutinizing his face.

He moves his chair nearer to the table. Nearer to Rose. 'Perhaps I'll find out.'

'That's what I'd like you to do, Theo.'

So this is why she's agreed to see him. The prickle of curiosity that's been nagging at him turns into a full-blown rash of inquisitiveness.

'I've been thinking of getting in touch with Daniel Deane too,' he says.

'If you do, our interviews are off. Wait until we've finished talking? Please?'

'Okay. It's a deal.' He really doesn't want to scare her off.

'Good. Shall we make a start?'

'What you've already told me in your letter is great stuff.' He pulls a pencil from his pocket. 'So vivid.'

Rose takes a deep breath and continues with the story of her first meeting with Abe Duncan's father. Hearing it from her lips, the cast comes alive, names on paper become real. Theo tries to take notes, but after a short time he lays his pencil on the table and simply listens.

8

Rose

29 March 1991

In the end, I took my time getting ready for my dinner with Daniel. I'd never made that much effort for Tom, who'd been in the hallway when I opened the front door. He'd seen Daniel waiting in the car but hadn't looked as upset as I'd thought he would.

Finally I made my way back outside. I pulled down the vanity mirror above the front passenger seat and dabbed at my red lipstick with a Kleenex, momentarily distracted by hair that had found its freedom. It had a life of its own, the reason it was always tied up.

Daniel turned. 'Wow. You look lovely. Where did you get that glorious hair from?'

'It's not glorious if you have to cope with it every day,' I said, laughing. 'I've the same hair as my mum. I'm sure my brother's pleased he doesn't.'

He flicked on his indicator, the car came to life and he pulled away, heading north out of Nottingham and towards the A60, easily overtaking the vehicle in front, which observed the speed limit.

'You'll have very beautiful and intelligent children,' he said, not taking his eyes away from the road.

'That's a very curveball compliment. Although I've exams to pass and a career to forge first.'

'Yes, you certainly do have a career to… forge.' He smiled.

'All right, a career to *build*.' He had a sense of humour. I liked that too.

'I'm assuming you're a student?'

'Med. Year four.'

'Ah, the dreaded year four. Lots of clinical exams.'

Year four was indeed a bit of a bastard year, which was only really a known fact within med school. 'So you're a doctor?' I asked.

'I am. But not practising. Never did really. Better at business, which is why I run the hospital.'

'Bluefields has a good reputation.' I paused. 'Did you not want to practise?'

He laughed, and I heard the contour of bitterness. 'I'm afraid I didn't, much to my father's disappointment. A lot of things I do, decide not to do or can't do disappoint my father.' Without me realizing, we'd pulled up at a pillared entrance. 'This is the Riverside Restaurant,' he said.

'Looks posh.'

He turned. 'I'm attempting to impress you.'

'Mission accomplished.'

'We can go somewhere else if you'd rather?' Concern crossed his features.

'No, this looks good.'

He parked up on the gravel driveway, and I peered out of the car window. The calm spring day of earlier had turned ugly. The wind had picked up in the last hour, and a fine rain was falling. The sky had changed from the eye-watering brilliance of just a few hours before to semi-darkness. I wrapped my thin linen jacket around my body and my stomach began to growl; I knew it was anxiety, but Daniel didn't.

'Come on,' he said, 'let's feed you up.'

As we got out, the sky started to properly unburden itself, and we hurried up the wide stone steps.

A well-dressed woman with a shiny tight blonde chignon showed us to a table. We took our seats and she disappeared, leaving us a menu with no prices. I wasn't a big drinker, but when a waiter came over and placed two gin cocktails on the table, I was glad to glug down what tasted like pure alcohol. I thought of grisly ends again, rape and torture, and decided that from then on I'd watch how much I drank.

'Rose, please relax.'

I sank into the upholstered chair. 'Okay. I will.'

'What do you fancy to eat?'

'I eat anything.'

'That's good.'

Despite having sworn to drink no more, I was helping him with a bottle of very good red that tasted like gooseberries and vanilla.

He sat back in his chair, studied me. 'Variety is the condiment of life. Maybe try something different to what you'd order usually.'

'I think I will.' I was already doing something different just being here. I hadn't been out for months.

Once we'd ordered, we chatted easily. I felt comfortable with him and tried to analyse why. I think it was because he appeared so open, so at ease, and I liked that, because often I was not at ease with myself.

I discovered he was half Moroccan. His father was a doctor, now retired, who had married an Englishwoman. They'd had two children – Daniel and his sister.

'Do your parents live locally?'

'They moved back to Morocco.' He looked at me, and I mean really looked. 'He said he was fed up of waiting for grandchildren. Family is important to him.'

'And your mother's waiting too?'

'My mother died.'

'I'm sorry.'

'Long time ago now.'

'You have a very English name,' I said, diverting the conversation away from what was obviously a painful memory.

'I took my mother's surname, and my parents gave my sister and me English first names.'

'Has your sister given your dad grandchildren yet?'

'Nope.' Suddenly he sounded sad.

'You'll be telling me next that he expects you to have a son to carry on the family name.' I didn't wait for his reaction and tried a smile. 'Although it wouldn't be *his* family name... Complicated.'

He didn't respond.

'I'm only kidding.'

His face cracked into an unadulterated grin. 'I know. People have such a stereotypical idea of other cultures.'

'Erm, you're second generation and as English as they come.'

He nodded. 'But, you know... it *would* be nice to have kids.'

I took another sip of wine and hoped I hadn't smudged my lipstick too badly. 'Anyway, back to parents. They can be funny, and I don't mean in the ha-ha way.'

He picked up an olive, swallowed it whole. 'They certainly can. Tell me about yours.'

'My dad left after my brother was born. My mum brought us up alone.'

'Must have been tough.'

'Yeah, I suppose.'

'But you've done well?'

'Not yet.'

'Are you close to your mum?'

'Not really,' I replied quietly. Mum was hard work, and if the truth were known, sometimes I didn't like her, even though, of course, I loved her.

He didn't answer, but a tender expression had settled on his features. He was so attractive when he smiled. So attractive when he didn't. My body was weight-free and in a state of anticipation just looking at him. His shoulders were broad, his neck long. He was sitting sideways in the chair, one firm leg crossed over the other, the outline of his thighs covered in dark brown linen. My eyes travelled upward towards his waist, and then quickly settled on the empty glass in front of me. He picked up his own and tipped it back, moving both legs safely underneath the table, not taking his gaze away from me.

'So why didn't you pursue an active career in medicine?' I said, breaking the pleasant silence.

'Not for me.'

'Fair enough. It's a vocation.'

'Your vocation?' he asked.

'My only vocation.'

'But room for other things?'

'Yes, eventually.' I lifted my glass and touched his.

-

It was nearly midnight when we rose to leave, and knowing how much wine had been consumed, my thoughts turned not to torture and rape but a drunken collision. The blonde maître d' went to get our coats. Being a waitress myself, I understood her attentiveness. The service charge was probably huge in a place like this.

Daniel turned to me. 'I'm going to get her to order a taxi. I've drunk far too much.'

'Good idea. I need the ladies', though. Be five minutes.'

I made my way to the door signed *Powder Room*. The restaurant was insanely old-fashioned. An enormous mirror took up the whole back wall. I considered my reflection; I was radiating happiness. I didn't think I'd ever felt like that before.

On leaving the comfort of the plush loos, I saw Daniel gesticulating to me. 'Taxi's arrived.'

'Thanks for bringing me here,' I said to him. 'It's so liberating to get away from my books, and Mussels.'

'Thank *you* for coming. I'll get the taxi to drop you home first.'

–

Inside the taxi, I shivered, and Daniel placed his jacket around my shoulders.

'Thanks, it's freezing tonight.'

'Yes, it's going to be a cold Easter weekend. Due to warm up next week, apparently.'

'That's good,' I replied, turning to look at him. After the copious amounts of wine and spirits we'd got through, he looked more his age. He *was* too old for me, and the minimal psychology I'd studied as part of my medical training filtered through my mind. My dad had left when I was seven – my brother had only been a year old. If I were looking for a father figure, Daniel wasn't a bad choice. I liked the way he was so in control. It meant I didn't have to be, and I was enjoying the feeling of not having to be sensible. I felt the corners of my lips lifting into a smile.

'What's caught your imagination?' he asked.

'Nothing.' That wasn't true, though, because it was Daniel who'd caught my imagination. A deep intuition was telling me that there was something Daniel needed rather than wanted. The veneer of him was gossamer, like a running stream – although I suspected he was broken water – and it was that which was stoking my interest.

I had the overwhelming desire to fix Daniel Deane. Sitting next to him in the taxi, a warm feeling bloomed in the pit of my stomach.

I didn't do crushes, but I was definitely doing one that night.

9

Theo

30 March 2016

The bell for the end of visit time rings sooner than Theo wanted as Rose talks about the end of her first date with Daniel Deane almost exactly twenty-five years before. She picks up the bottle of water sitting on the table, finishes it off and looks at him, nursing the plastic in slim fingers.

He crosses his legs. 'So you knew Miles from Mussels?'

'I did. I'd spoken with him lots of times because he always sat in my section. He asked me out once, but I said no. Told him he was too old for me. Then I went out with Daniel, who was the same age.' She scrutinises Theo's face. 'There was just something about Daniel that pulled me in, but I did genuinely like Miles. He was different to Daniel.' She places the bottle on the table and leans towards him. 'So very different.'

Theo pushes his chair backwards a fraction and uncrosses his legs, stretches them out. 'Maybe you should have mentioned to your barrister that you knew Abe Duncan's dad?'

'I didn't want people delving into my past. And it was clear back then that Daniel had no wish for anyone to know about our relationship.' She tilts her head sideways, keeping eye contact. 'I want you to know that I regret what happened. Every day. Every night.' She slumps into her chair.

Theo watches her intently. 'I do think you should have made that more explicit at your hearing, Rose.'

42

'There was no point. It was done. I admitted to Abe's murder. And that is that.'

Theo holds up his hands, a little like he used to do with Sophie when he knew he was getting nowhere in an argument. 'Thanks again for agreeing to talk to me,' he says, catching the eye of the custody officer, who's tapping his watch. 'I really will be able to get going on your story now. I look forward to the next visit, and the next instalment.'

'Thank *you* for listening to me.' She smiles and her whole face lights up. 'It's good to talk.' She unfolds those long legs and stands. 'I hope your next meeting with my mother goes well.' She hesitates. 'I'm sure she'll be a mine of information for you.'

He sighs and looks at her. 'What do you want me to find out from her, Rose?'

She digs her nails violently into the palm of her hand. 'Whether she's in contact with Daniel Deane.'

'Why would she be?'

'Just ask her.'

'How can I find out anything without knowing all the facts?'

She lifts her shoulders and begins walking away. Theo follows her with his eyes. There's something about this scenario, and what Rose has alluded to regarding her mother, that isn't sitting right. She turns again before disappearing through the security door, giving him a stilted wave and tucking that wild hair behind her ears.

He gets up and looks round at the other prisoners. None of them are like the woman he's come to interview, and he admits to himself his growing captivation with Rose's story. And with Rose herself. He's finding it almost impossible to accept the hard truth – that she killed Abe Duncan. Why is that so difficult to believe?

For the entire journey home, he thinks about the answer.

And he's not sure he likes what it might be.

10

Rose

I'm standing by the tiny window in my cell, thinking about Theo. He's already full of questions, and this is good. I saw his creative mind filling in the gaps. Gaps that exist and gaps that don't. It's what I want, although my head is still pounding with talk of my mother. I need him to speak to her, to find out if what Bella told me is true.

Theo wants his story but I sense he wants to help me too. He isn't stupid; if anyone can get answers, it will be him, and I know I've whetted his appetite. He's confident and assured but with a hidden seam of vulnerability. He reminds me a little of my husband in that respect. But no. Theo isn't like Miles. He's stronger, although he doesn't know it. I do, though, seeing it today in my first meeting with him. Theo Hazel is the sort of man I wish I'd met a long time ago.

I lie down on the bed and think about all these things. I think of Abe – I'm always thinking of Abe – and that terrible day.

The free association bell sounds and my door is unlocked and opened. I wait for Cathy. She's only asked me once about Bella Bliss's visit and I steered her away quickly, although this has only made her more inquisitive.

Now she sits on my bed. 'C'mon. Tell me about Theo Hazel.'

I'm safe for now. It's Theo who's captured her interest.

'Nothing to tell,' I say.

'I've signed up to his creative writing class,' she says. 'Is he as good-looking in the flesh as in his photo?'

'I suppose so.'

'Are you going to tell him? That's why you're seeing him, isn't it?'

'Tell him what?'

She swings her legs up onto the bed. 'The truth.'

'I tell you the truth, Cathy.'

She tilts her head back and her bottom lip drops a little, her eyes fixed on the cracked paint of the ceiling. 'You haven't told me about Bella Bliss.'

'Nothing to tell. I helped her with her research.'

She jumps up. Cathy is full of untethered energy. She leans forward and kisses me on the forehead, like the sister I never had.

I love Cathy, despite her enormous faults. I love her because she sees the best in me. She doesn't see me as the monster I know I am.

11

Theo

31 March 2016

Theo is sitting with his feet up on the study desk. He pushes away a pile of notes with his heel, managing to spill lukewarm tea down his clean shirt at the wrong end of the day. Since his visit to see Rose the day before, neither she nor Daniel Deane has been far from his mind. Abe's parents made no appearance at the hearing, which was understandable to Theo then, before he knew about Daniel and Rose's relationship. Not so much now. He should be requesting an interview with Abe's father, but Rose told him not to. He'll hold fire.

This story is truly a gift, and a way out of his crippling debt, or at least it was until he actually met Rose, because now he isn't sure he can write it with the hints of salaciousness he suspects his editor will want.

He gulps back the dregs of sugar-laden tea and puts the mug on his desk, then picks up the fledgling first pages of Rose and Abe's story. He's already made a start, with a dog-eared copy of Capote's *In Cold Blood* never far away. Using the information he gleaned from his initial Skype call with Natasha, he's begun with a snapshot of the victim's life, mirroring Capote's technique.

Good writers borrow, great writers steal; so said T.S. Eliot. So Theo doesn't feel too bad.

He's meeting Natasha for the first time in person later today, at the Premier Inn in Euston. She has an appointment with an editor tomorrow in Russell Square to finalise a deal for a children's book, and so their meeting fits in perfectly. He hasn't shared this plan with Rose – it didn't feel like the right time or place – but at least he's been honest about the fact that he and Natasha have been in touch.

He drops the pages back onto the desk, and his mind cuts away from Rose momentarily, his eyes finding the place they often do when guilt jabs at him. A single framed photograph of Elliot, taken a few days after his fifteenth birthday, four years ago, sitting on his brand-new bike and only months away from never sitting on a bike again. He leans forward and touches the glass with the pad of his index finger. A film of dust shimmers in the bleak early-morning light of the study, and he turns his head, desperate to get away. It is always the way. He wants to look at his son but doesn't want to feel the pain. He puts the photo in a drawer and kicks the filing cabinet back underneath his desk, allowing Elliot's memory to trickle into the deepest recesses of his mind. Best that way, most of the time.

Looking at the clock, he jumps from his chair. 'Shit.'

The taxi is due in half an hour to take him to Manchester Piccadilly station to catch the train to London, and he hasn't packed a bag.

12

The train gets into Euston fifteen minutes earlier than its sched-
uled arrival, and with only a rucksack to carry, Theo walks to
the hotel. At exactly 6.30 p.m., he's ordering a Budweiser. He
downs it in one.

'Thirsty?' the girl behind the bar says with a grin.

'A little. I'll have another. Thanks.' He places a generous tip
next to the empty bottle.

He is finishing the second when his mobile sounds an
incoming text.

I'm in the bar at the Premier.

He swivels around and sees Natasha waving; she's not smiling
exactly, but is close to it. How could you smile again after what
she's been through? Because she has Mia. He wonders if she's
brought her young daughter to the UK with her. Maybe not;
Natasha doesn't strike him as the sort of woman who'd leave a
child asleep alone in a Premier Inn bedroom.

He propels himself off the stool and makes his way over.

'Natasha. It's really good to meet you. Can I get you a drink?'

'I'd love a Bloody Mary. Make the most of Mia not being
with me.' Now she does smile.

He nods, returns to the bar, orders and then makes his way
back. 'Is Mia staying with a friend?' he asks, aware from their
Skype conversations that it's unlikely the little girl will be with
Natasha's parents.

The bartender comes over and places the drink in front of her.

'Thank you,' Natasha says, and then looks at Theo. 'My sister's looking after her.'

'Your parents haven't come around? Even after...'

'Not quite, although I'm sure they will. But I won't be waiting. They say that what happened to Abe is God's revenge.' She unbuttons her sheer black boyfriend cardigan. 'All bad things are down to God's revenge according to my parents.' Her tight smile indicates what she thinks of God. Theo thinks very much the same.

'I'm sorry,' he says, studying her. Natasha Duncan's skin is flawless. She wears very little make-up and doesn't need any. Long black hair that he guesses has been straightened. Small silver earrings that drop with elegance from her tiny earlobes; it's clear she aims not to overwhelm. Slim-fitting black trousers and a black polo-neck jumper twinned with the cardigan. Low-heeled boots. 'But it's great news about your book.'

'It is.' She looks up, her eyes vast pools of life, but he sees the shine of tears. 'I wish Abe were here to share my success. He was always behind me. Things were just beginning to look up for us.' She pats her flat stomach, as if her daughter still lies inside. 'We were both ecstatic about the pregnancy, and relieved when we found out that our baby wouldn't be suffering the same problems as Abe did with the EDS.'

'EDS?'

'Ehlers-Danlos syndrome. Abe was diagnosed just after his first birthday. He was late walking, a sickly child. He coped with it all well, though. It didn't stop him from achieving what he wanted. He carried a card; it's why the hospital was able to deal with him so effectively. Saved his life, only for...' Her voice trails off. Theo remains quiet. She twists her fingers together, pulls the sleeves of her cardigan over her hands, dabs at her eyes. 'His medical problem was an issue for his father.'

'In what way? Is it inherited?'

'It is, but only if both parents carry the gene; it's what is called an autosomal recessive disorder. Basically, that means that both Daniel and his wife are carriers, but don't show symptoms themselves.' She pauses. 'Daniel Deane is a perfectionist, Theo. He didn't like the fact that his son wasn't perfect. Liked it even less, probably, when he discovered it was half his fault that Abe had the disease. Abe was sick for most of his childhood. His relationship with his dad wasn't that great. Luckily, though, he was very close to his paternal grandfather, Zakaria. He loved Zakaria, and was devastated when he died.'

Theo jots down *Zakaria* in his notepad. 'You don't mind me making notes?'

She manages a gaunt smile. 'I'd expect you to.'

'Are you close to Abe's parents?'

'I'm not. I've met his mum several times, his dad only once. He was as opposed to our marriage as my own folks were.' She peels up the sleeves of her cardigan, revealing slim, smooth forearms.

'Are you planning to see them while you're in England?'

'No. And I have no wish to.' She takes a sip of her drink.

Theo contemplates telling her what he now knows about Rose, her relationship with Daniel Deane. It's been told in confidence, but this woman sitting in front of him deserves the facts.

'I've had my first meeting with Rose Marlowe, Natasha. And there could well be a motivation for what she did, though I don't want to betray her trust in me.'

A shadow of uncertainty falls across her features, but is replaced quickly by a look of acquiescence. 'Then don't tell me. I understand.'

'Let's just say that Daniel Deane was not a stranger to Rose. She knew him back in 1991.' He hopes Natasha will join the dots.

'Abe changed his surname to mine when we got married. That was the extent of his disgruntlement with his parents.

Daniel didn't visit him in hospital. Not once. So I don't see how Rose could have made any connection to Abe... If she did, it would have been through Abe's mum, Daniel's wife.' She leans forward, her forehead creased in concentration. 'Has Rose Marlowe admitted to you that that was her motivation... knowing his dad?'

'No, she hasn't, but there has to be a link.'

She nods, her expression sad.

'What was Abe's relationship with his mum like?' Theo asks.

'Not very close to her either. Pretty desolate childhood despite the relative affluence. Often the way, isn't it?'

'It is.'

She carries on. 'Abe told me that in the early days of the Deanes' relationship, before he was born, his mum worshipped Daniel. But that wasn't the case during his childhood. I don't know the details, but Daniel had a series of affairs that his wife was aware of and accepted. I don't know if that was because she adored him and would put up with anything just to keep him, or because it suited her. I think maybe they had... an open-style marriage. But Abe could never pinpoint the problem they both seemed to have in their relationship with him – but it bothered him, followed him around like a shadow.' She pauses.

'That was sad for Abe,' Theo replies. 'But then he found you.'

'He did. We were happy in America.'

He swallows. Sometimes the pain about Elliot comes from nowhere, and at the most random moments. 'Remind me, how old was Abe when he...'

'It would have been his twenty-third birthday in the September of 2015. Born in September 1992.' She pulls out a couple of photos from her handbag. 'This is him a few weeks before he left to go to England. The day I told him I was pregnant.' She begins to cry.

Theo touches her arm. 'We don't have to carry on...'

'It's fine, I want to.' She wipes enormous damp eyes with her cardigan sleeve.

Theo peers at the photo. A serious but good-looking man stares back. His hair is scraped away from his face, the full hairline of youth. He takes a look at the other photo. A profile shot. Abe's long curly hair is in a ponytail. 'A bit of a hippy?' he asks, smiling and handing her a clean tissue he's found in his jacket pocket.

'Maybe. I just think it was another way to be as different from his parents as he could possibly be. He was coming to the end of his medical degree. He was marked out to be a great doctor, would have been a great doctor.' She settles her gaze on him. 'Do you have kids, Theo?'

'One. He died.'

'I'm so sorry.'

A part of him wants to share more with Natasha, who's sharing so much with him, but he cannot.

She tucks a stray hair behind her ear, sits up taller in the chair and changes the subject. 'How do you plan to structure your book, Theo?'

'I want to tell both Abe and Rose's stories.' He watches for her reaction. 'Victim and—'

'Perpetrator? I can see why you want to do it that way. I think you'll do a good job.' She leans forwards, elbows resting on her knees. 'I like your work.'

'That means a lot.' He moves a little closer to her. 'Why *did* Abe come to England?'

'He wanted to try and smooth things out with his parents. His mum had wanted to come to America to see us after he told her I was pregnant, but Abe put her off. I don't think he could face it, but then he had a complete change of heart and decided to go to England. He wanted to make things up with them, now that he was going to be a father himself.' She pauses, and tilts her head. 'When I got the call telling me he was in hospital in Derbyshire, I was surprised. His parents' home is in Herefordshire. But he was in the Peaks, walking, as you know. He never mentioned to me that that was his plan, and we told each other everything.'

'Maybe he was there for another reason, not just the walking?' Theo conjectures.

'I think he was. To see Ed Madden.'

'Ed Madden?'

She nods. 'Ed Madden, yes. Back in the nineties, he and Daniel were as thick as thieves, although he was close to Abe's mother too. He lives in Derbyshire now. but he lived near the Deanes in Herefordshire until around 2003, maybe 2004. Looking through Abe's stuff after he died, I found Madden's address in Derbyshire. He didn't like Madden, but he probably thought he could tell him something about his mum and dad. Madden knew *everything* about his parents.'

'I see.'

Natasha picks up her bag and rummages inside, pulling out a clean handkerchief. 'I think Abe was on a mission to find out things about his childhood, his parents, and he believed Madden might be able to help.' She dabs her eyes.

'And that might be the reason why he returned to the B&B so upset that day… that's what the B&B owner told me, that Abe was upset.'

'Possibly.'

'Did you come over to the UK when he was admitted to hospital?'

'I planned to, but I couldn't get here immediately. I was quite ill in the latter stages of pregnancy; it was almost impossible for me to travel. And then when I called the hospital and they told me he had been taken out of the coma and was going to be okay, I relaxed a little.'

Theo takes a sip of his beer. 'Did you speak to either of Abe's parents during Abe's time in hospital?'

'I don't communicate with Daniel. I did speak to his mum on the phone several times, though. It had been touch and go for a few days, but once he was stable, she assured me I didn't need to come over.'

Natasha folds her arms tightly around her chest. 'There's something else. Abe was in hospital for ten days before he was brought out of the coma and moved to the high dependency unit. The last time I spoke to his mother on the phone, she sounded different. Distressed. I didn't think much of it at the time because I was so worried about Abe. But now I wonder. Why was she distressed? What had changed? After what you've just told me about Rose Marlowe's connection to Daniel, could it be a reaction to seeing Rose?'

'It's certainly food for thought.'

'Another thing. Abe recounted an incident to me that happened in his childhood, when he was staying with Zakaria in Morocco. He heard an argument between his grandad and his mum. Abe had been sleeping; he was ill with a temperature. He said he thought he heard them discussing something about him, but he could never remember what, and afterwards he thought it might have just been a nightmare. He was only six and he's mentioned the incident only twice, the first time soon after we met and the second time was the night before he flew to England. I'm sure that whatever it was that had happened in Morocco was the reason he came here. To speak to his father and go to see Ed Madden.'

Theo tips back the last of his beer. 'Abe knew something, didn't he?'

'I think he did.' She scrutinises him. 'It's Daniel Deane and his wife you should be talking to.'

'Rose has emphatically told me *not* to contact Deane. Not yet. Not until she's told me her story in full.'

'Then I think you must do as she asks.'

'I agree… Natasha, do you mind if I ask you a question?'

'Fire away.'

'How do you feel about Rose Marlowe?'

She sinks into the leather sofa. 'There's a small part of me that feels sorry for her. Stupid, eh?'

Her response tells him a lot about the woman sitting in front of him.

13

The next morning, Theo takes the 8.05 train back up to Manchester and is in his flat in Chorlton by lunchtime. He spoke with Natasha for four solid hours the night before and she gave him much more information about Abe and his early life, although it's their conversation about Ed Madden that continues to preoccupy him.

He flicks on his computer and googles Madden, which leads him to Companies House. Madden is a managing director of Bliss Interior Designs. The other director is Hugo Bliss. The company has a very nice website and a small showroom in a village on the outskirts of Derby, an image of which sits in the left top corner of the page. Theo jots down the email and telephone number.

He turns his attention away from the computer screen and picks up the opening pages of his book from where he left them the day before. He sits back in the chair and scans through the words. Not at all like Capote. Putting the sheets of paper back on his desk, he grabs his notebook where he jotted down reminders of what Natasha told him last night; events and thoughts Abe had shared with her.

Abe had certainly never adored his father, but in his early years he had admired him – until he was old enough to question, which was around secondary school age. It was around that time too that Ed had left the farmer's cottage near their house where he had been living. Abe had been glad when Ed disappeared from their lives. His mother had tried to persuade him to stay, but Ed's mind was made up. Ed held a power over his parents that Abe was unable to fathom.

Theo rests the notebook on his lap and then pulls out a file from the top drawer of his desk and reads its contents. He's written down everything that Rose recounted regarding her first meeting with Daniel Deane, and also everything she said about Miles and Ed. These are the main players in the story, though Theo strongly suspects that Abe's mother is also crucial.

Tomorrow Rose will hopefully carry on with her story, a tale that together with Natasha and Marion's input will form the solid basis for his book. Straight after seeing Rose, he'll go to Marion's house in Nottingham.

He scans his notes about Abe again.

To understand the crime, it's absolutely imperative to penetrate the victim's mind as well as the murderer's.

14

The next day, with the help of Google Maps, Theo navigates his way from Manchester to Peterborough in just over three hours.

He walks across the prison car park with a faint bounce in his step. His optimism is caused not only by the thought of moving on with Rose's story, but by the anticipation of seeing her again too. He's been in love only once in his life. When did he know it was all over with Sophie? Properly over? When she told him she'd met someone else? *We're getting married.* To a man five years younger than Sophie's forty and with two daughters, five and eight. He was crass enough to ask her how she felt about acquiring two new children. She didn't falter. *I love them already.* Theo told her he was pleased for her, and he was. One of them deserves to be happy.

After putting his pocket contents in the box, he makes his way through the prison's fluorescent-lit corridors, but is jolted when he hears 'Mr Hazel!'

He turns his head; Don Whiting, the counsellor Rose sees on a twice-weekly basis, is striding towards him. Theo met him briefly on his first visit but didn't have time to chat, as he was keen to get away to miss the rush-hour traffic.

Don seemed like a nice bloke, though. Theo takes a small detour towards him. 'Good to see you again, Mr Whiting.'

He nods. 'Please call me Don. Do you have time for a five-minute chat?'

'Of course.'

They sit down on the chairs lining this part of the corridor.

'How's it going with Rose?' Don asks.

'This is only my second visit, but I think the first went very well.'

Don leans back in the chair. His trousers are too short and he has quite possibly hemmed them himself. A flap of iron-on braid caresses a thread-veined lower calf. 'It would be good if you shared anything with me that she might tell you.'

'I'm not sure how Rose would feel about that,' Theo responds.

'I want to help her, Theo, not get a story.' Don bends forwards and pulls at the trouser hem.

'I'd like to help her too,' Theo replies. Don sighs, and despite the therapist's spiky comment, a wave of pity sluices over Theo. 'Of course I'll let you know if she tells me anything pertinent to her... well-being.'

Don relaxes. 'That's good. Obviously I can't share anything she divulges in our sessions.'

'I understand that. Although I'd like to ask you one thing, but I'll understand if you can't answer.'

'Go ahead.'

'Has Rose had any visitors recently, apart from her husband and mother?'

Don inclines his head fractionally and fingers the top button of his shirt. 'I'd like to know anything you know, Theo.'

'I will *absolutely* tell you.' A few seconds' pause. 'Don.'

'A student from Manchester University. Rose has been different since her visit.'

'Has she visited again?'

Don shakes his head.

'Does the visitor have a name?'

'I really can't say.'

Theo waits a few beats. 'I do feel, Don, that you might be well served looking into Rose's relationship with her mother.' He has to give him something.

'An English lit undergrad. Bella Bliss.' Don has the grace to colour. 'I did not tell you this,' he finishes, wiping his brow.

Bliss. A connection.

Don carries on. 'Has Rose mentioned her visit to you?'

'She hasn't.' It was good not to have to lie.

'Anything hitting you on the nose about Rose?' Don asks.

'To be honest, the only thing hitting me "on the nose" at the moment,' Theo says, 'is that despite media frenzy about the medical profession and such, it is, in fact, highly unusual for a trained nurse, a woman who was once at medical school training to be a doctor, to murder a patient in her care. There was no way Rose was sane the day she killed Abe Duncan, and it was a travesty that her defence didn't encourage her to pursue a plea of diminished responsibility.'

Don shakes his head with vigour. 'It's amazing what people are capable of. You can't go by what you see on the surface.' He smooths down the fabric of his trousers and glances at his watch.

Theo jumps up. 'Great to talk, Don.'

'It is, Theo.'

—

Theo lowers himself down into exactly the same chair he was sitting in a few days before, thinking how weird it is that habits form so quickly. Rose looks different today. Calmer, less agitated. Perhaps talking about the past is helping, although that's supposed to be Don's job. Theo has an inkling that Don isn't doing his job that well. Maybe if and when he gets to know Rose better, he can delve into this. And ask her about Bella Bliss too.

Today Rose is wearing a dress. It's long and black. Sophie would call it maxi length. Her legs are jutting out sideways from the table. It's a wrap-over style. He wants to think she's wearing it for him.

'Good to see you again,' she says.

'Ditto.' He knows he's looking too intently at her dress.

She smiles. 'I have an interview with the director later. A progress report. Old habits die hard, like making an effort for a meeting.'

'You look nice.' He cannot believe he's just said that.

Silence descends between them, although it feels companionable. It's Rose who breaks it. 'I'll carry on?'

'Please do. Daniel has taken you home in a taxi. I take it you saw him again?'

'I surely did, Theo.'

And Rose continues with her story.

15

Rose

From the depths of sleep I heard a gentle tapping on my bedroom door. I tried to rouse myself, but it was difficult. I'd hardly slept the past two nights.

'Rose, you awake?'

By then, I was. Totally. 'Come in, Tom.'

My ex-boyfriend but closest friend opened the door. 'You all right?'

'I'm fine, just tired.' And I really was. The reason I'd been unable to sleep was because I thought I wouldn't hear from Daniel again. After he'd dropped me home in the taxi, I was wired and sat up all night immersing myself in revision and drinking massive amounts of coffee. Morning had come and I'd done more revision, and that night I'd worked an extra shift at Mussels too. I'd wanted to go because I thought Daniel would turn up. Of course he hadn't, though Miles had come in for an early supper. I really hoped he hadn't seen my disappointment that it was him sitting at the table and not Daniel, although I surmised he must have guessed. He'd asked if I'd had dinner with Daniel the previous night. I tried to keep the conversation short, which was easy as it was a busy shift. When I nodded a yes, Miles had looked mildly agitated.

Last night I hadn't slept again.

'You shouldn't do so many shifts,' Tom said, leaning against Einstein's poster on my bedroom wall.

'I know, but it's busy, Easter weekend and all that. Noah asked me to pull an extra one.' I peered up at him from under the duvet, thinking of his ordinariness and his genius. It was appropriate that he was standing next to Albert.

'Is that where you met him?' Tom continued.

'Who?'

'C'mon, the bloke who was waiting for you outside on Friday night.'

I sat up in bed, picked up a stale mug of water, slurped at it. 'Are you jealous?'

He smiled, and his eyes skimmed over my desk. He wasn't, and that jolted me, though I was glad he was moving on. 'How's it going?' he asked.

'Revision? Like wading through treacle.'

'You'll be okay. Your photographic memory will help a lot.' He turned his head and studied me. 'Who is he then?'

'His name's Daniel. He manages Bluefields, the private hospital in the city.'

'You going over?'

'Meaning?'

'Pondering private work in the future?'

'Absolutely not!'

He nodded absent-mindedly. 'Is he a doctor or professional management?'

'Doctor, but doesn't practise.'

He inclined his head again, already bored with the conversation. 'Your mum called last night while you were at work.'

I pulled on a jumper. Nearly April, but it was still freezing. The useless landlord had never got around to fixing the heating. 'What did she say?' My mum always chatted to Tom. She didn't want me to end up with him because he was a student, and poor, but she liked him. Everyone liked Tom.

'That Sam isn't going to bother with his GCSEs because he wants to join the army, and you don't need GCSEs to kill people. Can you have a talk with him, your mum asked.' He perched on the edge of my bed. 'Oh, and why don't you live at home? You'd save money on rent.'

I swung both legs out. 'Christ, can you imagine?'

'No. Not really.'

I found my jeans and slipped them on. Tom looked away. When we'd shared a duvet, he wouldn't have felt the need to do that. He lay down on my vacant bed.

'You're still my mate, aren't you?' I asked, suddenly needing to know.

'Course I am. Bloody hell, Rose, I'm the one who acts as secretary for you with your batty mother.' He lifted his head from the pillow and grinned at me.

I worried about my mum. I knew that the factory where she worked had reduced the opportunities for overtime, and that for ages she'd been on a three-day week; and I knew this would encourage her to go back to her shoplifting habits. The weight of my family pressed down on me like an anvil sitting on my chest.

'Me and Casey are going to the cinema tonight,' Tom said.

'I'd love to come, but—'

'I'm not asking you.' He grinned again.

'Oh, I see… You and Casey?' He *had* moved on. Good for him. Perfect. And I loved Casey.

'She's fun.'

'She is.' I moved towards the bed. He was sitting up now. 'Can you help me with my clinical biochemistry and orthopaedics?'

'Course.'

I heard the doorbell. It was about the only thing in the house that worked properly.

'I'll get it,' Tom said.

He went downstairs and I finished getting dressed.

'Rose,' he shouted. 'It's Daniel Deane. The manager of the private hospital.' He emphasised the last two words.

Jesus, Tom, give it a break. But relief flooded through me. I rushed to the bathroom to brush my teeth and comb my hair, and then headed downstairs.

Tom was still standing in the hallway. 'Let me know when you want to go through the bio and ortho stuff.' He said it with an edge of humour in his voice.

'Thanks, Tom.' I watched as he made his way towards the kitchen.

'Sorry to just turn up,' Daniel said, watching Tom's disappearing form.

'I'm glad you did.' My gut flipped just looking at him.

'Will you come out with me again, Rose?'

I plonked myself down on the bottom step. He was dressed casually, but his jeans were ironed. How could I fancy a man with razor-sharp lines in his jeans? But I did. I really did. 'You're too old for me.'

'Don't be ageist.'

I grinned. 'Would you like a cup of tea?'

'Why don't you get ready and I'll take you out. Fancy a trip to Newstead Abbey? They're open over the bank holiday.'

'I like the sound of that. Haven't been there for years. But what makes you think I'm not ready?'

'Toothpaste on your chin.' He used his index finger to wipe it away. 'Perfect apart from that.'

'Go through to the living room,' I said. God, I hoped Tom and Casey had left it habitable. Casey was worse than Tom, and home more. An arts degree student with more reading time. Sometimes when I came home after a full day in lectures, it looked like she'd had a solo party while Tom and I had been out. I pushed open the lounge door with my foot. A whiff of marijuana too. I watched Daniel's nose crinkle. Quite cute.

'I'll wait in the hall,' he said.

'It's Casey, our housemate. She says it makes her philosophy original.'

He sat down on the step, looking out of place. 'Whatever does it for her. Pot's not good, though.'

I laughed. I couldn't remember when I'd last heard it referred to as pot. I stepped over him. 'You're right. I'll be ten minutes.'

Making my way back upstairs, I smiled to myself. Daniel was a bit old-fashioned, but he was right. I was always telling Casey to cut down. Casey and Tom. Brilliant. They were much better suited than Tom and me, and any guilt I felt about him flowed away. If anyone could wean Casey off her guilty pleasure it would be Tom, and she'd still write a phenomenal philosophy essay without it. Casey was gifted. And lucky. There was something about her I envied, and I was never quite sure what it was.

I looked in the tiny mirror that hung next to my bed. Manoeuvred my hair into a messy bun, wishing there wasn't so much of it; went into the bathroom and brushed my teeth again. Checked I had no toothpaste on my chin.

On the way downstairs, I pulled my puffa jacket off the landing pillar; Daniel was still sitting on the step, waiting. He turned his head and looked up at me, and again I noticed the stiffness in his neck. He wasn't as relaxed as he wanted to portray. Maybe he was nervous about being here. He stood, and a waft of aftershave penetrated the air between us. He smelt delicious, and a flammable mix of emotions laced through me. I fancied him like mad.

'Come on then,' I said. 'Tea at the abbey.'

At the gate, I turned and saw Tom and Casey looking through the front room window. I waved. Casey waved back. Tom didn't. Maybe he was a little bit jealous of Daniel, no matter what he'd said.

–

We walked and talked for hours, ate plastic sandwiches and drank vapid tea from the café. Daniel bought me a book of Byron's poetry and a Byron mug from the gift shop. He also bought me a totally overpriced multicoloured scarf too, as it had turned breezy.

It was three o'clock by the time we walked back to the car park. He'd parked under a massive oak tree, and as we approached, he peered at the bird droppings on the bonnet of his pristine vehicle and laughed. 'Bloody pigeons.'

In the car, he turned to me, took hold of my face gently and found my lips. His tongue was in my mouth, gradual and sweet, his hand on my ribcage, and beautiful stabs of pleasure travelled through my entire body, but too soon he pulled away.

'Beautiful, vibrant Rose, what am I going to do with you?' His voice was kind more than passionate.

I rested my hand on his thigh. He kissed me again, this time long and languid. When finally we parted, both of us stared through the car window at the afternoon sun as it shimmered like liquid glass through the trees, as if trying to work out what had just happened, because something had. And when I looked at Daniel, I knew he felt the same.

16

6 April 1991

I hadn't seen Daniel since the abbey visit a week before, although that had been my choice, not his. I'd told him I was full on with university work that I really needed to get done over the Easter holidays. I was, though, beginning to wish I hadn't been so adamant. I really wanted to see him.

I'd decided to go to my mum's, because despite our troubled relationship, I wanted to tell her about Daniel. I knocked on the familiar door. No response, so I put my key in the lock and let myself in. Inside it smelt as if the windows hadn't been opened for weeks, and before I even stepped into the kitchen I knew what I'd find. A tsunami of chaos. Dirty dishes, magazines and clothes strewn everywhere. It didn't help that Sam was often as messy as my mother. I flicked my eyes around. Worse than normal. I checked the clock, which had sat on the kitchen wall for years. How many times had I peered at it as a kid, wishing my mother would get out of bed? Too many. It had stopped at two o'clock. I looked at my watch; it was nearly ten. I heard noises upstairs; she was where I'd thought she might be. I began tackling the washing-up, wondering if Sam was home. Eventually my mum appeared in the kitchen wearing a grey dressing gown that had once been white, her hair a mass of activity, like an erupting volcano.

'Hello, love. Happy belated Easter.'

'You too, Mum.'

'Didn't hear you come in.' Her eyes swept around the kitchen. 'Was going to clear up this morning.' She looked at me. 'Sam's a nightmare.'

'Is he home?'

'Stayed out the last few nights.'

'Is he really not sitting his GCSEs?'

'That's what he says.'

'He'll hate the army.'

'But he'll be out from under my feet.' She pulled up the sleeves of her dressing gown. 'You talk to him, Rose.'

'I will,' I said. 'Do you have any work this week?'

'Just Friday.'

'Aw, Mum.' I went to hug her, but she moved sideways. Any show of affection between us was always awkward; it was as if in a split second we'd both decided not to bother.

'I've got a new job, starting next weekend. Full-time. Well paid,' she said, her eyes all over the kitchen and not once resting on me. 'So I'm giving up the factory. Work there's far too sporadic.'

'That's great. What doing?'

'Cleaning.' She began pulling at her hair, loose tendrils at first, but then great clumps of it. She wrapped her dressing gown tightly around her torso, and I noticed that its belt was from another dressing gown, another era. She sat down on a kitchen chair and then got up again.

'Really good news,' I said.

'Your tone of voice doesn't reflect what you're saying. Cleaning's a respectable job.'

'You're reading things that aren't there, Mum. As usual.'

'We can't all be like you.' She wasn't going to let it drop. But suddenly, she did. That was my mother all over. She carried on in a different tone. 'Leave the washing-up, love.' She put her hand firmly on my arm, which was busy scrubbing away at a dirty plate.

I pulled off the Marigolds. 'You taking your meds, Mum?'

'Course I am.' Her expression creased. She was only forty but often looked a decade older. It was the worry of everything and I really tried to understand. She wasn't taking her meds; the house and her demeanour screamed this fact. She picked up a glass that I'd just washed and filled it with water. Sipped, and then suddenly scrutinised me properly, flipping in an instant. 'You look different.'

'Do I?' I replied.

'You do.'

'I've met someone.'

She smiled, but it was lopsided and didn't connect with the rest of her face. My mother wasn't quite right today, and for the hundredth time I wondered if I should move back in. Coldness enveloped me just thinking about it. I couldn't do it.

'Thank God for that,' she said. 'Tom's a nice boy, but he wasn't for you.'

I pushed past her, accidentally clipping her shoulder. Why was she like that about Tom?

'Temper,' she said quietly, following me into the sitting room. I sat down on the old, worn settee and she plonked herself next to me. 'What's his name?'

My flare of anger had already subsided. That was the way she was and I told myself she only wanted the best for me.

'Is he a student?' she carried on.

I sighed. 'No, he's not.'

'That's a plus. Does he have a name?'

'Daniel.'

'Nice.' She grinned at me. 'Dare I ask what he does if he's not a student?'

'Does it matter?'

'No, it doesn't.'

'I'm pleased about your new job, Mum.'

'Me too. Cuppa?'

'No, I can't stay.' I shoved my hand in my jeans pocket. 'This is for you.'

She looked at the wad of notes. I'd had a good few weeks at Mussels.

'Take it.' No more hesitation; she took it and I saw her mentally counting. 'Eighty quid,' I stated quietly. 'Just make sure you're not tempted... to take stuff. It's a bad example to Sam.'

'Give me some credit.'

'I try to, Mum. I really do.'

She got up and began dusting the ornaments on the mantelpiece with the sleeve of her dressing gown.

I spoke to her back. 'Say hi to Sam for me.'

She didn't turn and didn't answer.

I left the house with the usual concave feeling. And although I'd told Daniel not to contact me for a while, I really was desperate to see him.

—

I caught the bus back to my digs in deep despondency. My mum wasn't right, she was unwell inside her head, and I wondered if she'd made up the new job to appease me. My brother was about to bomb out of his exams. And me? My up-and-coming exam prospects weren't looking too good either. I got off the bus and trudged up the street, then stopped dead when I saw Daniel's car. Gathering myself, I jogged the last few metres to the front door and let myself in, to be greeted by his smile. He was sitting on the bottom step of the stairs.

'What are you doing here?' I cast my eyes around. 'Who let you in?'

'Casey. She said she had to pop out for milk.' An anxious frown replaced his smile. 'Do you mind?'

'Mind what? Casey getting milk?' I was so glad he'd come.

'No, that I'm here.'

'Of course I don't mind.' I sat next to him. 'Are you on the naughty step?'

'I hope not. Just waiting for you.' He turned to face me. 'I've missed you.'

'You hardly know me.'

'I feel as if I've known you forever.'

I pretended to shove a finger down my throat, but he didn't laugh.

'I do, though,' he said, pulling me towards him.

It was me who moved away. I took his hand and led him upstairs, not believing I was being so forward.

'So, this is your den?' he asked, standing on the threshold to my tiny bedroom.

'It is.' I closed the door.

'I'm liking Albert on the wall.' He was standing in front of the poster attempting to admire the image, which was difficult as the room was so small.

I pulled a pile of clothes off my desk chair. 'Sit here.' I sat on my single bed, only a foot away from him. 'Why're you here, Daniel?'

'To ask you to... I'm not sure how to say this.'

'Just say it.'

'I want to be with you.'

'You're asking me to be your girlfriend?'

'I suppose I am.' He got up and sat next to me, gathered me to him, kissed me, the kiss feeling as it had done in Newstead Abbey car park. His hand moved beneath my T-shirt, unfastening my bra; his lips travelled to my neck, my chest, and all thoughts of my visit home disappeared as he pulled off my top. An overwhelming desire to forget everything – my mum, my course, my impending exams – flooded through me. And for many moments I did forget everything.

His face was nestled into the crook of my neck, his hot breath caressing my skin. His hand was gently taking off my knickers. I wriggled free and pushed my hips into his, and a rolling heat consumed me.

'I didn't want it to be like this, Rose.'

I looked into his soft brown eyes. 'With Albert looking on, you mean?'

A smile crossed his face as his rhythm increased. My quiet moan, and then his.

Many minutes later, he was lying at my side, his back squashed up against the damp wall, the palm of his hand cupping my cheek. 'What have you done to me, Rose Trahern?'

'I could ask you the same question.'

'I wanted it to be special.'

'It is special.' I traced a finger from his eyes to his lips and then rested my head on his chest, but despite the glorious feeling still filling me, the dawning realization of the mistake we'd made rose to the surface.

'Daniel, I'm not on the pill.'

He moved away from me a little, lifted my head, concern etched deep into his features. 'I meant what I said. I want to be with you.'

I propped myself up on an old flat pillow. 'This is my fault. I brought you up here...'

'It wouldn't be the end of the world, the result of me making love to you.'

'That is a lovely thing to say, but it would be pretty catastrophic for me. I need to take a morning-after pill.'

He nodded, his expression serious. 'But I want you to know that for me, it wouldn't necessarily be the worst thing ever.'

I punched him playfully on the arm. 'Is this your way of making our relationship kosher?'

'It is kosher.'

'Is it?'

'I think I'm infatuated with you, Rose.'

I didn't know what to say. I wasn't naïve, and I wasn't a dreamer, but I believed him. He wasn't lying. He didn't have to, not then. It was me who'd practically seduced *him*. He drew me to him, cradling me until we heard the front door and Casey returning with the milk.

Later, Daniel chatted with Casey and Tom in our tiny kitchen, and I liked to think Tom had thawed a bit towards him. He was just being protective, and part of that entailed him being suitably sceptical of Daniel. I got that, and to be honest, I thought it was quite sweet.

That night Daniel stayed over, both of us wedged into my bed. We didn't make love again, but somehow this made me feel closer to him.

The next morning we woke to the banging of a loose gutter against my bedroom window. Daniel said he was going to contact our landlord, and I was happy to let him, glad that I didn't have to do it. Maybe the bastard would take him seriously because he was older. I was less happy at the risk we had taken, though, and with this thought I jumped out of bed.

'I need to go and see my GP.' The words felt clinical and stilted, but the consequences of the day before had been with me all night as I'd lain next to his warm body.

'It's Sunday, though. You won't get an appointment. I've been thinking about this. Let me call Miles. He can write a prescription and then get it for you from the pharmacy at Bluefields. It'll save a lot of hassle.'

'That sort of feels wrong.'

'Miles is a doctor. It's a hospital. This is part of what we do. If it makes you feel better, you can register as a private patient, but I'll make sure it's Miles who sorts out the prescription or you. A lot of morning-afters are prescribed in the course of a month. We're very proactive with... prevention.' He smiled at me. 'Make your life easy, not difficult, Rose.' He paused. 'Write down any conditions, medical history, anything Miles should know about, but he may well ask you to go in and see him. That's Miles all over. Proper and by the book.'

'I like that he's like that. Okay.' I wrote down my medical history and gave him the piece of paper.

'Pristine health record,' he said with a grin. 'And give me your landlord's number too. I'll sort the house stuff out for you. Sounds as if he needs a good kick up the arse.'

'He does.' I threw my address book onto the bed. 'His details are under B.'

'B for what?'

'Bastard.' He laughed. I pecked him on the cheek. 'I'm going for a shower.'

Miles was okay doing the prescription, but only on the proviso I booked an appointment to see him as soon as I was able. Daniel drove me to Bluefields to pick it up, although Miles had left before we got there.

None of this felt very romantic, but it was the sensible thing to do. And we were doing it together.

17

9 April 1991

Tom was calling me. 'Rose! Daniel's at the door.'

I jumped up from my desk, snapping closed *Gray's Anatomy*, glad to get away from the list of nerves that supplied the muscles of the hip joint. I hadn't seen Daniel for a few days, although I had seen Miles; I'd made an appointment at Bluefields, as Daniel had suggested, and thankfully it hadn't been as embarrassing as I'd thought it would be. Miles had been the consummate professional.

I was halfway down the stairs as Daniel stepped into the hallway.

'Good to see you again,' Tom said as he passed him. He meant exactly the opposite.

I'd reached the bottom step and the front door was still open. Tom was already jogging down the road.

'I don't think Tom likes me,' Daniel said.

'He's protective.' I smiled at him. 'But don't worry, Casey loves you.'

'That's good. How are you feeling?'

'Okay. No side effects. I haven't been sick. So all's well.' I kissed him on the cheek.

'Good.' He paused. 'I'll be more careful. I'm sorry, Rose.' He moved a strand of hair away from my cheek. 'You took me by surprise.'

'You took *me* by surprise.'

He delved into his jacket pocket and took out a pack of Jiffys. Held it out.

'Strawberry flavour?'

His cheeks filled with colour. It was the first time I'd seen him embarrassed, and it was then that I realised how fast it was all going.

'You're in luck, I like strawberries,' I said.

His face lit. 'I'd love you to come over and see my house, Rose.'

'I'd like that.'

'C'mon, then.'

Daniel's home was situated in the elevated north part of the Green Estate in Nottingham. A Georgian building, not enormous, but still large for one man.

'You live here alone?'

He nodded and pulled up to the kerb. 'I do, but a mate's staying with me at the moment – not permanent, though.' He turned to me. 'I can't wait to show you inside, the work I've had done.'

As he spoke, a man appeared at the driveway entrance. I guessed this was Daniel's friend. He wore grey flannel trousers and a light purple shirt with the sleeves rolled up to the elbow. Around fortyish, I thought, and although I didn't have a dad to compare him to, he looked like a dad; a bit crumpled, and wearing an annoyed expression that was similar to the ones I'd seen on the faces of my friends' fathers over the years. He could even have been Daniel's dad; but of course he was too young for that. Also, Daniel's dad didn't live in England, and the man in front of me didn't look like a doctor. Stupid thought; what did a doctor look like? Maybe Daniel had wanted to be a proper doctor, and he'd tried to be and failed but didn't want to admit it. I'd sensed acrimony somewhere between father and son, mirroring the underlying antagonism between my mum and me. This imagined bond warmed me towards him even more.

It was then that I spotted the small sports car, gleaming red and wet, a bucket of water sitting beside it. The man with the rolled-up shirtsleeves had clearly been washing it. I assumed the red beauty belonged to Daniel.

'Looks like you're doing a great job on the car,' I said to the man.

He totally ignored me, and I wondered if it was a social faux pas on my part because Daniel hadn't formally introduced us.

Daniel cleared his throat, which was a louder noise than it had to be. 'Ed, mate, thanks for doing this for me. She is a bit ditched.'

'No problem. All part of the service.'

He took hold of my arm. 'Ed, this is Rose.' He turned and glanced at me. 'With whom I've fallen head over heels, so be nice to her.'

Ed didn't even look at me. It was a pretty impressive total snub.

'You've had three calls from Herefordshire while you've been out, Daniel,' he said, still ignoring my presence. 'And a call from the carpenter saying he can't make tomorrow.'

Daniel nodded. 'Sorry to lumber you with my calls.'

'No probs,' Ed said, and then finally his watery blue eyes settled on me.

People think that to be a good doctor you need to be objective and pragmatic and sensible, and you do, but as my pharmacology lecturer said, the best and most effective doctors possess innate intuition about the human psyche too. A diagnosis is not solely about quantitative facts. A good doctor peels the qualitative onion too. My lecturer told me I had the ability to do that.

I could tell that Ed didn't like me.

'I've nearly finished,' he said, gesticulating towards the car. 'Then I'll be off.'

Daniel inclined his head. 'You have everything you need?'

'I do,' Ed replied.

Daniel adjusted the collar of his black polo shirt and smiled. Ed picked up the bucket and made his way to the front door of the house.

'Cute car,' I said.

'1967 MG convertible. My indulgence. Like it?'

'Very much.'

'I'd take you for a spin, but I'm lending it to Ed. He's off for a few days to see his parents, for his mum's birthday. It needs a long run, good for the engine.' He smoothed his hand over the car's bonnet.

'How did you meet Ed?'

'Met him in the early eighties. My mum and dad had moved back to Morocco, and I'd just started the job at Bluefields. I wasn't living here then – bought this place a few years ago. Ed was a door-to-door salesman; he knocked on the door of a house I was renting, flogging hoovers.'

'You're kidding me, right?'

'No. It's true. We became friends. Ed's unemployed at the moment, so he's helping me out. I'm swamped at Bluefields. He's a good man. Keeps me organised. Pretty domesticated, too, probably why he was selling hoovers.'

'You do make me laugh.'

Daniel's expression dropped into seriousness and he carried on, 'Soon after I met Ed, I met his sister too.' He scrutinised me. 'We started dating.'

'Ah...'

'I just want you to know about me.'

'What happened?'

'We went out together for a year, and then split. But Ed and I stayed mates.'

'What happened to her?'

'She went to live overseas. Lost contact with Ed. She was a troubled soul. Why it didn't work out between us.'

'Did you love her?'

'I thought I did at the time.'

'I thought I'd end up with Tom when we first started going out, but I realised we're better as mates. And him and Casey are much more suited.'

'Some things just aren't meant to be.' He leaned against the car. 'But I was meant to meet you.'

'Yeah, I think so.' I grinned. 'I really need to go to the loo.'

'Through the door, there's a toilet on the right.'

As I walked into the house, I turned and saw Daniel putting a pink envelope on the MG's passenger seat; a birthday card for Ed's mum, I assumed.

I shoved open the door to the toilet, my bladder pushing at the waistband of my jeans. I walked towards the window and poked my head out; Daniel was standing very near.

'It doesn't close,' he said. 'I'm waiting for the carpenter to come and fix it. Just pull the blind down,' he added with a smile.

'Will do. A lovely house, but the bog window doesn't work!'

'Love your humour, Rose. It's what this house is missing.'

I flushed the loo and returned to the hallway, finally seeing the inside of the house properly. It was impressive, and all newly decorated.

Ed appeared as if from nowhere. He'd put on a grey jumper. His thinning short back and sides was Brylcreemed, with a parting down the left side so straight it was as if he used a ruler to achieve it. He moved his feet further apart, as if increasing his base of support. Crossed his arms over his chest. He did all the movements slowly.

'Don't get too comfortable.' He peered at me as if I'd been brought in by the cat. 'Rose.'

'It looks as if *you* have.'

The statement had fallen out before I was able to censor it.

Much later in my life, I'd question if those six words secured my fate.

18

Theo

Theo is deep in thought as he makes his way back to the car, so deep that he goes in totally the wrong direction. He swears under his breath and does a U-turn, finally locating his Fiesta.

On leaving Rose, he wanted to touch her, but all contact is totally restricted on these visits, and it would have been inappropriate anyway. He's only just met her; she's in prison for the premeditated murder of a young man in the prime of his life, and yet...

Because of a fire drill, visit time was unexpectedly cut to an hour rather than the allotted two. They were told to finish up their conversations quickly, so there'd been no time to talk at the end of the session.

He gets in the car with the last part of today's story hanging heavily in his mind. Ed Madden is definitely a key player in the tale; everything is leading him to this conclusion. He was also – if Natasha's thoughts and conjectures have any veracity – one of the last people to talk to Abe before he fell unconscious and was taken to hospital.

Marion is an important ingredient too.

He pulls out his notebook from his rucksack and starts scribbling.

> *Rose's U-turn about seeing me – connected to Bella Bliss's visit? WHAT?*

Rose's obsession with her mother

Is Bella related to Bliss owner – Hugo? Check out

Hugo is Madden's business partner...

Abe sees Madden (?) before taken ill – what does he discover? Anything?

He closes the notebook, puts his seat belt on, enters Marion's address into Google Maps and heads to Nottingham.

–

When Theo reaches Marion's house, he parks up and surveys the detached property. It's well kept and smart; he estimates the 300 K bracket in today's climate. The impressive front door opens; she must have been waiting by the huge bay window. She waves and makes her way down the path. 'Good to see you again, Theo.'

They shake hands and he studies her. A short woman, mid sixties and with too much flesh on her bones. A creased face, with visible patches of dry skin above each over-plucked eyebrow. Well dressed in a self-conscious way, but as at his first meeting with her at the café, she seems uncomfortable, if not in her skin, then in her outerwear. Her clothes, although clearly expensive (the label of her black Jaeger jumper sticks out like a square white ear), don't sit quite right on her.

'It's nice to see you again too, Marion, and thanks for inviting me.'

'Come in. I've put the kettle on.'

'Perfect.'

He follows her through the front door, picking up the strong smell of her perfume. Nice. One he used to buy Sophie on her birthdays, before they were skint. Through the conduit of Rose's story about Daniel Deane, he's aware of her impoverished childhood. He glances again at Marion's outfit.

'Visit went well with Rose?'

'It did.' He pauses. 'Are you planning another visit yourself, Marion?' he asks, although he knows she probably isn't.

'Things are a bit hectic,' she replies. 'I feel for Rose, God I do. But she doesn't want me there, not really... I will go. Soon. I have to be in the right headspace to cope with it. And, you know... life goes on.'

'It does,' he says, casting his eyes over the hallway, which is all hard-wood floors and perfect decor. He suspects Farrow & Ball. 'Nice place,' he says. 'Shall I take my shoes off?'

She laughs. 'No need for that. Let's go into the kitchen.'

He follows her. 'Really nice place.'

'You sound surprised. Did Rose lead you to believe I live in a hovel?'

'No, she didn't.' Marion can so easily, and disconcertingly, see-saw from mild to brusque. They are now standing in the kitchen, with its white units, aqua tiles. A huge skylight on the left. 'We don't talk about you,' he lies.

She doesn't reply.

He carries on. 'I think she was disappointed you weren't with me.' That's another lie.

'I'm sure she wasn't.' She sighs heavily. 'It's difficult for Rose and me.'

'I understand,' he says although he doesn't. Not yet, anyway.

She fusses around as she makes a pot of tea. Takes off the silk scarf wrapped around her neck. Puts it back on. Takes it off again and throws it onto the elegant jarrah-wood table. She adjusts the sleeves of her jumper and fingers a tight grey corkscrew curl that's flopped over her right eye. Finally she hands him a mug.

'Are you driving home today? You'd be more than welcome to stay here the night. Plenty of room.'

It's a nice offer, but he concludes she might be mortified if he takes her up on it. 'I'll be driving back, but thanks for asking.'

She moves her head a fraction. Yep, she's relieved.

'You got a wife and kids up in Manchester?' she asks. 'Nice-looking bloke like you, bet you have.'

Fortunately the landline rings out, taking away the need for him to come up with the answer that always tears away another piece of his heart.

She lets the call go to answerphone, and a male voice leaves a message.

'Mum, can you call me? It's urgent, about Majorca.'

She looks at him. 'My son, Sam.'

'You can call him back, I don't mind.'

'It can wait.'

'Rose says she hasn't seen Sam for a while. He doesn't visit her?' Theo stops short at the 'either'.

'No, he doesn't. It's the way it's been for a very long time.'

'Can I sit down?'

'Please do. Look, Theo, I didn't want to say much when we met before, but don't let Rose pull you in. Take what she says with a pinch of salt.'

'She appears… balanced, considering.'

He watches for Marion's reaction. She holds out her arms, palms up, and shrugs at the same time.

'Does her husband visit regularly?' he asks.

'I believe he does. I have nothing to do with Miles, and never have, as I've already told you. Rose and I haven't seen that much of each other since…'

Not at all, Theo is beginning to understand. 'Since when?'

'Since she married Miles,' she finishes.

'You must have known him a little?'

'A little,' she agrees. 'It was a bit of a surprise when Rose married him. Anyway, that's when she moved away and changed completely.' She takes a slurp of tea. 'I was just glad she'd found someone. Miles was a good catch. She was lucky to get him.' Marion could never be described as a modern feminist.

'Whatever the reason, it's good that you and Rose are making up now, when she needs you.' He turns to look at her, giving what he hopes is his most sincere smile.

'I *will* go and see her again.'

He nods. 'I'd like to talk a bit about Daniel Deane. Rose has told me about her relationship with him. She really should have told her defence team.' He takes a breath. 'You knew him?'

'I did. It was obviously Rose's choice that she didn't mention her connection with him. Her prerogative, Theo.'

He shrugs.

'You said you wanted me to fill you in on Rose's early life?' There's a hint of brittleness in Marion's voice. 'For your book? The book that will tell Rose's real story. I want to help as much as I can.'

'That's good,' he says. 'That you want to help.'

She shakes her head. 'She's bewitching you already, isn't she? Beware, Theo. She'll embellish everything she tells you. Look, Rose was not sane when she killed Abe Duncan. She should have pleaded insanity, but she didn't.' She looks at her watch. 'I think we were at the secondary school part of her childhood? She aced her O levels. Eleven A's, one B.'

'Impressive.' He isn't surprised.

'Yes, it was. But she was always hard work, from the beginning. A three-day labour. Cried a lot as a baby. Demanding. Her brother was so different.' She stops and sighs loudly. 'Yes, Rose has always been a slog. I think it's girls.'

Theo examines her as she speaks and wonders about her own childhood. 'Rose mentioned you were born in Ireland,' he says, trying to open up the subject.

'I was. Met my husband there and we moved to England. And then he left me.'

'Do you miss Ireland, your family?'

'God, no. My dad died when I was two. My mother was difficult and probably the reason I got pregnant young, and therefore married young. To get away.' She peers at Theo. 'My childhood was dismal, so whatever Rose might tell you about hers, it was a dream compared to mine. My mother was a drinker. I've never had a problem with alcohol.' She rubs at her neck. 'And I never had the chances Rose had, the chances she threw away.'

84

'I'm sorry to hear that, about your childhood.'

She huffs and carries on telling him more about her daughter.

—

On leaving her mother, he feels even more sympathy for Rose. A sense of sorrow swamps him too, and he's not sure quite why. But Rose *did* plead guilty to Abe's murder. There was no trial, only a hearing. Her defence wanted to issue a hybrid order, Section 45A of the 2008 Mental Health Act (Theo looked that one up), whereby she would have been hospitalised for a short term in a psychiatric unit and then spent a shorter term in a mainstream prison. A term more like seven years, rather than the twenty that the judge was compelled to give with a straightforward guilty plea. But she refused.

It is a haunting tale and he suspects there's much more to come. The mystery hangs at the periphery of his mind, enticing and not quite tangible, but there. Rose's journey is fascinating him, as is Rose herself, although Marion's role within her daughter's jigsaw is intriguing him too. He guesses that Rose knew it would.

He tries not to think about money and debt, the stack of unopened envelopes back at his flat, and pushes away the terrifying thought that he might well have to move back in with his dad. Not that he doesn't love his dad – he adores him – but for Christ's sake, he's forty-four.

No, he won't let himself think about his financial situation today. He forces his mind back to Rose. Something has changed in her world.

He flicks on the car radio and his thoughts beat to the music.

—

After an hour, he stops at a service station to get drinks and a sandwich. He takes his stash back to the car and shovels it down. Looking at the dash clock, he realises he hasn't eaten since five o'clock this morning – twelve hours ago – but as he contemplates his ravenous hunger, he has an idea. He picks up his mobile from the passenger seat and punches in Marion's number. She answers immediately.

'Hi, Marion, Theo here.'

'Are you all right?'

'I'm fine, sorry.'

'Oh, I thought something terrible had happened, seeing as you've not long been gone.'

He hears some distraction in her tone, maybe even a little irritation. He's beginning to recognise her mood swings. Sometimes she'll talk nineteen to the dozen, on the ball, missing nothing, but other times, she's sluggish and forgetful.

'If it's not convenient, I can call back tomorrow?'

'It's fine. I'm organizing a trip to Majorca. Getting excited and thought you were the travel agent calling.'

'Ah, sorry! But a holiday? Nice.'

'It will be. Really lovely villa near Magaluf. It's been a tough time.'

'I'm sure it'll be good for you to get away,' he replies.

'Yes, and Sam and his wife are paying for everything.'

Why does she feel compelled to give him so much detail?

She continues, a hint of anxiety in her voice. 'Perhaps better you don't mention anything to Rose about us going away.'

'Of course I won't. Maybe you can come with me on my next visit?'

'We'll see.' She clears her throat. The line goes quiet.

'Marion?'

'I won't be around that much in the coming months. Sam's in the process of actually buying the villa. It's up in the hills, you know?'

Theo doesn't know; he's never set foot on the island in his life.

Marion is blundering on. 'Him and his wife'll need my help getting it ready, as it's quite big – four bedrooms and a pool. I said I would, and Sam's keen I don't sit around here getting depressed.' She manages to say it all in one breath.

'That sounds like a nice thing for you.' He waits, thinking she'll say something more. When she doesn't, he carries on. 'Anyway, next time we meet, and I hope it's soon, I'll take you to the new restaurant that's opened in Nottingham city centre. Lunch on me. That's why I called.'

'Scandal, you mean? Ooh, I'd love to go there. It's got a Michelin star.'

'How about next Wednesday?'

'Won't they be booked up already? I hear they get jammed. It's expensive too.'

'It's no problem.' His mate from long-ago university days knows the chef. 'I'll pick you up at midday.'

'Do you already have a deal for your book, Theo?'

Marion is most definitely on it today. 'I do.'

He doesn't. Not yet. But he will. He has to. He's three months behind with the mortgage payments on his flat; the fourth will see the bank foreclosing. He was desperate to find somewhere to live after his divorce from Sophie, and wasn't functioning properly when he bought the overpriced property. Sophie told him to wait, not make a snap decision, but he ignored her and bought it anyway. Then she offered to give him back some of the settlement, which he refused. He wanted her to have all the money. It was as if, by doing this, it absolved him a little in some way. He would always feel crushing guilt about Elliot's death.

'See you on Wednesday then,' Marion says, breaking into his thoughts.

'Looking forward to it, and sorry to have bothered you again.' He disconnects.

How can Sam, a self-employed lorry driver (Rose told him he never did make it into the army), afford a villa in Majorca?

The question taps at him until his thoughts return to the jigsaw of Rose herself. He cracks open the can of Fanta he bought in the service station, trying to clear his mind of her face.

It will take more than a fizzy drink to achieve this aim.

19

Rose

Theo has left and I'm walking to the meeting point where we've been instructed to gather in the event of a fire. I think as I walk. I wonder how Theo's chats with my mum are *really* going, because I suspect he's not telling me everything, although that's probably because he thinks I won't want to hear everything.

I'm divulging my past to him and so he's gaining an insight into the me I once was. He sees beyond what is in front of him; I believe it's a gift he has. But I sense he's having problems with my story. As with the judge at my hearing, he knows there's something I'm holding back, and my mind travels to the place I try to avoid. I was twenty-two, holed up with books and studies, looking after my mum and Sam. Daniel was the manager of a private hospital affiliated with the city's NHS hospital. I try not to clutch at the scenes of us making love, but I do. Snatches.

I was so stupid. What did Ed call me? *Unseeing.*

The day in the unit scatters through my mind. How I felt touching Abe's skin; how I felt afterwards. I shake my head, attempting to get rid of the unsettling feeling that began on that day and was reignited by Bella's visit.

My session today with Theo was too short, and I'm sad about this because I do really like him. His visits are a relief after Miles's, which are full of empty silences and things unsaid. But still he comes, every week without fail. And every week he asks me if I've made an appointment to see the prison doctor. *Please change your mind, Rose.* Miles and I are connected by much more than our wedding vows.

Finally I arrive at my destination, and together with around sixty other women I wait for instructions on what to do in the event of a prison fire. It's a bit chaotic, and no one seems to know what's happening, but then the fire drill is cancelled and we're instructed to return to our cells.

All I can think is that Theo could have stayed longer. One of the prisoners from the cell next to mine makes a joke about it being April the first. I don't think the director possesses that level of humour, or that degree of unorthodoxy.

An officer opens my door and I step into the room. I glance at the calendar pinned to the wall and realise that in fact it's 2 April. Time is an odd thing in prison. Moments later I hear him turning the key. I fall onto my bed, my mind going through the story I've just recounted to Theo. I noticed how intently he listened when I got to Ed Madden and me in Daniel's hallway. He really is taking everything in.

I inhale deeply. I know that often I am not calm and that my temper can get the better of me. With this self-awareness an unwanted flashback to the high dependency unit burns inside my brain again. I tried to stay calm, but his mother's words were too much, her utter lack of compassion breath-taking.

He looked so peaceful.

I flip over onto my stomach and push my head into the pillow, as if I'm trying to suffocate myself.

Going to Daniel's house was the beginning of the end for me, although that end had begun in the house I shared with Tom and Casey, in my tiny bedroom, with Albert Einstein looking on.

20

Theo

6 April 2016

Naked and facing the bathroom mirror, Theo admires the return of some abdominal definition. Not bad for forty-four. Not bad at all, although since starting this new project, his exercise regime has come to a dead halt, not helped by the fact that he's had to let his health club subscription lapse.

His mind has been on Marion all morning, trying to formulate the best approach with her, but it's also on Rose and the last part of her story. An image of her and Daniel Deane making love is one he'd rather not linger on for too long. Obviously she didn't go into detail about her first intimate association with Daniel, but he felt her passion, obsession even. Rose is a woman well into middle age, a woman in prison, a woman who appears to have given up on life, yet despite all these factors, he sees the essence of her; it's still there, even now. She was a woman who seized her sexuality, revelled in it; she was not ashamed of it, nor ashamed of what she felt for Daniel.

He accepts he's connected with Rose on an intellectual level, but there is absolutely no doubt that his feelings for her are physical too. No denying it.

In an indefinable frustration, he moves out of the bathroom and takes the two short steps towards the bedroom. He pulls on a pair of underpants, puts on a clean pair of jeans and the shirt he ironed last night. He takes a grey linen jacket from the clothes rail (he still hasn't got around to buying a wardrobe, mainly because he can't afford one) and makes his way to the front door. His old university mate assured him they'll get a quiet table. *Customers are always thin on the ground midweek*, he said.

Theo puts his phone and his wallet in his inside pocket and leaves the flat.

–

Three hours later, he pulls up outside Marion's house. She must have been loitering by the impressive front bay, as within a few minutes the door opens and she emerges. Her hair looks as if she hasn't combed it; tight grey ringlets fall across her temple. She's wearing a camel coat. A red skirt pokes out from underneath, flopping around her ankles. She's make-up-free, her face creased in anxiety. A totally different Marion to the last time he saw her. Maybe she's had some bad news, he thinks, perhaps about Rose, and a ripple of anxiety shoots through him.

She opens the car door and gets in. Today there's no waft of perfume; in fact as she closes the door, Theo smells something much less fetching.

He looks across at her. 'Hi, Marion. You okay?'

'Fine. Bit of a morning.'

'Nothing connected with Rose?'

Putting on her seat belt, she replies, 'Rose? No, nothing to do with Rose. What makes you think that?'

'Nothing. Nothing at all.' He rearranges himself in his seat. 'We can cancel and do this another time if you'd prefer.' He really doesn't want to do this another time.

'I'm looking forward to it,' she says.

He smiles at her. 'Good.' Flicking on the ignition, he pulls away from the kerb, giving her time to recover herself.

It isn't until he's parking up in the restaurant car park that he speaks. 'Anything you want to talk about?'

'Just some news this morning.'

'Bad news?'

'Yes.' She places her middle fingers on her temples. 'I'll be fine.' She pulls down the sun shield for the mirror and peers into it. 'I look terrible.'

'No you don't.'

'Have you been to see Rose again?' she asks, still examining herself.

'I'm seeing her again next week.'

'That's good.' A pause. 'How are you getting on with your research?'

'Good. I met with Abe Duncan's widow.'

'Oh, I didn't know…'

'She's filling me in on Abe's story. I did tell you, didn't I? That it's his story too, the book? About his childhood. That's what Natasha Duncan is helping me with.'

'No, I don't remember you telling me that.'

She seems even more despondent at his admission; he didn't tell her and he feels bad.

Opening the car door, he makes an attempt to cheer her up. 'You need that holiday. Some time in the sun will be good for you.'

'The sale of the villa's fallen through. We're not going on holiday now.'

'I'm so sorry. Difficult buying abroad, I'd imagine.' He doesn't know what else to say. Things appeared to have crashed for Marion.

She nods and gets out.

He moves around the car and takes her arm. 'Come on, let's go eat and drink some wine. You'll feel better.' She stumbles. 'You okay?'

'Just distracted.'

Theo questions whether her distraction is a reaction to seeing Rose in prison, and after so many years of estrangement. Perhaps it sent her hurtling towards a mental health crisis. Or is there another reason?

Once they're seated in the restaurant, at the promised table, the chef makes a quick appearance to say hello, then disappears back into the kitchen. Marion is oblivious, though, and has already knocked back the complimentary cocktail that was waiting for her. Theo pre-ordered the non-alcoholic one for himself. He needs to stay on the ball, and he's driving. He motions to the waitress to bring another for Marion.

'I don't normally drink in the day,' she says, fingering her empty glass.

'This is my treat. Go for it. Booze is good sometimes when you're wound up.'

The waitress places the martini glass in front of her. Marion pushes it to one side. 'I can't drink more than one.' Inside Theo's head is a screenshot of the prices. Eight quid a pop for the cocktails, even the non-alcoholic.

'No problem. I'll have a sip.' He takes a small one and then slides the glass to the edge of the table.

He begins by attempting to engage Marion in conversation about the mysterious Majorcan villa purchase, although he suspects he's still only getting half the story, if that. Sam has had problems with the finance, apparently; some agreement he had with his wife's father has fallen through, and the father's now decided against helping them buy the place. This information at least sorts out Theo's problem in understanding how Sam could afford it.

'The old man might change his mind,' he suggests.

She nods absent-mindedly, not buying into his optimism.

'Is something else bothering you? Is it Rose?' he presses.

'Rose always bothers me.'

The waitress comes over to take their order, and Theo waits for her to leave before saying, 'Why did you agree to help me with my research about Rose?'

'I've nothing to hide, you know.'

'I don't think for a moment that you do.'

'Rose isn't who you'd like to think she is. She *was* devastated after what happened to her... back then.'

'What happened "back then"? What am I missing?'

'It's not for me to tell you. I'll leave that to her.'

He nods and waits, sure there will be more.

'Everyone has their burden, but Rose milked hers a bit too much.' She plays with her necklace. 'Even Daniel Deane had problems. It wasn't easy bringing up a child with Abe's medical condition.'

Theo only found out about Abe's EDS after speaking to Natasha. The information wasn't in any of the newspapers at the time. After a little more research, he discovered that not only is it a reasonably rare condition, but it's also not widely recognised and acknowledged. He decides to keep this to himself for the time being. He doesn't want to alert Marion to his growing suspicion about her relationship – a potentially on-going one – with Daniel Deane.

Is his guile today instigated by his need to crack this story, write the book and secure the large advance, or is it because of the engulfing feeling he already has towards this woman's daughter?

'No, it couldn't have been easy,' he says finally, studying her expression.

Is Marion still in touch with Daniel? He pushes the basket of premium bread towards her, the pats of truffle-infused butter too, and then goes in from another angle. 'How well did you know Ed Madden?'

'Ed Madden?' She looks away from him, fixing her gaze somewhere towards the kitchen door, where waitresses are coming and going furiously. 'Ah, you mean Daniel's mate? God, I haven't thought about him for years. I didn't know him at all really. I met him a few times when I was cleaning at Bluefields; he sometimes came in with parcels and correspondence. It was a long time ago, though.'

He had no idea that Marion had worked at Bluefields Hospital. 'I didn't know you worked for Deane?'

'I worked at Bluefields, not for Daniel. And it was a long time ago.'

Interesting. 'So you haven't seen Ed Madden recently?'

'Why would I?'

'No reason at all. Did you like him?'

'I hardly knew him.'

'Marion, why *did* you agree to help me?'

'Because Rose suggested it.'

He nods. 'Fair enough.' He takes a sip of water. 'When did you move to the house you're living in now? It's a lovely place.'

'I can't remember exactly.'

'Rose says it was around the time she got married.'

'Yes, probably around then.'

'So the back end of 1992?'

'That sounds about right.'

'Did you carry on working for Daniel after he and Rose split?'

'Of course. It was a good job, paid well.'

'It certainly did.'

She gives him a hard stare. 'I've lost my appetite. I'd like it if you'd take me home.'

Sweat pools at the base of his spine and underneath his arms. This isn't how he planned this lunch. Or is it? As a journalist, he often operated this way, his intuition leading, but Marion won't see or speak to him again after today, although he's found out all he needs to know.

Marion did know Ed Madden.

After Rose's split from Daniel, she moved to a much larger house.

What he can't understand is why she has agreed to have any contact with him. And the villa in Spain? The story about the money isn't hanging together.

Theo is confident that he's the sleaziest bastard alive doing this, until he thinks of Rose. She needs his help, and somewhere in the folds of this story is the reason she agreed to talk to him. A puzzle she expects him to work out.

'No problem. I understand.' He lifts his hand to get the waitress's attention. It's always effective in films.

It doesn't work, so he stands and puts on his jacket, his hand in his pocket fingering the wallet holding his last usable credit card, and goes off to find the maître d'.

21

15 *April 2016*

Theo has become a little more au fait with the prison's routine because the previous Friday, two days after his lunch with Marion, he was here to take the first creative writing seminar. His class was fully subscribed within twenty-four hours. Everyone wants to be a writer, and what better place to have a go? No shopping to do, limited internet access, regular meals provided. Contemplating all the pluses, he began to think it might be a good idea to get himself put away. Until he saw what incarceration did to a human. The loneliness, the impotency, the time these women had to mull over their lives – and the mess most had made of them. He was aware that not all the inmates contemplated their navels, but it was obvious in his first class that those who did were the ones who wanted to have a bash at writing.

For today's visit he has brought a nicely packaged array of pencils, which have already been confiscated. So much for knowing the routine. He spent a good hour in Paperchase picking the ones he thought would please Rose, settling on a nest of ten, beautifully presented and setting him back fifteen quid.

He makes his way to the visits hall.

Today Rose wears jeans and a grey jumper, which he recognises as the clothes he bought in Next. It satisfies him that they fit perfectly, although she appears deflated and flat. It seems it's only as she tells her story that she comes to life, as if that helps her come to terms with what she's done. It's then she becomes the Rose Theo sees in his mind's eye. The young Rose with so much vitality.

He plants a smile on his face, hoping he can encourage one from Rose. 'How's it going?' he says, pulling out a chair.

'Oh, you know, can't complain.' She lifts her head but doesn't move.

'I bought you new pencils, but unfortunately...'

'Confiscated?'

'Yep, sorry.'

'You have to package stuff up and leave it in the visitor reception, then it will be given to me.'

'I know that now.'

'Never mind. But thanks for the thought.' A trace of a smile shadows her face. She was hunched forward in her chair, but now, quite suddenly, she sits back and looks almost relaxed.

'I'll bring some more next time,' he says.

'Just remember the rules, eh?' Her cheeks lift fully; her dark brown eyes brighten. She presses the pads of her index fingers into her temples, squeezes her eyes shut, then quickly opens them. 'Your writing class is popular. The good-looking novelist.' She does the thing with her fingers and temples again, but this time those liquid eyes stay open.

Theo's stomach clenches, and a long-ago feeling floods through his body; of attraction and anticipation. Warmth consumes the skin on his face, and he dips his head as he pulls out the chair so she can't see the result, although he catches her amused smile.

'Yep. I thought I'd dislike doing them, but I don't.' He studies her. 'You're okay with me being here, aren't you? Just say if you change your mind about this.'

Please don't change your mind.

'It's all good.'

He continues in a quieter tone. 'Rose, I hope you don't mind me being direct, but it does feel as if there's something missing from your story.'

Her defined jawline tightens – only a little, but he sees it – and his objectivity kicks in. Perhaps this is a hint of the rage Rose experienced that day on the unit. The day of Abe's death. What caused that fury? Was it born out of the crushing realization that Abe was Daniel Deane's son?

She's watching him, and as quickly as her displeasure erupted, it dissipates. Like a transient madness.

'What was your motivation, Rose? Tell me.'

She doesn't answer, and Theo rummages in his pocket to find chewing gum. Takes a packet out and offers it to her. She unpeels a stick and places the wrapper on the table.

'It'll all become clear,' she says finally. She slides the packet back across the table towards him. 'Shall I begin where I left off last time?'

'That'd be great.' He opens his notebook and fishes inside his pocket for a pencil. The same officer is on duty as on his last visit. The man watches him. Theo holds out the pencil and the officer nods; he missed the chewing gum.

'I want to hear about you too one day,' Rose says.

'All in good time. Your story first.'

'Underneath your bravado, you're sad, aren't you?' she says, doing something origami-like with the chewing gum's wrapping.

'I was born a bit sad, I think.'

'I wasn't, despite the uphill struggle with my mum. Tom said that deep down I was the happiest person he'd ever met. Why didn't I stay with him? We'd be married and probably have zillions of children.' She yanks at her thumbnail. 'He's been to visit, with Casey. He married her as soon as he finished his finals.' She looks at Theo. 'I didn't go to their wedding. I always regret that.'

Theo doesn't reply. Waits for more. 'Casey had their first baby when Tom was still a junior doctor. Went on to have three more.' She smiles. Such a sad smile. 'Tom's an orthopaedic consultant now. Top of his game.' She pauses a moment. 'It's nice they came. Tom didn't know what to say, but Casey did. I'm glad he married her.'

Rose told him in one of her first letters that she was unable to have children. He didn't delve deeper, but the gaping fact of her childlessness is raw. The pain evident within her features as she talks about her old friends' kids is heart-breaking.

'I don't believe you are capable of murder, Rose.'

'Oh Theo. You're a lost cause.'

He leans over the table and from the corner of his eye sees the custody officer shaking his head. He sits back. 'Will you carry on with your story? I want to know all of it.'

'I will, but first tell me one thing about you. One sad thing. There are many sad things for *me* to tell.'

'I'm a bit of a liar and a fake, to be honest,' he says.

'We all are. That's the truth.'

She waits for him to expand, picking at the edges of her nails, rocking side to side in her seat. Rose is never still, never immobile. Prison must be killing her.

'I've come here under false pretences,' he says eventually.

'And what are they? Go on, shock me.' She laughs. Deep, penetrating. Disturbing. 'Except, Theo, nothing can shock me any more. Absolutely nothing.'

'You agreed to talk with me,' he replies, 'because I wanted to write a non-fiction book about you and about Abe.'

She nods; her laughter has slipped away.

He carries on, 'This book I plan to write about you is pure exploitation.'

'It's not exploitation of me if I know about it, is it?'

'I suppose.'

'I can't wait to read it.' She leans forward, cupping her face in her hands, elbows wedged onto the table. 'Tell me something else.'

'I had a wife, and I let her down very badly. But I let down my son more than anyone.'

Rose's eyes soften even more, if that were possible.

His hand moves to touch hers, but he stops himself. 'I'd like to tell you.'

'And I want to know.'

Theo talks as he's never talked before about Elliot. About his own work, his obsession, that caused, he's always felt, the death of his son and ultimately the collapse of his marriage.

He has not said the next words to anyone for a long time. 'My fifteen-year-old son committed suicide.'

'I don't know what to say... I'm so sorry.'

'You don't have to say anything. Elliot was being bullied at school. Sophie was out all hours working to keep the family afloat, as my job didn't bring in enough money to pay the bills. Neither of us saw the warning signs, though I should have done, seeing as I was at home all day.' He pauses. 'My body was, anyway; not sure where my brain was.'

'It's easy to judge yourself retrospectively.' She squeezes those beautiful eyes closed, then opens them. 'This underpins everything about you, Theo. It defines you.' She's staring at him. 'It's what led you to me.'

She pulls up her knees, lodges her heels on the edge of the chair and continues with her story, picking up the thread in Daniel Deane's hallway, just before Ed went off in Daniel's MG to see his mother.

If she had never seen Daniel Deane again, perhaps she wouldn't be in prison for murder. But she *did* see him again and she *is* in prison for murder, and having glimpsed the beginning of her story, the sense of despair spearing through him causes Theo to question many things about himself and his own life: his destiny, the unrolling of events, either in your control or not, chance, luck. Stupidity. But more than anything, he begins to soberly examine the incidents that led up to the death of his son. Signs and events he ignored. Perhaps as Rose had done all those years before.

22

Rose

9 *April 1991*

Daniel was making me a cup of tea in the kitchen.

'Sugar?'

'Please.' My stomach began to grumble, and not through hunger. My encounter with Ed in the hallway had unsettled me.

'Hungry? I'll make you an enchilada? Mine are much better than what they serve up in Mussels, you know.'

I tried to smile. 'Maybe not. I'm sick of the sight of them.'

'You feel uncomfortable, I can see that. Is it Ed?'

Had he heard my exchange with Ed in the hallway? 'He doesn't like me.'

'He can be a bit obtuse. It's just the way he is. Take no notice of him.'

My eyes swept around the kitchen. 'I've got so much work to do, exams soon. I should be home revising.'

He moved closer. 'Have a few days off, with me.' He touched my arm and a galvanic current cracked through every molecule. He turned to the two mugs and stabbed the tea bags with a spoon. I was surprised he was a cup brewer. 'I'll help you revise. I outperformed Miles in most exams.'

I managed a tight laugh. 'You outdid Miles?' I'd imagined Miles as a conscientious and excellent medical student, despite the haziness I'd sometimes seen in Mussels.

'I did. Milk?'

'Yes please.' I took the mug from him. His face fractured into a grin and he slicked back a strand of thick dark hair. I liked how he wore his hair long, tendrils curling well below the nape of his neck. 'Miles is nice.'

'He's one of the best doctors we have.' He scratched his head. 'Although sometimes we see things differently.'

'What sort of things?'

'Most things really.' A smile stretched across his features again. While he'd been talking, he'd knocked up a cheese and pickle sandwich. He pushed the plate towards me.

'Thanks,' I said. 'My favourite.'

He sat down on a kitchen stool. 'Tell me about you. About your mum, your brother. I want to know.'

Suddenly I wanted to tell him everything. Exams were pressing, everything was pressing, and I needed a valve. 'My mum works in a factory part-time. Well, she did. Recently she's found another job. She's divorced from my dad. She has a few... issues.' I glanced at him; he was listening intently.

The tears came then, I couldn't stop them.

'It's all going to be okay,' he said, his voice soft. 'What's your relationship like with your mum?'

'A little splintered.'

'And your father?'

'I only saw Dad once after he left. He'd gone back to Ireland, where both my parents were born. About a year after he'd deserted us, he came over to England and took me out for tea, with his new wife. Sam didn't come with us; he was still so little, not even two years old. I hated every moment. I was rude, and when I wasn't being rude, I was silent. The afternoon went on forever. I bet they couldn't wait to drop me home.'

I stopped talking and gathered myself. He let me be quiet, and I remembered the rest of that day.

Dad, Mum and the new wife all thought I'd gone straight upstairs to my bedroom, but of course I was listening on the landing. It was then that I heard Dad say things to Mum that I pretended weren't true: about Mum being made to leave her job because of money that had gone missing in the factory where she'd worked; about *inside your head*, and how she was always promising she'd take the tablets but never did, *never for long enough anyway. It was never a marriage, and you never even tried.* None of these things made much sense to an eight-year-old. I refused to see Dad again, and after a few years he stopped trying to visit. Of course I remembered the conversation – every time she forgot to do something important for us, dental or hospital appointments, parents' evenings. Every time a policeman knocked on the door.

I continued, sharing more with Daniel. 'By the time I was thirteen, I was the one looking after Sam – and looking after my mum too. She was supposed to be on medication. Anyway, by that time it had become obvious from my school reports that I might be able to do okay in life, so she tried harder with me and our relationship evened out a bit.'

'Parents, eh?' He pushed the plate nearer. 'Is your mum on meds now?'

'When she remembers to take them.'

She still had a propensity towards a spot of theft, though, when she thought she could get away with it. It was one of the reasons I gave her as much money as possible.

I decided to change the subject. 'Is your dad proud of you?' I picked up the last sandwich and started to nibble on it.

'He's still a little pissed off that I'm not a practising doctor. A consultant. I don't think he ever saw me as management. He thought I should be saving the world. That was what he tried to do.' His gaze moved away, fixed somewhere in the far corner of the kitchen, and I detected that same hint of sadness I'd seen in the restaurant. Probably why he couldn't make eye contact. People never can when talking about something that bothers them. I was the same when anyone asked me about *my* dad.

He picked up a dishcloth and began wiping a countertop. 'Is he proud of me? He will be, one day.' Folding up the cloth, he placed it squarely on the windowsill.

I jumped up. 'I'd love to see the rest of your house, Daniel.'

'It's a work-in-progress. I've been renovating it for a year. These things take time. Hopefully I'll make a good profit when I sell it.'

'So it's not a home?'

'It could be.' He grabbed hold of my hand. 'C'mon, let me show you around.'

23

Daniel took me through to the lounge, which was Middle Eastern in its decor, with sideboards and multicoloured lamps. Two lime-green sofas sat facing each other. Huge brightly coloured silk cushions were scattered thoughtfully and – I smiled – a little too symmetrically across both. The walls were covered in oak panelling, and to the side of the room was a set of patio doors painted dark green; red curtains hung on each side, held up by intricately welded iron hooks. It really worked.

I walked towards the doors and looked outside, spotting an outbuilding to the right side of the garden. Daniel told me it was where he indulged in his hobby of carpentry. The doors led to a small terrace, a wooden table sitting in its centre. From there, a twisted set of steps snaked down towards the lawn, which was surrounded by mature flowering shrubs, silver birches and an oak so old its roots were exposed, its branches thick and gnarled like an old man's fingers.

I thought of the house I shared with Tom and Casey, of damp and rot and things that crawled into your breakfast bowl if you left it in one place long enough. Despite that, our shared digs held security and love. Daniel's house was beautiful but empty. Daniel was lonely.

He joined me at the doors. 'C'mon, I'll carry on with the tour.'

I followed him through the hallway and towards a smaller sitting room, which was filled with books. A rocking chair sat by a set of smaller French doors.

This was where Daniel spent his time. I looked for signs of his life and spotted several images of two kids, a boy and a girl, in a country that I guessed wasn't the UK. I pointed to the photos. 'Is that you and your sister?'

'Yes, in Morocco, visiting.'

I moved closer. 'You both look happy.'

'We were. Our childhood was particularly idyllic.' The tone of his voice wasn't coordinating with what he was saying, though, and I saw the veil of grief somewhere within his features. He bent over the rocking chair and rearranged a cushion.

'I'd love to meet her one day,' I said.

'And you will, although she doesn't often move out of the twenty-mile radius of her home.'

'Do you see a lot of her?'

'I do, but it's mainly me who goes over there. She rarely comes here.'

'Nice brother!'

'Just the way it is.'

I moved over to the inbuilt bookshelves, which were filled with medical books, novels, biographies, books on every subject imaginable, including quite a few I wouldn't have envisaged on a bloke's shelf. Daniel had eclectic taste. I decided I liked that. I liked too that he enjoyed reading.

'I have a lot more medical books, but I keep most of those in my office at the hospital,' he said.

Looking at the textbooks brought a sudden anxiety. I had a biochem clinical assessment as well as written exams soon, and didn't understand half of it. I should have been at home, sitting with Tom on the deflated and tatty sofa, going through it all. I reached up and pulled down a couple of textbooks on biochemistry and clinical reasoning.

'Is that what you struggle with?' Daniel asked.

'As well as other stuff.'

'I'm guessing you want to be a GP?'

I threw the book onto the sofa in mock disgust. 'No, I don't. Why does everyone think every female med student wants to be a GP?'

He grinned. 'Orthopaedics?'

'Sublime to ridiculous. Paediatrics.'

'Noble.'

'I love kids.'

'Do you?'

'Yes, I do.' And then I wondered if there was some psychology thing going down here about finding the mate you knew was going to take care of you. Because that was how it worked. At the primeval level, a woman could sniff out the perfect breeding mate, and it wasn't always the most faultless physical specimen. It was the one she believed would stay with her to bring up the kids. Not very feminist, I knew that, but I was certain there was a lot to it. On the male side of things, it was a little different. They looked for a mate who showed good health and the potential to bring perfect kids into the world. Okay, we've moved on, but deep down that was how we all operated: looking for good gene matches, and the reason why you didn't fancy your brother or sister; nature's way of varying the gene pool. I liked to think it was why we were attracted to our polar opposite. I thought about lovely Tom; our kids'd be screwed. If him and Casey got it together, though, it would be a brilliant mixture. But I did want kids one day. A brood of them. With the right man.

Daniel put his arm around my shoulder. 'I'm sorry about what happened. It was stupid of me.'

'I don't want you to be sorry. We dealt with it. I'm as much to blame as you.'

I watched him sitting in the chair, legs crossed, and my stomach rolled. He attracted me like an industrial-strength magnet.

'C'mon,' he said. 'I'll show you the bedroom.'

I rolled my eyes.

'Ah, Rose, I didn't mean that. It's where the carpenter's been doing his thing. Come and have a look.'

'At your etchings?'

He burst out laughing. 'Yeah, those too.'

Upstairs, he pushed open his bedroom door and I walked in, my bare feet sinking into carpet of deep pewter grey. A sash bay window at the front of the room faced the door, with a sofa sitting adjacent. To the left, another door, leading into a white-tiled bathroom with towels the same leaden grey as the carpet.

In the centre of the room was Daniel's bed. The headboard and the foot were made of a deep mahogany wood with intricate carvings. Women and babies. The detail was stunning. I moved closer and stared.

'Nice, don't you think?' he said.

'Beautiful.'

'A work of art.' He stepped closer and inspected the craftsmanship. 'Nearly perfect.'

'This is what the carpenter's been doing?' I asked.

'Yes, it's taken him months.'

'Why?'

'Because it's a work of art, like I said.'

'I mean why've you had it made?' The women were carved to a theme. The same woman. It was the hair that caught me. The artist had captured it brilliantly. Masses of corkscrew curls, standing proud. I swore it could be me, only the images were of an older woman. There were two babies, and the artist had made it clear that one was a boy, one a girl.

'It's taken from an image I loved as a boy from a church in Morocco. My father took us there as kids.'

'You and your sister?'

He perched on the side of the bed, almost lost in the sea of the creamy luscious bedding. 'Yes, me and my sis.' He stroked the wood. 'To be honest, I had the bed made for my dad. A belated seventieth birthday present. I know he'll love it. I'm trying to work out how I'm going to ship it over to Morocco.'

'That's a lovely idea.' I sat down next to him. 'You know, I always wanted a sister.'

I scrutinised him and again sensed that unhappiness. *Was* he lonely? Was his relationship with his sister not all it should be, or could be? I could understand that. Family relationships were tough. What was missing in Daniel's life? Except I knew, because it was probably similar to the gaping loneliness I often felt.

He turned and cupped my face gently in the palms of both his hands. They were smooth and I smelt the cream he'd used. The ripples of the carpet caressed my feet, and as he leaned forward and kissed me, I scrunched the loose weave in between my toes, turning my body into him. We fell backwards onto the marshmallow duvet and I traced my hands down his back, feeling the bumps and curves running parallel to his spine – that was the doctor's part of my brain always at work, working out why Daniel sometimes had problems turning his neck. Tension, maybe stress.

With my eyes closed, my hand slid away from his spine and inward. I felt the touch of his fingers on my cheek. I opened my eyes and caught his tender, illuminated expression. He reached sideways and opened the bedside drawer, pulled out an already opened condom packet.

'No more scares.'

I smiled at him and he gently pulled off my blouse. His hand moved downwards, his fingers touching and probing deep. I bit into his shoulder.

He reached for the condom, handed it to me. 'You put it on.' I looked at him. 'Like this.' He stretched the latex over himself and placed my hand there, then buried his face in my neck.

I pushed my hips upwards, and a short but intense curl of pleasure engulfed me. His rhythm became faster and the building tension began. As the seconds flowed into minutes,

I felt his release, and as he rested on my chest, I lifted my hips again and more waves of pleasure overtook my body.

He smiled down on me. 'I—'

'Shush,' I said, kissing his nose.

We lay there in the fading afternoon sun. Maybe we slept for a while. I didn't know. All I remember was the feeling of absolute contentment.

Darkness had fallen when Daniel retrieved the biochemistry book he'd put on the bed on first coming into the room. He moved himself towards the headboard and sat back, the wooden hair of the woman close to his left shoulder. He patted the space next to him and opened the book.

'You're kidding, right?' I said.

'I don't want you to fail.' He gave me a sideways glance and adjusted the cushion behind his head.

'Now?'

'Yes, now.' He studied the table of contents. 'Shall we start with the basics?'

I scrutinised him side on. I liked how he was doing this. I liked him so much. 'Yeah, why not?'

We worked for two hours and I couldn't believe how much I learned. Daniel got up and went downstairs to fetch some food, returning with a laden tray. Tinned tuna and salad, freshly baked bread. We ate sitting on the bed. He'd brought beer too. Then we carried on trawling through work. After coming to the end of the final chapter we'd agreed to look at, I lay back, and remembered nothing more until he woke me.

The sun was shining outside and I'd slept the whole night. Daniel was standing next to the bed, dressed. He caressed the carving as he looked down at me.

'I didn't even brush my teeth,' I said.

'I've put a new toothbrush in the bathroom. I always keep a spare one. And luckily my sister left an unopened pack of M&S knickers from her last visit.'

Leaning on my elbow, I peered at him. 'Thanks.'

'When you're ready, come down, because after a superb supper of tinned tuna, this morning we shall feast on scrambled eggs.' He left the room.

I closed my eyes.

I was a little in love, and most definitely wholly in lust.

24

I was nestled in Daniel's kitchen wearing one of his old shirts, eating scrambled eggs and drinking percolated coffee, the smell dousing the air. It felt so civilised.

'Fancy a nice bracing walk later?' he asked.

'Sounds good.'

I was finishing the last of the coffee when the doorbell chimed. I looked down at the shirt and really hoped it wasn't Ed.

Daniel made his way out of the kitchen.

A female voice in the hallway. Thank God, not Ed.

Daniel returned with a middle-aged woman, small in build and with a mop of grey hair, watery blue eyes, a small upturned nose and high cheekbones. As she moved closer, I saw that her features were furrowed in acute anxiety.

Her eyes shot to me. 'I'm sorry, Daniel. I didn't know you had company. I was wondering why you were home on a Wednesday. I'd planned to talk to Ed, to be honest.'

'I'm taking a bit of time off. Lots of holiday owing to me. And it's fine, Mrs Finsbury, always lovely to see you. This is Rose, my girlfriend. She's staying for a few days.' He looked at me. 'This is Mrs Finsbury, my wonderful cleaner. A woman I cannot do without.'

Mrs Finsbury's face crumpled further. 'It's Rob. He's been arrested again.'

'Tea's in order. Sit down.'

She nodded. 'He broke into a house on the estate. I can't believe it.'

I glanced at Daniel, who was busy making tea in a teapot. No mug brew for Mrs Finsbury.

'Dirtying his own doorstep?' He placed a china cup in front of her and then rubbed her shoulder. 'Your son's not the brightest button in the box, if you don't mind me saying. How long's he been out of prison this time?'

'Less than a year. With this stunt, though, he'll get a longer sentence.' A shard of a smile touched her features. 'No, he's not the brightest, Daniel. Gets that from his father. But he's all I've got.'

'Have you a good solicitor?'

'That's the thing. I can't afford one. He'll have to accept the duty solicitor assigned to him.'

'Give me the details and I'll sort out a decent one. And don't worry about the money.'

She began properly crying now. 'I don't know how I can thank you.'

'Just by carrying on cleaning my house beautifully.'

She smiled at him through her tears. 'How's Ed?'

'He's gone to see his mum.'

'Aw, that's lovely. Tell him I have a new recipe for him to try out when he gets back. He's so good at cooking. I thought he could have a go at it first and then tell me how to improvise a bit.'

Mrs Finsbury seemed so nice, even if her son was a burglar.

'I will, Mrs Finsbury,' Daniel replied. 'Rob needs to change his ways. He needs a job, too. Keep him out of trouble. With a good solicitor he should only get a few months.'

'You're wonderful. When I see him later I'm going to give him a clip around the ear, I tell ya.' She swigged back the tea, into which Daniel had heaped three sugars – clearly he knew exactly how she took it – then got up. 'I'm sorry to interrupt you two lovebirds.' She looked at me. 'You're a lucky girl, Rose.

There's no one like Daniel. No one.' And with that, she left, finding her own way back to the front door.

'Wow,' I said.

'Wow indeed. Bloody Rob. If he will insist on burglary as a career, I wish he'd get better at it.'

I laughed. 'Poor Mrs Finsbury.' But then my expression became serious. 'She likes you.'

'I like her.'

'It's nice that you're helping her.'

'It's not nice. Known her for years. Rob is a bit of an albatross around her neck, but he's her son. Family.' He jumped up. 'Make yourself at home. I've got a few calls to make.'

And off he went to the small sitting room, I was guessing to sort out Mrs Finsbury's errant son.

I went back upstairs, padded along the landing and into his bedroom, making my way to the shower. I let the water encase me for a long time, and then wrapped myself in a thick grey towel. The M&S knickers sat on the floor in the corner. I pulled a pair out. They looked as if they'd fit. Daniel's sister was obviously the same size as me. I opened the large cabinet above the sink and searched for deodorant. Three cans sat in perfect alignment on the top shelf. I reached up and took one out, then noticed the one on the right was a different brand. Without aluminium. The sort I preferred. Better for women, doesn't mess with your breast tissue. I rolled it on, and then returned both to the cabinet.

Daniel had said he was going to drop me home to pick up an overnight bag, and I was fine with that. I wanted to stay a bit longer.

I returned to the bedroom and picked up the textbook we'd been going through the night before, plonking myself down on the sofa. Sunlight spilled into the room. I leaned back and tried to read, but accepted that my concentration just wasn't there and tossed the book on the floor. I immediately relented, but as I fumbled to retrieve it from underneath the sofa, my hand touched paper. I abandoned the textbook and slid the paper towards me with my heel, then picked it up.

Speak with Miles

A's b'day DO NOT FORGET

I put the note on my lap. Looked at it for a minute and thought about the pink envelope sitting on the seat of the MG. Daniel really hadn't wanted to forget Ed's mum's birthday. What a thoughtful man. Then I pushed it back where I'd found it. The last thing I wanted was Daniel thinking I was a snoop.

Retrieving my clothes from the back of the chair, I decided to hang them up for a while to get the creases out (was I as anal as Daniel? I asked myself). I looked towards the two wardrobes and went to open the one nearest the bed, hoping to find a spare hanger. Locked. I glanced around for a key, none to be seen.

The other wardrobe was open. I was confronted with a neat row of shirts, in colour order, starting with white on the left and moving towards black on the right, with many shades in between, all in a similar style. I grabbed a hanger and then glanced at my watch, wondering how long Daniel would be, because it did look like a glorious day. A walk was just what I needed.

'You find everything you need?'

His voice startled me. 'I did, thanks.'

I was still standing in front of the wardrobe, and I held out my arm towards the line of shirts. 'I think you're a tiny bit compulsive.'

He moved closer and took me in his arms, the thrum in my groin pulsing down into my inner thighs. 'I'm hoping you'll cure me of it.' He paused. 'C'mon, let's make a move, or we may never again leave the bedroom.'

We turned and made our way towards the door. As I passed the bed, I ran my fingers over the carvings. The wood was sleek, warm and soothing.

25

I'd crammed with a lot of help from Tom, and in the end felt reasonably confident about my written exams. Daniel had left me alone, as he'd promised he would. I'd only seen him a few times since the end of April, although he'd called regularly. So when I was summoned to Professor Wilkins' office three days before the results were posted on the main noticeboard, and a day before the anatomy viva exam, I wasn't worried, saving my anxiety quota for the placement. I was dreading that.

Wilko – as he was known throughout the school – was famous for his total lack of social etiquette, manners and humour, so I braced myself, knocked and waited. It took him about twenty-five seconds to tell me to enter. He was known for that too. Making you sweat. He was a bit of a bastard, but then all the lecturers were. All men, all old, all dinosaurs, and all more than a little annoyed that women were allowed onto the course, let alone let loose on an unsuspecting society: the hysterical woman – what good can she be in such an objective profession?

Our course was fifteen per cent female, so generally we women stuck together, although sometimes I thought that some of the female students were worse than the men in their misogynist attitudes. I'd noticed how the boys would, without question, cover each other's backs, but for the girls it wasn't quite the same scenario. There were five female students in my year, and only one I talked to, although you could never call us friends. The last four years had been lonely, and sometimes I wondered if I'd feel like that my whole career. Was that why I'd fallen for Daniel so quickly? Because as different as we were, we were similar. Lone wolves. Rogue elephants. I liked the second analogy better.

I walked into the stuffy room; Wilko never opened the window. It smelt of stale cigars and old man. He must have been at least seventy, although he looked a hundred and six, and very like the cadavers that littered the anatomy room. It was common knowledge that he'd donated his body; we were all quite pleased that with a bit of luck – or not; it depended which way you looked at it – it wouldn't be on our table.

I took in a gulp of thick air and the nausea rose in my stomach; I'd felt off for days, and all through the exams. Wilko had his back to me, pulling an ancient book off his bookshelf. Dust filtered through the heavy atmosphere of the room.

He spoke, still not having turned around.

'Miss Trahern, do sit.'

I sat and crossed my legs, and another wave of nausea spun through me. I saw a jug of water on his desk. Dare I ask for some? I did. And to my surprise, still with his back towards me, he said, 'Go ahead.' I gulped back a whole glass, and by then he'd turned around.

'Miss Trahern, there is some concern about your exam results.' He coughed. 'And your general attitude at the moment. It's come to my attention that you have not completed the pre-placement study, which Mr Warner was expecting to receive in the post last week at the latest.'

'I sent it, sir, two weeks ago.' Daniel had posted it for me. He'd come round for a cup of tea and to see how I was doing. He hadn't wanted to stay long, didn't want to bother me just before the exams, and had taken the package to the post office. 'I sent it, sir,' I repeated. Wilko hated repetition.

'Well, Mr Warner has not received it, and I'm sorry to inform you, but your written examinations are not looking as we'd hoped they would.' He peered at me then with what I thought he believed was compassion. A tortured expression, as he had no idea how to achieve the one he was searching for. 'It can be challenging, medicine. It is a vocation, a calling. It demands total attention.' I waited; knew it was coming. 'Difficult for the female to focus sometimes—'

I jumped up; the glass catapulted off the table. 'That is utter bollocks. And if you don't know it's utter bollocks, it's time you retired… sir.' *God, Rose, what are you saying?* Just the truth. It had been building for four years. Longer.

I had to hand it to him, his expression did not change one iota.

'You have your viva anatomy tomorrow. Be prepared.'

'More prepared than the men in my class?' *Let it go, Rose.*

'Lip does not make a good doctor.' He paused. 'And neither does failing written year-four exams.'

The vomit had made its way into my gullet. I stumbled towards the door. 'I have a copy of my pre-placement study to send to Mr Warner. I'll hand-deliver it tomorrow to Leeds Infirmary.' I would take it there after the viva exam. I'd ask Tom if his dad might give me a lift.

'See you promptly at nine a.m., Miss Trahern.'

Sweat poured down my cleavage. My breasts ached. Daniel had told me he'd posted it. Maybe it had got lost. I hadn't asked him to do a recorded delivery. Why hadn't I?

And my exam results. It was unusual to call a student in to discuss them before they were officially posted on the board. I must have bombed spectacularly. I walked quickly down the corridor to the ladies'. Kicking the door open, I rushed into a cubicle, bent over the toilet and heaved. As I flushed and saw the sand-coloured projection swirl down the bowl, I watched my life flush away too.

–

Somehow I made my way home and called Daniel. I knew I wasn't making much sense, but I heard him juggling the phone at the other end, asking Ed to take my pre-placement study to Leeds.

'No!' I yelped into the receiver.

'Calm down, Rose. I'll be over in half an hour and *I'll* take it.'

'Like you posted it?' I said.

By then Tom was standing next to me, and I think he'd got the gist of what was happening. He'd sent his pre-placement study off to his supervisor way ahead of the deadline, received a receipt of submission too. Why hadn't I checked if I'd got a receipt? I was totally losing it.

'You okay?' he asked.

'No, I'm not. I think I've failed the writtens too.'

'Jesus.'

'Daniel'll be here soon. He's going to take my pre-placement study to Leeds for me.'

'I can ask my dad.'

'It's okay, but thanks for offering.'

He shrugged in surrender, then said, 'You need to calm down for tomorrow. You know the Old Guard have a way of eating female students for breakfast in the viva.'

'I know. I'll be fine.'

'You don't look fine. You look ill.'

'I think I have a bug. Going to grab a few hours' sleep after Daniel's been and gone.'

'I'm off to the library. I'll check in on you later.'

'Thanks.' A sweep of nausea hit me again and I pushed past him to the loo.

–

Daniel turned up exactly half an hour after the phone call. He took me in his arms but said nothing.

I handed him the package. 'Make sure it gets there, Daniel.'

'I will. And it *was* posted.'

'Did you post it?'

'I gave it to Ed. He took it to the post office with all my other correspondence.' He looked at me. 'It was sent, Rose.'

I didn't answer; there was nothing to say.

He carried on. 'Don't worry about your exams; they're just trying to put the pressure on. He didn't say you'd failed. Bastards. Get ready for the viva tomorrow.' His eyes swept over my face. 'You look pale.'

'I'm very anxious, in case you hadn't noticed.'

'I'll call you tomorrow after the exam.' He kissed me on the cheek, took the envelope and left.

I was glad to be alone. I hauled myself up the stairs like a zombie and fell onto the bed, slept for two hours and then sat at my desk doing last-minute revision on the shoulder girdle complex. My eyes settled on the notes – *the triangle of auscultation,* I read, and pulled the plastic model of the shoulder from my shelf. Studied it, studied the names and the alignment, the spacing of the intricate muscle groups that held the shoulder together, and the nerves that innervated those muscles.

The names danced in front of my eyes, *ulna, radial, brachial, median.* My stomach had settled down. I went downstairs and ate toast. Carried on revising until late evening. Daniel called the landline and left a message. The package was with Mr Michael Warner. Safe.

I went to bed, my head full of anatomy and Latin names.

Full of the mistake Daniel and I had made.

26

'Miss Trahern,' the senior anatomy lecturer said, peering blatantly at my breasts before his gaze moved upward. My hair was scraped back and I wondered if he was scrutinizing the frown lines that had appeared overnight above my nose. 'Can you please explain, briefly, the general configuration of the muscles, together with the main nerves around the shoulder complex, and then illustrate your answer by using the skeleton in front of you.'

I stood tall and gave my explanation. 'The triangle of auscultation has the boundaries of, superiorly, the inferior portion of the trapezius muscle; inferiorly, the latissimus dorsi; and laterally, the medial border of the scapula. The rotator cuffs are the important muscles giving the glenohumeral joint its stability.'

'Give me the names of the rotator cuff muscles, Miss Trahern.'

Easy. 'Teres minor, supraspinatus, infraspinatus and…' I tailed off. It had gone, the last one.

'Easy question. Please answer.'

I rooted around my super-crowded and fuzzy mind. It really had gone.

He sighed. 'Subscapularis, Miss Trahern. Remind me not to include you in my surgical team.' I knew I'd gone bright red. I hated blushing, especially in that situation. 'Now, please carry on and tell me about the other muscles in the upper thoracic dorsal region.' A pause. 'If you can remember them, that is.'

I took a huge breath and told myself not to allow him to rile me. The next fifteen minutes went okay, I thought. In fact, I was sure the esteemed professor had a fact wrong about the rhomboids and their synergy with the levator scapulae muscles, which elevate the medial border of the scapula, and also downwardly rotating the scapula with respect to the glenohumeral joint, and I told him so. Which of course, being a woman, was totally the wrong thing to do. He scowled, and I saw him glancing at the *Gray's Anatomy* sitting in front of him. If I was a male student I knew they'd be having good-natured banter about it. Not with me, though. Daniel was right. They were all bastards.

When I left the room, the student due in after me was sitting on the edge of one of the rock-hard chairs that lined the corridor. Gary Bolton. Nice guy. He nodded and didn't ask how it had gone. It was a kind of rule between us all. Never ask. I saw Tom sitting at the end of the corridor. He smiled at me thinly but didn't ask either. I touched his shoulder as I walked by at speed, desperate to get outside and away from the smell of the uni, of medicine. Of failure.

–

Two days later, I got confirmation that Warner had received my pre-placement study. I also found out I'd failed two clinical-based papers (I thought they'd gone okay), though I'd managed a distinction in the anatomy viva. Re-sits it would be. At least they were allowing me to.

I threw myself onto my bed; I felt terrible. The phone rang and I let it go to answerphone. Daniel had been leaving messages on it all morning. It was him again. I didn't get up.

Tom and Casey had gone to the gym. Tom had distinctions in virtually every exam. I suspected he'd gone out to get out of my way. He felt bad for me and couldn't cope.

I hauled myself up from the bed and made my way downstairs, debating whether to call Mum, ask her to come over. I thought about it for at least half an hour. Then I picked up the phone. She didn't question me when I asked her to drop in to Boots to pick something up for me.

She arrived at the house within an hour and a half looking completely together and in control. I didn't bother telling her about the car crash of my exams. It was irrelevant at that moment.

'I can't believe this,' she said as she walked into the hallway.

'I might be wrong.'

She handed me her purchases. She'd bought two. 'Go on, I'll wait down here.'

–

Half an hour later, I joined her in the kitchen. She was washing up. Why couldn't she be like this all the time? She turned and lifted her brows.

'I am.'

'You're a medical student; how could you have been so stupid?'

There were times when my mother's ability to aim right into the centre took me by surprise. That was one of those times, and the heat of anger threaded through me. 'Just for once, can't you attempt to control what comes out of your mouth?'

'It's your life. You should have gone on the pill.'

'I took a morning-after. We used condoms. This shouldn't have happened.'

'Is it your new boyfriend's?' she asked quietly.

'Of course it is.' I faced her. 'Please go. I need some space.'

Without another word, she got up and left.

I went back upstairs and lay on the bed. Less than an hour later, I called Daniel.

'It's all going to be fine,' he said.

'This is just the wrong time, so completely the wrong time.'

'We'll get you through the exams and the placement. Will you tell your tutor?' he asked gently.

'That I'm having a termination?'

'No, Rose. I want you. I want the baby.' He went quiet on the other end of the phone. 'I love you.'

I began to cry. It was what I'd wanted to hear. What I'd needed to hear. I had no problem with the ethics of abortion, but I could not have one.

'I'm coming over,' he said.

'You *really* want a baby?'

'It's not a problem, Rose.'

'Can you come over now?'

'Already in the car.'

Leaving the front door off the latch, I returned to my bedroom and waited. A baby. I couldn't think.

I heard the door open and then close, Daniel coming up the stairs. I shouted from my bedroom and he came in, lay on the tiny bed next to me. We didn't say a word. At last he kissed my forehead and I turned sideways, looking at him. 'You really are a surprise, Mr Deane.'

'So are you, Rose.' He buried his head in the hollow of my neck.

And I could not see his face.

27

17 June 1991

Daniel left late the evening before. I'd told him I wanted to be alone a while to think.

I got up and called my GP surgery and managed to get an appointment that evening. The doctor confirmed the positive test, and despite my thoughts of the previous night, despite Daniel wanting our baby, I told him that I wasn't a hundred per cent sure about going through with the pregnancy. *I have to finish my course*, I said, with an uneasy feeling in my gut betraying my uncertainty. *I have to qualify.*

He was a youngish doctor, maybe around Daniel's age, maybe a little older. I studied him. No older than forty. He understood my dilemma completely, and handed me tissues. He'd been my GP for ten years and knew about some of my problems, all related to my home life and my mother. He gave me strict instructions to discuss it all with the baby's father, and then made me an appointment at the main NHS hospital for the following morning; the appointment that could set in motion the road to a termination. I cried as I left the surgery.

I had no intention of discussing it with Daniel. This was my decision.

–

The next day, Daniel called early and I could hardly bear to listen to the excitement in his voice. He wanted to meet later that afternoon; I told him I had uni work to do.

My appointment at the hospital was at 10 a.m., and I was sitting in the waiting room at 9.30. Luckily, and astonishingly, they were running ahead of schedule, and I was inside a sterile consulting room at 9.50. It smelt of Dettol and antiseptic cream. I cast my eyes around; the paint on the wall was peeling, and one of the lights on the ceiling didn't work, so it was too dark. The room had no window to the outside.

The doctor who would be advising me had a long, lean face that didn't appear to lend itself to smiling.

'Please take a seat,' she said.

'Thanks for fitting me in so soon,' I replied, sitting down.

She looked at my notes. 'Time is of the essence,' she glanced up at me, 'as you will understand, being a medical student.'

I nodded.

'Year four?'

I nodded again. My situation would be positive for the outcome I wanted. Being in the fourth year of a medical degree was a viable and understandable reason to want a termination. But *did* I want a termination? Now there, I wasn't so sure.

'I'm here, Miss Trahern,' she carried on, 'to explain about having a termination, and to assess whether it's something you really want. After our consultation, and if you still want to go ahead, another doctor has to agree with the decision, and then we can book you in for a termination. I'm sure you're aware of this protocol?'

'I am, yes.'

'And you are aware of the procedure? What it entails?'

I wanted to say *of course I am*, but bit my tongue.

She carried on, 'Is the baby's father aware of the pregnancy?'

'He is.'

'And is he in agreement to a termination?'

'It doesn't matter what he wants; this is my choice.'

It was her turn to nod. 'Yes, indeed. But I suggest you discuss it with him again before making a final decision.' She paused, and finally I saw some compassion in her expression. 'It's the best way forward, trust me.'

'Yes.' I didn't want to discuss a termination with Daniel because... because... Why didn't I? Because I didn't want him to think badly of me and I knew in that moment, if I were to go through with one, I would forever think badly of myself. In my third year I'd observed an abortion. I was a big advocate for women making their own choices regarding their own bodies, I was very much pro-abortion, but the surgical procedure was brutal. I was staring at the doctor sitting opposite me and she smiled back; it changed her whole face.

She then went through the itinerary of a termination – all of which I was aware. My stomach began to turn over, as if the bundle of cells forming inside could hear her. My mind reached back to being with Daniel, how I felt about him, how he made me feel, and his complete and unconditional acceptance of my bombshell pregnancy news.

I can't do this.

'So, Miss Trahern, I will discuss this with my colleague, and I'll be in contact with you within seventy-two hours.'

Still thinking of Daniel, and the surgical abortion I'd once witnessed, I stood. 'I can't do it.'

She stood too, took my elbow and gently pressed me back into the chair. 'Does the father want you to keep the baby, Miss Trahern?'

'He does.'

'You can defer a year on your course, you know. You are young.'

'I know.' I looked at her. 'This is all in confidence, isn't it? You won't discuss this with my school? My head of faculty?'

'Of course not.'

'I've changed my mind,' I said in a whisper.

'Go away and think about it for a week. We have time; you are well within the limit.'

'I don't need to think about it.'

She studied me. 'No, I don't think you do. But contact me in a week in any case with your final decision.'

I got up again. 'Thank you for your time.'

Her facial expression had settled back to the way it had been at the beginning of our appointment. 'It's my job, Miss Trahern.'

On the bus home, I felt much lighter than I'd felt on the way there.

My decision was made.

28

Daniel picked me up late the next morning and took me to Newstead Abbey. We talked a lot but I mentioned nothing about my previous day's activities. By the end of the afternoon my decision was cemented. There was no way I'd go through with a termination.

Back at Daniel's house, he made me tea and toast, and after watching some inane TV, we had an early night. We didn't make love; he just held me, and I slept the whole night through. The following morning, I called my mum to tell her I was bringing Daniel over, but she didn't pick up.

As we drove to my childhood home, I wondered if the house would be in total chaos when we arrived. It was early, so she might still be in bed, though I hoped not. Daniel parked the car and took hold of my hand.

'I'm not sure,' I said. 'My mum's not keen on impromptu visits.'

'Go and check. If it's not convenient, I won't come in.'

'Okay.' I got out and made my way up the path. Outside the front door, her shoes were neatly laid out on a piece of newspaper with an umbrella resting inside one of them. A good sign. She'd been out for an early walk. She'd been organised: she'd left the dirty shoes outside and had remembered to take a brolly. I pulled out my key and opened the door. Thankfully the house smelt of strong air freshener. I sneezed.

'Mum, it's me,' I shouted.

She poked her head around the kitchen door. 'Hello, love.' It was as if the day she'd come over to my house, the pregnancy test and our argument hadn't happened. That was often the way.

'I've brought Daniel to meet you. He's waiting outside.'

'Bring him in then. Have you told him?'

'Of course I have.'

'And he knows I know?'

'Yes, he does.'

I made my way back to the car. Daniel opened the window. 'Come on in,' I said.

He gave me a thumbs-up and I managed a smile.

Mum was waiting in the hall, and her eyes opened wide as she saw Daniel for the first time.

'So nice to meet you again,' he said.

I stabbed a look at her, then at Daniel; lifted my shoulders in question.

'Mr Deane, what a surprise. Please, come in. Don't stand in the doorway.'

'You two know each other?' I directed my question at Daniel.

'I met Mr Deane at the end of my interview,' Mum interjected.

'Interview?' I asked.

'At the hospital,' Daniel replied for her.

'Your cleaning job?'

'Yes, Rose,' Mum replied. 'The cleaning job.'

I turned to Daniel. 'You knew?'

'I bumped into… Mrs Trahern in the waiting room.'

'That's right,' my mum said with a huge grin. 'After my interview with Personnel.' I'd forgotten she was in the hallway with us.

'You didn't think to tell me?'

'I didn't know Marion was your mum, Rose,' Daniel said. 'I only caught her first name.'

Mum took hold of his elbow. 'Come through to the kitchen. I'm just about to make a brew.'

'How's the job going?' he asked her.

'Well,' she replied.

'Great to hear. I know we've been struggling to get someone reliable.'

'Well, despite some initial problems with the background questions,' she replied quietly, 'I think we got it all cleared up.'

I wondered if she'd come clean about the shoplifting. If she had, it was a step forward.

Daniel said, 'I should have put you two together immediately. That hair.'

God, she looked bashful. 'Our meeting was very brief,' she said.

I couldn't believe we were standing there talking about this.

We drank tea in the kitchen. My mum was comfortable with Daniel. Finally I addressed the elephant in the room.

'Mum, I'm keeping the baby.' I glanced at Daniel. 'We've decided together.'

She moved closer to me. 'You need to get it confirmed with your GP, Rose.'

I squirmed a little, hating to lie, although I wasn't lying exactly, just not telling the entire truth. 'I have.'

'Mrs Trahern, you don't have to worry,' Daniel interjected gently. 'I know this is all very quick, but I love your daughter and I want our child.' He leaned forward in his chair. 'I haven't asked her yet,' he glanced at me, 'but I'm booked to go to Spain in a few weeks and I'd love it if she came too.' He glanced at me again. 'I know you'll kick back at this idea, but you should consider it… and I hope your mum agrees.' He was being so proper, and despite everything, it made me smile. I liked it.

'Seems like a good idea to me,' Mum said. Her easiness with Daniel was wrong-footing me a little. 'Give you time to think, love.'

'I'll take good care of her, Mrs Trahern.'

She glanced at me. 'What about your placement?'

Wrong-footed twice. She never remembered the finer details of my course. I looked at Daniel. 'I do have to prepare for my placement.'

'You can revise and work by the pool at the villa,' he said.

'Is it *your* villa?' my mum chipped in. I stopped myself doing an eye roll at her response.

'My dad's actually, Mrs Trahern,' he replied.

'I'll come to Spain with you, Daniel. It'll do me good,' I said.

'It'll put some colour into those grey cheeks,' my mum said, grinning at Daniel.

I checked my watch. 'We have to be going.' I got up and Daniel followed suit. 'Say hi to Sam when you see him.' But then I heard the front door.

'Bloody hell!' Sam shouted from the hallway. 'Whose car's that outside?' We'd come in the MG. Sam was a car fanatic.

He blundered into the kitchen, all gangly and uncoordinated like a colt. God only knew how he'd fare in the army.

He clocked Daniel first, then me. 'Hi, sis.' He peered. 'You look… good.' His eyes flicked to Daniel and his grin widened. 'Your car?'

'It is. I'm Daniel. Fancy a drive in it? I mean, me drive you up to Junction 23 and back?'

'Now?' Sam asked with enthusiasm.

Daniel took his car keys from his pocket and they left.

'You could do worse,' my mum said.

'I'm going up to my old room. Some stuff I want to take with me.'

'As you will.'

–

Back in the car with Daniel, I felt exhausted. It was always that way after spending time with Mum.

'Did Sam like the car?' I asked.

'Loved it. It's a bloke thing.'

'I can't believe my mum's working at Bluefields.'

'I really had no idea she was your mum. I only met her briefly. I don't remember everyone. What I do remember is Personnel being delighted that we'd found someone who spoke good English.'

'What does that mean?'

'Just someone who could understand instructions properly. It's a medical institution. We have to be strict about cleanliness. We need someone with good English.'

'Do you know about her... history?'

He glanced at me. 'The shoplifting convictions? Yes, I was told about them.' He took a corner quickly. 'She's only human, and she deserves a chance. Anyway, on to more important things. You're really coming to Spain with me?'

I glanced sideways at him: hair dishevelled, colour on the defined bones of his cheeks, a day's worth of dark and appealing stubble. I nodded.

Everything would be fine. Life was all about flux. I'd made my decision. I sat back in the seat and laid both hands on my stomach.

'So you've already seen your own GP, to get confirmation?'

'I have.'

He inclined his head a little. 'I've taken the liberty, and really hope you don't mind, to make an appointment for you at Bluefields for tomorrow.'

'Of course I don't mind. Thanks for doing it.' Would I have to come clean with the obstetrician at the private hospital about my appointment with the NHS doctor who had found it so difficult to smile? No, I'd keep quiet. I didn't want Daniel to know that I'd even contemplated a termination. I stroked my stomach. I felt too guilty.

Daniel placed his hand on mine. 'This is perfect. You are perfect.' He grinned. 'And finally I have a reliable cleaner for the hospital.'

29

20 June 1991

I'd stayed over at Daniel's house and woke up with a wooden curl right next to my nose and Daniel putting a mug of herbal tea on the bedside table.

'It feels early.' I looked at the clock: 7.43 a.m.

'I'm making a flying visit to Herefordshire to see my sister. Something's come up that she wants to talk to me about. To do with our dad.'

I hauled myself up. 'Does your dad ever come to England?'

'Rarely.' He moved hair away from my eye. 'I'll take you to see him in Morocco when we get a chance.'

'I'd like that.'

He checked his watch. 'Gotta go, I want to miss the traffic. I may well stay over. Stay here if you want to. The fridge is stuffed.' He paused. 'And I told Ed not to come round. I know you two rub each other up the wrong way.'

'We do. I'm sorry, but I find him really odd. Thanks for the offer, though. If you don't mind, I'll raid your fridge and take its contents back to my place.' I winked at him.

'That's fine. See you tomorrow, and good luck today.'

He kissed me on the forehead and left.

–

I took the bus to Bluefields, which was located in the centre of Nottingham, although nestled away from the hubbub in a small patch of green. The sign, *Bluefields Hospital*, was huge and sat neatly on the iron railing surrounding the building.

An efficient-looking middle-aged receptionist took my name and didn't bat an eyelid, although I suspected she had no idea about my connection with the hospital's manager. She indicated the waiting room, but Miles intercepted me before I got there.

'Rose, it's good to see you.'

'You too, Miles.'

'How's it going?'

'It's going well. I'm here to meet my obstetrician, Dr Mark Stephens.'

'Excellent,' he replied, although his voice was flat. An awkward silence sank into the space between us. He took my elbow and led me to a door with his name on. 'You can wait in my office. I think you're a little early. Would you like a drink? Water, juice, tea?'

'I'm fine, thanks.'

'Please, take a seat.'

'It's a buzzing hospital. Bigger than I thought,' I said, maybe for something to say.

He nodded, and suddenly an exquisite discomfort spread through me. 'Will the morning-after pill have any effect on the foetus, Miles?' I asked. 'From what I know, I think I'm fine, but a qualified doctor's reassurance would be good.'

'It's not my area of expertise but I do keep up to date with research, as a number of my patients are from obs and gynae. All the data suggests not.' He paused and crossed one leg over the other. 'I'm sorry it wasn't effective.'

The on-the-nose comment unsettled me. 'Don't be. I've got my head around it… and I'm happy about having a baby.'

'What about your course? Your career?'

'I can carry on, or defer a year.'

He took a long breath. 'You know… you don't have to stay with Daniel just because you're pregnant, Rose.'

I looked at him, his kind eyes, his uncomfortable posture. 'I love him, Miles. And I already love my baby.' I coughed, my throat suddenly dry.

Miles opened his desk drawer and pulled out a bottle of water. 'Here you go.' He handed it to me.

'Thanks.' I unscrewed the lid and took a huge swig. It was so stuffy in the room.

'Rose…'

'Yes?'

'Nothing. It's fine, not important.' He uncrossed his legs, allowed his knees to splay apart. Suddenly he looked relaxed, as if he'd made a decision. 'Let's get you to Mark's office.' He glanced at his watch. 'He'll be ready for you now. I think today is more a chat and introduction. Get your blood pressure checked, an examination, a full medical history. You'll be out within an hour. Is Daniel picking you up?'

'No, he's gone to Herefordshire to see his sister. I have lectures this afternoon.'

'Ah… okay.' He got up and opened the door, but avoided eye contact.

Not for the first time since being with Daniel, I felt some guilt that I'd turned Miles down. He was a lovely bloke and I really hoped he'd find someone who deserved him.

–

Dr Mark Stephens was a small man, around five foot six, and I towered above him. His movements were small and jerky, his features much the same. His manner was optimistic and a little over the top, but he was professional, and although I didn't warm to him massively, by the end of our session I trusted him. I'd told Daniel that morning that I was more than happy to go the NHS route, and of course I would if any complications arose with my pregnancy – because you never knew. But for now, we'd decided that going private was the best thing. Now that I'd made the decision to keep the baby, I wanted everything to go as smoothly as possible, so that hopefully my studies would go as smoothly as possible too.

When we'd finished, Mark sat back in his chair. 'I have you booked in on the twenty-fourth for your twelve-week ultrasound scan. I know Daniel is keen to be here for it.'

'That's great. Thank you, Dr Stephens.'

'Please, call me Mark.'

Four days later, I was back at the hospital with Daniel, lying supine on the bed, my T-shirt pulled up to my bra.

Mark Stephens placed the ultrasound head on my stomach and I nearly shot through the ceiling. I glanced at him, smiling. 'I think maybe warming up the gel would be a good idea, Mark.'

He grinned tightly. 'Sorry, the midwife usually does that for me.' He checked his watch, and as he did so, there was a light knock on the door. 'That'll be Cam, your midwife.'

The woman who entered had shoulder-length red hair, a face full of freckles, and an energetic demeanour. I put her in her mid thirties.

'Miss Trahern,' she said, bustling towards me. 'The big day!'

I smiled. 'It is, isn't it?'

She picked up the fat tube of gel. 'Mark didn't put it on the radiator to warm. Sorry, Miss Trahern—'

'Call me Rose, please.'

'I'm Cam Bradley, and I'll be looking after you.' We shook hands lightly. She turned to Daniel. 'Exciting, eh, Daniel?'

Daniel's face lit up. I was sure he was more excited than me about today, and a warm beat of contentment vibrated through my body.

Mark flicked on the ultrasound machine and glanced at Daniel and Cam. 'Okay. Off we go.'

I couldn't see the screen, but all I hoped for was a healthy baby, and not looking would put off the moment when Mark might tell me there was something wrong. Daniel and Cam's eyes, though, were glued. Mark pressed a button to capture a static image of my baby, and it was then that I asked, 'Can I look?' Cam took my hand and squeezed it lightly.

Mark moved the monitor nearer, and I saw a black and white image of a live human being. I couldn't stop the tears then. I'd had no idea I'd react like that. I was already changing. Had already changed.

Daniel stepped away from the monitor, rested his palm on my stomach and grinned, handing me a tissue with his free hand. I wiped my eyes. Mark coughed, then walked to his desk and began scribbling on my notes.

30

Theo

15 April 2016

After talking about her first ultrasound scan, Rose stops and probes Theo's reaction by examining his face. She holds his gaze, and it's he who breaks eye contact, noticing that many of the other visitors have already left. He didn't hear the bell signalling that time was nearly up.

He turns back to look at her. 'Why haven't you ever mentioned this? A baby with Daniel… Why, Rose?'

'It was a long time ago. Another life.' Her arms are crossed over her chest, palms grabbing at each shoulder.

'Did you lose the baby?' She doesn't answer, and he carries on. 'I'm sorry. It's not my place to ask. But your mum did mention something.' He catches her eye. 'She wouldn't tell me. She said it was up to you to tell me.'

Rose only nods.

He moves closer to the table, his forearms resting on the surface.

'Does that position make you think better, Theo?'

He wants to ask more about her baby, but he knows it will be futile. All in good time. He smiles. 'Not really.' He pulls at the lapel of his jacket. 'Rose, what made you change your mind about seeing me?'

'I trust you.'

'And you *can* trust me.'

'I had a visit from someone.'

'Bella Bliss?'

'Who told you that? I bet it was Don. He shouldn't have divulged that information to you.' Her tone is low and he detects some fear in her voice too.

'I know,' he says.

'Bella told me things about my mother,' she continues. 'I wanted you to find out if they were true.'

'About Marion keeping in touch with Daniel?'

'She knows something. Something I should know. But Bella wouldn't tell me what. She was scared. She's so young... she reminded me of myself at her age.'

He nods. 'What makes you think that what she said is true?'

'She didn't have to come.' She reaches over the table, lays the palms of both hands on its surface. 'Please... please stay with me on this, Theo.'

He grins. 'How could I not?' His grin slips. 'There's more than I know, isn't there?'

'There's more than *I* know.'

'I'll stay with you.' And he will. This is not about the story, or the money. Not any more.

'Good.'

He heaves himself from the chair. 'Time's up.'

'It is.' She stands and holds out her hand.

He takes it and squeezes gently, but reluctantly unclasps when he sees the custody officer shaking his head.

Walking to the car park, he acknowledges that he's in deep, in thrall to a convicted murderess – like those mad people in the States who write to diabolical killers on Death Row and then profess undying love for them. But Rose isn't a diabolical killer. He's sure of it. And he's not one of those mad and deluded people.

He really isn't.

31

Rose

Theo left a few hours ago, and now I'm sitting in the little room that backs onto the recreational area, one of the few spaces in the prison that has a window bigger than a foot square. It's where I met DI Alison Greenwood, but today I'm waiting for Don to appear. I check the clock on the wall. He's late. He often is for our sessions. And he obviously divulges things to people that he shouldn't. Maybe Cathy is right about him.

Discomfort scuttles through my right breast. Not sharp, and not really a pain, and if I didn't know what I know, I'd ignore it. I wait for it to abate. It means nothing. Only anxiety. It's the thought of talking to Don, I tell myself.

'Hi, Rose.'

I didn't hear him come in. He sits down. He looks awkward, a little fraught, and I don't know if it's because of me or connected with other stuff going on in his life. Intermittently I feel sorry for Don – I have no idea why – but I suspect he doesn't return the feeling. Today, though, my pity towards him is lean.

I watch him. Yes, he's very uneasy, and preoccupied, perhaps feeling guilty that he disclosed Bella's visit to Theo. When he finally looks at me, I try to give him a smile. I hate these sessions, but there's no way out of them.

Don squeezes his eyes shut, then opens them again and the concerned therapist appears. I'm relieved, because now we can get on and get this over with.

I know a fair bit about my therapist's existence outside the walls of the prison. In our early sessions he said very little about himself, but it didn't take him long to begin unburdening himself; he doesn't even know he's doing it. I'm good at asking the right questions – it's a shame I didn't have the same ability in my youth. I was so naïve when I met Daniel, although I didn't think I was. I thought I knew it all. I thought I was sassy and streetwise. I thought Daniel Deane was a man I'd love forever.

My thoughts return to Don. He's uncertain where he's going with me. I'm not giving him much to work with. I can't: Don is not the man to unravel the puzzle of my life. Theo has been honest with me about Natasha, and I appreciate that. There, I've said her name. I've even looked at the photo of her that Theo showed me. But it was as if he knew not to mention the child, and he certainly didn't get out *her* photo.

I knew from Theo's very first letter that he could, and would, help me. You can glean a lot from people's written words, and even more from spoken ones. My skill at getting information dates back to taking medical histories. The root of any problem, physical or mental, is all in the history. And I should know. That I didn't ask the right questions all those years ago hounds me, trails me. I wear it like a lead coat.

It was the embarrassment, horror, confusion, visceral hatred I experienced on the hospital unit with Abe lying unconscious that has led to this: sitting in a small room in a prison in Peterborough, talking to a therapist about a young man who has had his life ruthlessly taken from him. The emotions I felt that day on the unit and the resentment that penetrated me like a knife smashed, destroyed, annihilated me. Took away the last small remaining piece of me.

Don sighs, coughs and clears his throat. I think he's had a bad chest for weeks now. I want to tell him to cut out the fags. 'Okay. Let's start, Rose.' There's an edge to his voice. He's really fed up. The session will be short. 'Let's talk about your husband.' He leans forward in the prison-themed electric-blue chair and picks up his glass of water, swigs it back in one go. Coughs again. 'Do you discuss your feeling with Miles… about being in here?' His hands gesticulate, taking in the room, the prison, although he doesn't say *and what you did*.

Abe's death is never talked about openly; only, it seems, by Theo. Theo can take it. Theo is real. I think he is the most real person I've ever met in my life. I want to see him again. I don't want to be here with Don. I want to be sitting opposite Theo. That would be enough for me, just being near him. But it will never happen. The thought floors me for a moment, and I hear my own gasp for air.

'You all right, Rose?'

'I'm fine.'

'Let's talk about Miles.' Don always wants to know about Miles, but I cut him off there every time, and he knows I will do the same today. But he tries anyway. Miles is somewhere I won't go. Every time I cut him off, Don does exactly the same thing – pushes back imaginary hair from his forehead. I think he is the sort of man who lost his hair early.

He closes the open file that sits on his knee. I know he'll bring up my mother next, because like clockwork he always does. He is so out of his depth.

I'm so out of my depth.

I say, as I always say, 'I don't want to talk about Miles.' And it happens.

'Let's explore your feelings about your mother.'

'I have very few feelings about my mother,' I say. It's what I always say.

'You love her?'

I don't answer. He always asks me this too, just in differing sentence constructions.

'You blame her in some way?' he presses.

'My mother is my mother. As you know, we are… estranged.' I pause. 'But you know, Don, not every flaw we have can be traced back to a parent.'

'Indeed, Rose.' His vowels are stiff. 'Yes, your mother has only visited you once. I'm sorry.'

'It's fine, Don.' I should mention him telling Theo about Bella's visit, but it's pointless. It's done and perhaps it's a good thing Theo knows.

He does something unprecedented now. Stands up. Walks towards me. Sits on his haunches, very near. I can smell his breath, a hint of his morning smoke and coffee. I'm sure this is Don attempting to look sympathetic.

'Do you want her to visit more?' he asks finally.

'No, Don. I don't.'

He sighs loudly and I'm supposed to hear it. 'Why are you talking to Theo Hazel? What do you hope to achieve?' he asks.

What he really wants to ask is why I won't talk to *him*.

'It seems like the right thing to do.' I smile, and Don's back to standing. Given up.

'Your mother bothers you, Rose?'

'I *really* don't want to talk about her.'

'But you mentioned her in one of our early meetings. This is key. I've been seeing you for some months now, and we need to talk about this.' He wrings his hands. 'Talk to me.' He's sounding desperate. 'It will help you come to terms with what you did, and why you did it.' He's sitting again, legs splayed apart, an unusual posture for Don. 'You didn't plead insanity, but clearly—'

'I knew what I was doing, Don.'

He snaps his folder closed. He feels the need to be out of here quickly. 'Let's have another session tomorrow,' he says without enthusiasm.

I've already stopped listening. My mind is on Theo again, and guilt sweeps over me about my husband – that I feel something I should not for Theo. But I have loved Miles.

Without me realizing, Don is ushering me from the room. I have half an hour before I start work in the library, where I'm cataloguing medical reference books and teaching biology to several inmates who signed up for the GCSE. I return to my cell for half an hour's peace. And as I sit hunched on the bed, I cast my mind back twenty-five years. To my baby.

My body shakes. Someone is walking above my grave – or is it Miles's grave?

Or am I walking over Abe's?

32

Theo

16 April 2016

Since leaving the prison and Rose the day before, and with only a few hours' sleep, Theo has been tightly ensconced in his study, blinds closed, the desk lamp throwing out shadows he hasn't noticed before. The weather outside is abysmal. Torrential rain and wind. A branch of the old birch outside is tapping incessantly on his flat's third-floor window. A stack of bills sits on the left-hand side of his desk. He opens the latest letter from the bank that lent him too much money and scans the words. Folds it up again and returns it to the envelope. He stares at the other correspondence, still sealed. Three credit card bills that he can't pay. He doesn't bother opening them to view the eye-watering balances, or the even more astronomical amounts of interest.

He does the ostrich thing and thinks of Rose. All in all, the visits are going well, very well. He didn't fully appreciate the underlying acrimony between mother and daughter, but after his lunch date with Marion, and Rose's own words, he certainly does now. Remembering Marion's expensive clothes, the nice house in the right part of Nottingham, intrigue is gathering. And somewhere inside the unfinished equation that Rose has given him is her husband, Miles.

Her story is unrolling.

He picks up his notes. He planned his book to have three separate strands: what Rose is telling him, her story; a second layer with his own independent findings; and Abe's sections, which are forming as Natasha reveals more about his early life. He's allowed himself some artistic licence with Abe, experimenting with faction, but may well change his mind. He'll see how he feels when the first draft is written, if ever he finishes the first draft. Over the past days he's lost all enthusiasm, not in finding out the answer to the puzzle, but writing the book for possible publication.

Checking his mobile, he decides he has time for a shower and a quick bite before going to see Miles. In the kitchen, he pulls out an M&S salad from the fridge, wolfs it down and heads to the bathroom, taking off his clothes on the way. He lets the water run, waiting for it to heat up, and leans forward onto the sink, holding its edge. The image of Rose – either then or now, he isn't sure which – is powerful.

Half an hour later, he is standing by the door of his flat, ready to go. The drive from Manchester to Derbyshire, although not long, will be gruelling today, and the bad weather is translating into early dark evenings; he wants to be there and back before nightfall. Rose asked him not to bother Miles, but she wasn't so vehement in this request as she was in her warning not to contact Daniel Deane. Her husband will probably tell him to sod off, and it won't be the first time he's been turned away by someone who doesn't want to talk to him.

He picks up his car keys.

–

Rose and Miles have lived in a place called Old Whittington for the last eighteen years. When they first got married, they lived in London for a while, during which time Miles was working for a private clinic in Harley Street. Rose called it his wilderness years, but she didn't expand.

Theo arrives in Derbyshire in record time, but the maze of streets around Old Whittington catches him off guard, and without the aid of his stolen sat nav or Google Maps (there's no signal), he gets lost. He pulls up on the kerb and attempts to find his elusive sense of direction. Catching sight of the River Whitting in the distance, he knows he has to be close, and after quickly checking the street map spread on the passenger seat, he decides he should be heading west. Pissing off the driver behind, he does a six-point turn and five minutes later finds himself where he needs to be.

The house is a double-fronted Victorian. Theo turns off the ignition and sits back in the uncomfortable car seat. Now that he's here, he isn't so sure. He opens the car door, pushes out stiff legs and surveys the front door. Solid and reliable, like the man inside. More guilt pours through him.

A dead plant sits in a scarlet pot on the porch's Victorian tiles. He pulls the iron rod on the right-hand side, which sets off a loud and deep ringing inside the house. No movement. Maybe Miles is out, but a sky-blue BMW is evident in the cramped off-road parking space. Finally Theo senses activity, and the door opens.

Rose's husband. A tall man with a mild lantern jaw. Older than Rose, as she said. Perhaps nearing sixty, although it's difficult to give an exact age. Slate-grey eyes, even emptier than in the newspaper images. This man's life has imploded. Theo shouldn't have come here unannounced, and feels uncomfortable and devious.

'Can I help you?' Miles's voice is low and level. He peers over his shoulder towards Theo's parked car. 'You're not a journalist, are you?' Before Theo has time to answer, Miles carries on. 'Because if you are, you can sod off.'

Theo wants to smile at that. The phrase is so out of keeping with the man's appearance. 'I'm not a journalist, no, Mr Marlowe... not now, haven't been for years. My name's Theo Hazel.'

'I recognise that name.'

'I'm a writer, an author.'

Miles stares at him. 'Thought it rang a bell. Unusual name. Why are you here?'

'I've been visiting your wife... in prison.' Where else would he be visiting Rose? Inane thing to say.

Miles doesn't appear too perturbed at Theo's revelation, or that surprised; in fact Theo sees what looks like an expression of relief pass over his face. He doesn't move away from the front door, though, and despite now thinking this really wasn't his best idea, Theo's neck elongates and he peers into the hallway. A staircase on the left, carpeted in a mustard-yellow pile. Victorian green and blue ceramic tiles cover the hallway floor, a coat stand to the right with one solitary jacket hanging from its metal curves. Utterly organised, and utterly empty. No sign of life. Rose hasn't said much about her life with Miles, but what has come through to him loud and clear is their grief at not being able to have children.

No, Miles doesn't look angry about Theo's unexpected appearance on his doorstep, only unoccupied, like his hallway.

'Could I come in?' He might as well ask. The man can only tell him to piss off, although he suspects Miles wouldn't ramp up to that vocabulary.

'I'm about to go out.'

Miles retired soon after Rose's hearing and imprisonment, so Theo knows he isn't going to work. It's the one thing Rose has mentioned about him – that she wishes he'd found a job in another hospital, because clearly (and this is Theo's thought) he couldn't have stayed at the one he was working at; the hospital where Abe died. Theo wonders what Miles does with himself apart from going to see Rose, which he does every week.

'I'd really appreciate half an hour of your time,' he says.

'I like your non-fiction. Read all of those. Not so keen on your novels.' Still Miles hasn't moved from the door.

'Nice to know someone reads my work.' Rose mentioned that Miles might well have read one of his books, and her quick comment pleased him more than it should have done.

'I thought your last one was the best,' Miles carries on. 'Come in.'

Theo's whole body lapses into mild euphoria, a reaction both to Miles having liked his last book and being invited inside. He's trying to ignore the novel comment. He steps into the hallway, which although a pleasant space smells strongly of mould. 'Thanks.'

He follows Miles through to the kitchen, noticing on the way the continuing sparseness of the hallway, although the kitchen is a very different space. The late-morning sun streams through a large window, blatantly illuminating the chaos that's in such contrast with the orderliness at the front of the house. Every countertop is filled with mugs, plates encrusted with old food, used cutlery and piles upon piles of newspapers. He catches sight of Rose's image in one of them. Taken in her youth. Dazzling. The sink heaves with washing-up, the intensity of the laser-like light catching months of dust and debris. He scours around looking for photographs, pictures, anything personal, anything to show Rose, anything to show her husband and their life. There is nothing. He surmises that Miles has removed everything. This is a place where Rose's husband eats and drinks, reads old newspapers. Where he exists as opposed to lives.

Theo is a voyeur, watching and assessing someone else's bleak life, and the feeling mounting inside him is the same one that galvanised him into giving up journalism and taking up the writing of investigative non-fiction. As curious as he is regarding the human condition, as detached as he can sometimes be, he doesn't like nosing around people who have no wish for him to be prying. And that was never a good trait for a journalist. Standing in Miles's kitchen, observing the everyday life of a man whose wife has admitted to and subsequently been imprisoned for murder, those long-ago feelings of awkwardness surface again.

Miles cuts into his thoughts. 'I'd offer you a cup of tea or coffee, but I've run out of both. Water?' He picks up a pile of newspapers from the small chaise longue that runs parallel to the kitchen table. 'Please sit down.' In the harsh sunlight, he looks older. Theo notices his stoop and the way he doesn't seem to look at him directly, his eyes downcast.

'Water's good. Thank you.'

Miles nods and walks to the sink, washes out a glass, doesn't bother drying it, fills it and hands it to Theo. 'How are you finding Rose?'

'Well, considering. I've only made a few visits so far,' he says, glugging the water. 'It's good of her to agree to talk with me.'

'She didn't tell me a writer was visiting her.' He perches on the end of the chaise. 'You're intending to write about her, I take it?'

'Yes, that's the plan.'

'A take on Capote's *In Cold Blood*?'

'That's right.'

'Why are you here?' Miles asks.

'Background.' Theo turns to look at him. 'Although Rose suggested I didn't bother you.'

'But you came anyway?'

He nods.

'You're no Capote.'

'No,' Theo admits.

'Have you spoken to anyone else, apart from Rose?'

'Her mother, Marion. We've met a few times now.' Theo tries to gauge how much to reveal. 'And I'm also in touch with Abe Duncan's widow.'

'Getting the victim's story through the victim's wife?' He detects an edge of sarcasm in Miles's voice and hates himself a little more.

'I don't think Rose wants you to know she's talking with me, Mr Marlowe.' He looks at the broken man.

Miles pulls at the sleeve of his mohair jumper. 'I'd do anything for my wife, Mr Hazel. She shouldn't be...' His voice tapers off as quickly as the look of pain on his face appeared.

'Shouldn't be what?' Theo's heart beats in rhythm with the rapidly dripping kitchen tap.

'I'm very surprised she agreed to see you. What did you say that caught her interest?'

For the first time, Theo catches a flicker of amusement pass over Miles Marlowe's features. 'I obviously charmed her with my wit and genius,' he says. 'Are you angry she's talking with me?'

'No. I'm not. I'm really not.' Miles leans forward. 'What do you want from me, Mr Hazel?'

'I'd like to know more about Daniel Deane.'

'Ah, Rose has told you?' His concave cheeks seem to collapse even further. 'I haven't seen Daniel Deane for years. Not since I resigned from Bluefields in 1991.'

'She's told me, yes, about her relationship back then.' Theo glances up at him. 'Why did you resign, Mr Marlowe?'

'I didn't like what Daniel was involved in.'

'And what was that?'

Miles lifts his shoulders in futile submission.

Theo watches this man who is clearly desperate to talk. A man he guesses isn't a talker.

Miles continues, his voice a whisper. 'Daniel asked me to resign.'

'Why?'

'Because he wanted me out of the way.'

'And you didn't question why that was?'

'I didn't.'

Theo ploughs on. 'Mr Marlowe, to be perfectly honest, I've no idea how Rose could have done what she did.'

'I love her,' Miles says, staring at the floor, his shoulders hunched so far forwards that he looks as if he's about to retch. He gathers himself, shakes his head. 'The worst thing I could have done after Rose went to prison was retire. She knew my career meant everything to me.' He swallows hard. 'It is Rose's story to tell. And I hope she *will* tell you.' He pushes his fingers through thinning hair. 'I think it's time for you to leave.'

'Mr Marlowe, why did Rose train to be a nurse and not carry on at med school? From what she's told me, I sense that her true vocation was to be a doctor... a paediatrician.'

'It *was* her vocation.' His eyes move away from Theo's face. 'This is for Rose to tell you.'

Theo inclines his head. 'Rose didn't know that Abe Duncan was Daniel Deane's son, did she?' He waits a few seconds. 'Was it *you* who knew?'

Miles's head moves vigorously from side to side. 'No, I didn't know.'

The heat of frustration consumes Theo. 'Will you talk to me again, Mr Marlowe?'

'See how it goes with Rose. See what she says.' Miles gets up, walks to the window and peers out, his back to Theo.

Theo gets up too, but loiters.

Still peering into his garden, Miles says, 'My hands were tied, Mr Hazel, and have been for years.'

'Was Daniel Deane blackmailing you?'

'Our conversation is over.'

'Can we talk again?'

Miles dips his head, and Theo takes it for a yes.

33

Theo gets into his car and drives a couple of streets away from Miles and Rose's home. He parks up, takes out his notebook and pencil from the glove compartment and begins to scribble.

Miles – was he being blackmailed by Deane?

He flips to the back page. Rose's photographic memory hasn't faded with her life. She still remembers what was written on a scrap of paper all those years ago in Daniel's bedroom, and the note saying *A's birthday DO NOT FORGET.* A stab of intuition jabs at him, but it's a ridiculous thought and he sweeps it to one side. Rose and Miles are both hiding something; they are working in some sort of weird harmony to give him information yet not give him anything. It's as if both want to talk and both dare not.

Ed Madden will know something, he's sure of it.

He picks up his mobile and presses the contact *Bliss.* A female voice answers. Young, perky and with a strong Derby accent. 'Bliss Interior Designs, can I help you?'

'I wondered if I could speak to the managing director?' He hears a sigh on the other end of the phone, maybe even the young woman blowing a chewing gum bubble.

'Can *I* help? That's what Hugo employs me for,' she says.

'I was under the impression that there was another director?'

'What's your enquiry about, Mr…'

'Theo Hazel. I'm looking for some cutting-edge interior design for my flat in Manchester, and your company came highly recommended, but if I'm blunt, I was told to only have the director do the work for me.'

'Blunt's fine, Mr Hazel. It's Hugo you need to speak to.' Theo hears the clicking of keys. 'No free consultation slots for a month.' A pause. 'Manchester's a long journey.'

'I want the best job done and I was told Bliss would do the best job. It's not a big project. Okay... what about his business partner? Ed... Madden?' Theo has really thought about how he will approach this.

The girl on the other end of the line splutters. 'Ed? He's not a designer. I think you'd call him a sleeping partner.'

'Oh, I see.' There's an edge of dislike in her voice, as well as a hint of boredom. His call is probably the highlight of her morning, sitting at her desk in a shop in Derby that's likely often empty. Selling ideas and creative expertise is tough – he should know. Not much through traffic. The girl will talk for as long as he can keep her interest, and he's getting the distinct feeling that talking about Ed Madden is doing the job. 'So Mr Madden has no input into the business?' he asks.

'Ed comes over on a Saturday. He likes to take Hugo out for lunch. That's where they are now. Having lunch.'

'Ah, I see.' He thinks he does see.

'Ed is Hugo's boyfriend.'

'Lunch out of the office is always good, especially on a Saturday.'

'That's what Ed says.'

'Wise man. Do you work full-time...'

'Bella. My name's Bella Bliss. No, just Saturdays. Every fifth one off. I'm here next Saturday.'

Bella Bliss. Rose's visitor is talking to him on the other end of the phone. The line has gone quiet.

'You write books?' she says finally.

'I do. Are you googling me, Bella?'

'I am. Sorry. Says here you write non-fiction as well as literary fiction?'

'I do. And no need to be sorry. At all. I'm flattered.'

'Mr Hazel…'

'Please call me Theo.'

'Theo, Hugo's at the top of his game in the interior design business. If you're looking for the best, Hugo's the one.'

'I'll pop over next Saturday to have a look around the shop. Get ideas.'

'He has an hour just after lunch. He has a long lunch. Like I said, Ed takes him to the bistro.'

'Local?'

'There's only one.'

'Any good?'

'Not bad.'

'Might give it a try before I drive back.'

'I'll tell Hugo. So, he'll be here around two. Have to go, the other line.'

'Thanks, Bella. Catch you next week.' A second's pause. 'I really look forward to meeting you.'

Since Bella gave him her name, and he's connected the huge dots, his heart has been sprinting at the speed of Usain Bolt in the last fifty metres. Theo likes to think he's a man who is up on technology, but a phone call, real contact, always works, and certainly has done in this case. He puts the date in his digital diary with an alert for the day before, although this appointment he won't be forgetting.

34

On his drive to Bliss Interior Designs, Theo goes through in his mind what he's found out about Ed Madden. Born in Doncaster in 1945; his father was a miner, his mother worked as an administration clerk at the local railway station. Ed has one younger sister, but Theo hasn't been able to find out anything about her after she dropped off the radar in the mid seventies. Maybe she emigrated. Madden was a door-to-door hoover salesman. Before that, and after completing a City & Guilds course in Sheffield, he was a sous chef for a while. Odd career change.

It's more than clear that Rose never liked him; her hatred when talking about him is visceral.

Theo is keen to meet him. And Bella.

Bliss Interior Designs turns out to be easy to find. It's on the main shopping drag, although he counts only six shops. He circles the tiny town a couple of times, looking for somewhere to park, and whilst doing so spots the bistro where Ed and Hugo will be having lunch. At last he finds a car park.

He looks at his watch. Nearly one. He takes a walking detour to the bistro. Small and busy. He opens the door and noses inside, wondering if he'll spot the pair. He counts twelve tables. Four families with kids; five with groups of women, shopping bags littering the floor next to them; two tables of different-sex couples, and then, at the back, he sees two men. Bliss is easily recognisable, as he's at least thirty years younger than his companion. Dressed to perfection, and Theo finds himself wondering where he got that shirt. Loud pink and electric blue, the sort he'd love to wear himself. Gelled spiky jet-black hair and a face made for the front of *GQ* magazine, and although he's sitting down, Theo sees he's in good shape. He obviously takes care of himself, and Theo reasons that he'll be as fastidious with the quality of his work as he is with his appearance. His gaze moves to Ed Madden. What does Hugo Bliss see in him? Madden is ancient compared to the young, good-looking boyfriend. Several empty Desperados bottles litter their table.

A tall waiter is moving towards him, and quickly Theo turns to leave.

'Should have a table in about ten minutes,' the waiter says.

From the corner of his eye, Theo catches Ed Madden peering in his direction, shoving back his chair a little, his face puckered in inquisitiveness. Hugo Bliss, oblivious, is trying to gain the attention of the waiter; he does the writing thing with his index finger in mid-air, which never works for Theo.

'It's fine, but thanks,' Theo says, exiting quickly but feeling Ed Madden's eyes still boring into him.

That wasn't smart. He begins making his way to the shop, hoping it'll take a while for the pair to get their bill.

–

Bella is sitting at a modern desk; the shop is divided into four show sections: a bedroom, a kitchen, a lounge, and a bathroom. It is impressive, and Theo immediately sees Hugo Bliss's talent. She glances up from a Mac laptop, looking very much as she sounded. Young, no more than twenty-two or three, dark hair that hangs like an ironed silk curtain, unblemished white skin, and as he moves closer, piercing violet eyes glance up at him. Bella looks as original and striking as the designs surrounding her. A book lies spread-eagled next to the laptop. A George Saunders.

She grins. 'Mr Hazel?'

'It is.'

'Hugo'll be here soon. I have you booked in for an hour.' She pushes back her chair. 'He's often late after lunch with Ed, though, so have a look around, get a feel for what you might want.' She points to a rack of neatly filed brochures on the back wall. 'Have a nose through those. Would you like tea, coffee?'

'Tea'd be great, thanks.' He spots a crate of Desperados behind her desk; obviously Hugo's tipple of choice.

'On it.' She's on her way to a door situated to the left side of her desk, but stops and turns to him. 'I've read all your books.'

'You have?'

'In the last week, yeah. Onto a Saunders now.'

'Impressive.'

'My tutor says I should read stuff not linked to my course.'

'What course are you doing?' he asks, even though he knows.

'English lit. Manchester Uni.'

There's pride in her voice, and there should be. Theo picks up the Saunders. 'He's a much better writer than me.'

'I agree.' Her eyes sparkle like bluebells in a harsh spring frost.

'You're not supposed to say that.'

'You like fawning?'

'No, not really... well, maybe a little.' He grins. 'What are you doing here? It's a way from Manchester, as I know.'

'Hugo's my brother.'

Ah. The connection.

'I help him out on Saturdays,' she continues. 'And in the holidays. I stay with him, and Ed.' She spits out the name.

A waft of cool air blows past them, and Theo turns around. Ed Madden is striding into the shop as if he owns it – which, Theo's now thinking, he probably does.

'All okay, Bella?' he barks.

'All great.' She looks over his shoulder at her brother. 'Your two o'clock's here, Hugs, Theo Hazel.'

'Brilliant.' Hugo glances at Theo and smiles effusively. 'Give me five and I'll be with you.'

Hugs. Theo likes that.

Ed Madden loiters in the shop's entrance. He's one of those blokes who looks as if he's constantly grumpy; probably a trait he's always possessed. The worst of your characteristics seem to become more entrenched with time, and eventually supersede any good ones you might have. Theo speculates on what Ed's good ones might be.

Hugo lightly touches Madden's arm, a familiar and companionable gesture. Hugo seems like a nice guy. There must be something not immediately obvious about Ed Madden that encourages such loyalty and love. Theo is unsure if his own reaction to Ed is due to Rose's dislike for him, or because of what Abe thought about his father's old friend.

Ed smooths down the lapels of his jacket, a relic from sometime in the nineties. He wears a blue shirt and a tie. Theo's eyes scan down. Ed Madden is very thin. Drawn, his skin pasty. Madden catches his eye and Theo looks into his, which are rheumy. Standing next to Bella only accentuates his lack of vitality.

'You're the bloke who was in the bistro earlier.' Ed jerks out the words.

Bella chips in. 'This is Hugs's two o'clock client.'

Ed ignores her and continues to stare at Theo. 'What were you doing in there? I saw you looking at our table, then scarpering.'

Hugo's expression is one of indulgent exasperation. 'Give it a break, Ed,' he says. He checks his watch, a very nice Cartier with the signature sapphire; it glints in the unforgiving spotlights hanging over Bella's desk. 'Don't you need to get home?'

Ed nods, a small but definite movement. 'I do,' he replies, narrowing his eyes at Theo. 'Do I know you?'

'He writes books, Ed,' Bella says. 'About crimes committed in the past.' She turns to Theo. 'You investigate them, don't you?' Her violet eyes search his. Bella is not stupid. Maybe she's already made the connections. He's certain she has.

'I do write books like that, yes,' he replies, and takes a quick glance at Ed, whose countenance has slipped even further into waspishness.

'You're a journalist?' he asks.

'A writer, Ed,' Bella says. 'Do you need a hearing aid?'

'You really are a bad-mannered brat,' Ed snaps. He gives Theo the once-over and finally the muscles in his face spring to life. The pale eyes become smaller, the creases on his forehead deeper. 'You don't look like the sort to be employing Hugo's services.'

'Nor do you,' Theo replies instinctively. Ed doesn't appear at all ruffled by the quick retort. Bella smiles.

'I'll see you at home, Hugo,' Ed says, touching the younger man's arm affectionately. 'I'm doing a salmon en croute tonight – your favourite.'

'Fab,' Hugo says. 'I won't be late.'

Ed turns to leave, but not before giving Theo another glare. Then he rotates, literally, on his heels and exits the shop.

'I'm sorry about that,' Hugo says. 'Too many beers at lunchtime don't agree with him. Not carrying enough fat to take it.' He smiles indulgently.

'Was that all about the Marlowe thing?' Bella says to her brother in a conspiratorial tone.

Hugo nods, although his expression is now both serious and anxious. Lodging his behind on the desk, he places the heels of both palms on his temples and pushes hard for a few seconds. Then he pulls at his belt, tucks in his shirt more securely, rakes through his hair and checks his Cartier. At last he speaks. 'Are you writing about Rose Marlowe?'

Theo nods. 'Yes, I'm visiting her in prison with a view to writing a book about her case.'

'Ah.' Hugo crosses his arms over his chest. 'I see.' He pauses, unravels his arms. Darts a look towards his sister.

Bella gives him a gentle smile and nods her head gently.

'Okay,' Hugo sighs. 'I hope Bella told you to bring photos of your flat, the rooms you're interested in me working on?'

Bella shrugs. 'I'm sorry, Hugs. I forgot.'

Hugo slides his behind off the table. 'This isn't going well, is it?'

'It's going fine,' Theo says. He likes Hugo. Hugs.

'Look, Mr Hazel—'

'Please, call me Theo.'

'Theo, I'm happy to take on the job. I'm pretty booked up but I have to be in Manchester next week.' He glances at Bella again. 'Visiting my sis. I could come by your flat? We could do a consultation there… maybe have a chat? How does next Thursday sound?'

Christ, Theo really can't afford this. But to get Hugo Bliss alone can only be a good thing, and he is getting the impression that Hugo might be willing to tell him something. Maybe even wants to tell him something. 'That would be great,' he says. 'My lounge…' He may as well go for it. 'And the kitchen's a rat hole, need to do something with that too.' His gaze sweeps around the shop and the display. 'You definitely have an eye, Mr Bliss.'

'Call me Hugo. Have a look around the shop; anything takes your fancy, fabrics, furniture, ideas, jot it down and we can talk about it. Is that okay?'

'Really okay.'

'I'm sorry, but I have to go. Bella'll take your address, and email you prices and so on.' Hugo is staring at Theo. 'See you next week,' he finishes in a confident tone, as if he's made a decision, before turning and jogging from the shop.

Bella sits back down and pulls what looks suspiciously like a Primark handbag from underneath the table (Theo knows, because he bought one for his eleven-year-old niece only weeks before). It certainly doesn't fit in with the rest of the shop. She takes out a book and he recognises it immediately. His first published work: *Jane Toppen and the Sexual Thrill of Murder.* He still feels shame about that title. His editor insisted.

'Hugs is embarrassed about Ed's behaviour,' Bella says quietly. 'Without Ed, he would never have got a loan from the bank.'

'It's okay. I've had worse encounters.'

'Ed was in love with Daniel Deane, you know. It irks Hugs.'

Not wanting to come across as too hungry for info, Theo says as casually as he can, 'Why is Hugo with Ed?'

'He loves him. And as I said, Ed made all this,' she takes in the shop with her arms, 'possible. Hugs's dream.'

Theo nods. 'That's what you do for someone you love.' Time to take another chance. 'I know you went to see Rose Marlowe, Bella.'

Fear crosses her pretty features, and he feels really bad.

'Did she tell you?'

'No,' he replies softly. 'She didn't want to get you into trouble.'

'Sorry you came all this way for nothing today,' she says, touching his book.

'I didn't, though, did I?'

She shakes her head and her hair shimmers like Russian amber in the light. 'No, you didn't. I'd like it if Hugs could talk.'

'I do need my flat updating.'

'Can you afford Hugs?'

He can't, and the fourth credit card won't take the heat on this. He makes a mental note to apply for a fifth – the sort that charges a zillion per cent interest. His stomach contracts and his brain disengages.

'I'll email you the details then,' Bella says, cutting into his thoughts.

'Great.' He pauses and shifts his weight from one leg to the other. 'I didn't know you'd be here when I called to make this appointment.'

'Look, I shouldn't have gone to see Mrs Marlowe. It's up to Hugs to say something. I think he wants to say something.'

'Perhaps he does. I think that whatever the reason was you felt compelled to go and see her, she appreciated it.' He smiles at her.

'Good luck with Hugs next week.' She hesitates. 'I couldn't tell Rose what I wanted to tell her. I just couldn't. I waited for days after visiting her for the police to come. They didn't. Thank her from me.'

'I will, and I look forward to the email, and seeing Hugo.'

'You haven't looked around the shop.'

'I don't need to.'

'No, I don't think you do,' she says, her pretty forehead scrunching into what on anyone else would be a scowl. 'If you give Hugo a few Desperados, it'll loosen him up.' She searches his face, her own expression serious. 'He needs to unburden, and not just to me.'

'I'll bear it in mind, Bella.'

'I hope you do.'

He touches her arm lightly, then turns and leaves.

Walking back to his car, he has the uncomfortable and alarming feeling that Rose's story is about to get a lot darker.

35

25 April 2016

It's 9.30 on Monday morning and Theo's been up since four, thinking about Bella, Ed Madden, Hugo's impending visit, his lack of money, his failure, Elliot, and Rose. Always these days thinking about Rose.

He logs on to his bank account, and as he studies his negative balance, he tries to figure out how he can possibly pay for the services of an interior designer for his poky flat. It's untenable. A cold sweat breaks out and encompasses his whole body. He pulls his T-shirt from the waistband of his jeans and flaps it, the cool air circulating around his midriff. If, though, he's able to extract information from Hugo, information that he suspects Bella wanted to share with Rose in her prison visit, he won't have to follow through with work on the flat. He can easily pull out of the deal, whatever the outcome. He looks up and takes in the dingy room. He'd like to get something done though.

His landline rings out, bringing him away from his thoughts. Must be a cold caller; no one calls the landline.

Or rather, only one person these days.

He lurches around the flat looking for the phone, managing to get to it before it stops bleating. He returns to his study, the phone glued to his ear.

'Theo. Glad you picked up. I have good news that I didn't want to relay in an email.'

Yes, his editor. 'I like good news, Greg. Go on.'

'Acquisitions love your proposal for the Marlowe book.'

Theo's heart is beating inside his throat. 'That's good.'

Love is always preferable to *are interested in* or *like*.

'Two-book deal. This one and another non-fic.'

Greg is stringing it out, and although Theo is desperate, he's also desperate not to appear so. He waits.

'One hundred and fifty.'

'Pounds?'

'Stop dicking around, Theo. Thousand.'

Theo's heart is now in his mouth. 'Brilliant.'

'You're welcome. Publication date February 2017. Oh, and an outline for book two by the end of July this year. Non-negotiable.'

'No problem.'

The image of Greg inside Theo's head becomes less wolf and more owl, and he berates himself for swaying with the wind. His immediate financial problems are over. Maybe having Hugo, or someone like Hugo, revamp his flat is a possibility.

Does he really think he'll get any info out of Hugo? Bella seems to think he can. He isn't so sure, although if he did it would make him a more fulfilled man, and thinking of Rose, a happy man too. Elliot not dying would have made him happiest, but that isn't on the cards. Elliot is gone. Forever.

Yes, Rose could make him happy, a woman he's about to exploit. The beginning of a headache threatens; he rarely gets them these days and can guess why one is forming now. The advance. His bank balance. The conflict. Rose. Before anything else, before he tries to fix inside his head and make a decision about the way forward, he needs to find out the truth. The truth about Rose, the truth about Daniel Deane and his wife.

Having come back down to earth after Greg's call, he opens the notebook containing Natasha's information about Abe and carries on going through it.

At eighteen, Abe was desperate to get away from his parents, particularly his father, and made plans to pursue his medical studies in America. To the fair-haired young man, the dark-haired doctor turned businessman didn't seem like a father at all. Sometimes when things were very bad, and his parents argued well into the night, he would smell the aroma of cigarettes pervading the house; the only time his mother smoked. In his darker moments, he would fantasise that he'd been adopted. These thoughts permeated the most during the long nights when he couldn't sleep, when a jagged sense of something bothered him, although he looked just like his mother – everyone thought so.

His father didn't support his desire to become a doctor, but luckily his grandfather did. Abe loved his grandfather, and all the more because he knew Zakaria loved him back. He adored the time he spent at his grandfather's riad; sometimes his mother went with him to Morocco, and these were the happiest memories he possessed of her. She became a different person in the laid-back ambience of the North African country.

The determination to become a doctor lay in Abe's genes, together with the aptitude to easily pass exams, and it was only in the depths of his depression that he questioned whether people thought him cleverer than he really was. That was when he plunged deeper into the abyss.

He felt like a fraud. He felt as if he didn't belong.

He felt like an imposter in his own life.

He had believed his mother and Zakaria got on well enough, until the day – he would have been around eight – when during his afternoon nap in the bedroom that backed onto the courtyard of his grandfather's riad, he heard raised voices. The shutters of his room were closed, but the sound was loud. He opened the shutters and listened to his grandfather and mother arguing, the sound echoing. He was never sure if he'd heard properly, but what he did hear imprinted in the depths of his mind. He tried to forget, and over time he *did* forget, or pushed it so far away that it became a dream. It wasn't until he was expecting a child of his own with Natasha that the dream, the nightmare, came back.

When Abe fell in love with Natasha, it was only to his mother that he sent a photo. *Your father will not be happy*, she wrote back. But Abe married his love, only returning to England occasionally, and always alone.

Theo flips the pages, rereads, sits back in his chair and thinks. Was Abe adopted? It's something to think about. And what sort of parents were the Deanes? Not particularly good ones, it would seem. Natasha told him that as soon as Abe started his medical studies in the States, he made it his mission to find out more about his condition, which had become less severe and more manageable as he got older. He would never have been a top athlete, but he was stable, and probably healthier than most.

Theo swivels around in his chair, wipes his blackboard clean, and writes in pink chalk.

Ed, Rose, Abe

What is the connection? Daniel Deane

What did Bella want to tell Rose?

What does Hugo know?

Taking a swig of tea, he opens up a Word document. He has a creative writing class at the prison in the morning and is seeing Rose immediately afterwards. He loses himself in preparing, but eventually his mind jerks back to her. Her life, and Abe's, is embedded beneath his skin.

He wolfs down three slices of cheese on toast doused in Worcester sauce, then goes to the bathroom, which still has three boxes piled up in the corner, taking up at least a quarter of the floor space. Once he has brushed his teeth, he makes his way back to his study, where his mobile is alerting to him to a text from Sophie.

> Hope your new project's going well. Think about our offer. You gave me everything when we divorced. X

He did give her everything. Because he had no wish to keep any of it. Does he regret it? No, he does not. Money, possessions mean nothing to him, never have, never will. His mind flips to Marion Trahern, and Daniel Deane. Yep, he's a different creature to Marion and, he thinks, Daniel too.

To them, he suspects, money means everything.

36

26 April 2016

Theo leaves his flat at 7 a.m. to get to Peterborough prison for his 11 a.m. class. He stops off at a service station halfway to fill up with petrol.

In the shop, he uses the wrong credit card. It's declined. The woman behind the counter is staring at him with a vacant expression. As he fumbles inside his wallet for credit card number three, he feels an awkward lopsided smile form on his face. Finally he manages to pay.

'You need a VAT receipt?' she asks, her expression not cracking a fraction.

He nods, hoping he looks like a man who pays VAT.

Less than two hours later, after driving through incessant bulbs of rain for the entire journey, he arrives at the prison. Finally knowing the routine, he sails through security, but not before witnessing the confiscation of a folder containing a wad of innocuous-looking blank paper. He watches the security officer ripping a piece off and putting it in his mouth. The officer grimaces. Theo guesses that it's permeated with either spice or LSD.

Another officer says to him, 'Mr Hazel, you're in the canteen today for the class. Then at two, I have you down for a visit to Rose Marlowe.'

'That's right. The canteen?'

'There's no other room available. The staff have promised they'll be quiet, but they'll have to turf you out around twelve thirty to be able to serve the lovely fare.' He grins.

Theo nods, knowing there's no point in arguing. He'd better get a move on.

When he arrives, a kitchen worker is silently setting up the serving station. She inclines her head towards him and puts a finger to her lips, indicating that she'll try to keep the noise down. He smiles at her.

A group of women are already sitting around a large table. Everyone from his first session is here, and he notices a couple of new faces too. He ensures that his smile encompasses every one of them, remembering the writing course he signed up for when finally, more years ago than he wants to acknowledge, he decided to ditch journalism to write books. The tutor who ran the course seemed to get great satisfaction from playing off each desperate student against the others. Theo hated that course, a waste of a good grand, and at a time when he and Sophie needed the money. Elliot had only been four. Sophie's income wasn't supporting them, and Theo had just given up his day job. Bad move.

'Ladies, good to see you all again, and some new faces too.'

He moves towards the table and heads to sit next to Cathy. She was in his first class and he tagged her as the natural leader. A good-looking woman in her late twenties with a mane of jet-black hair – not dyed, no roots – who's been in here three years. She pulls out a chair for him. Theo retrieves her crime from his memory bank. She abandoned her three children for a four-week holiday in southern France. Her youngest child, who was only four, died whilst she was away – an underlying heart condition that Cathy knew nothing about. Her opening piece of creative writing in that first class was an excellent one thousand words on the death of her child, and the architecture of a rural village in France.

Theo likes Cathy, but she is utterly without remorse for what she did, or didn't do. There's something missing inside her brain that means she has no sense of right and wrong. And yet she's able to write quite beautiful prose. This has given him a lot to think about when he isn't thinking about Rose.

173

'What's on the cards today, Theo?' Cathy asks.

'Yeah,' says the woman sitting next to her. She's small, anxious-looking. Thin grey hair but with skin texture that tells him she's only in her thirties. Theo can't remember her name, but she was at the last session too. 'We all going to start writing a novel today?' she says a little too loudly.

'Sorry, remind me of your name?' he asks her.

Her narrow face falls into an expression of disappointment, and Theo hates himself.

'Emma,' she replies in a tone that reflects her hurt.

'I have a terrible memory for names, Emma, but a great one for faces. You were in the last session. I liked your work, I remember it.'

She gives him a dazzling smile and he tries not to notice the missing incisor on her left upper jaw.

He carries on. 'Today we're going to talk about tension in a story, and how to achieve it.' Taking off his coat, he places it on the back of his chair.

Cathy turns to him. 'Lots of tension in Rose Marlowe's story, don't you think, Theo?'

'Do you have a lot to do with Rose?'

'I like her.' She scrutinises him, her eyes alerting him to the fault that lies at her centre. 'She couldn't have done it, you know.'

'She told you that?'

The table descends into silence. Everyone listening.

'I never wanted kids,' Cathy says randomly.

More silence heaps into the space of the canteen. He waits for Cathy to expand.

'Rose did, though,' she continues. 'It's been everything to her. Not being able to have them. She wouldn't kill someone else's.' She takes off her trainer and begins picking at the heel of her left foot.

'Any idea who did, if it wasn't Rose?' he asks.

Cathy looks at the floor and doesn't answer.

Theo looks round the table. All the women, bar a few, are grinning at him with amusement. He will leave this for now.

'Okay,' he says. 'Today I'd like you to write a one-thousand-word story. Just spew it all out. The theme is finding out you are unable to have children. Does it make you happy, sad, angry?' He pauses. 'What potential conflict could this lead to? I want you to show me feelings, and then we'll go through a couple of individual pieces.'

He gives some direction on what he wants them to do and then sits back while they scribble, mulling over Cathy's words. He asked at reception earlier if Don Whiting was in the prison today. He is. He'll try to get to talk to him before he sees Rose.

When the time is up, he chooses three pieces of work, including Cathy's and Emma's. Within Cathy's story it isn't the female protagonist who is distraught at being unable to have children, but the protagonist's husband. It is the best piece, by far.

'Next week then, ladies? Either here or in the meeting room. For homework, I'd like you to write a poem.' A collective groan. 'Poetry allows the writer to explore and understand how every word counts. It's good practice.'

'Theme?' Cathy asks. 'You have to give us a theme, Theo.'

'Concealment.'

'Huh?' Emma says.

'A poem about the result of hiding something,' he explains. 'It can be hiding an emotion, a fact, keeping a secret. Go for it, ladies!'

The kitchen worker is now making a lot of noise; it's time to leave. All the women troop out, apart from Cathy. Theo turns in his chair to look at her. She peers at him, directing her gaze just above his head. 'Does Rose talk to you about what happened, what she did?' he asks.

'She's not a killer,' Cathy says.

'Look at me, Cathy.' Finally she finds his eyes, if only briefly. 'You think it was her husband?'

She shrugs. 'If he was the way Rose has talked about, then I could see him doing it, yeah.'

'What way does Rose talk about him?'

'He was into pharmaceuticals. He was a doctor, you know. Easy to get hold of.'

'I see.'

'Don't listen to me, though. I'm not quite right, am I?'

'You are unique, Cathy.'

He thinks he sees a smile loiter on her lips. She grabs her jumper and leaves the canteen.

Drugs. Miles. Theo sees a potential connection with his blackmail theory.

Picking up his own stuff, he makes his way to the communal meeting area with the coffee machine, in the hope he might bump into Don. He doesn't spot him and plonks himself on a chair; it's a while yet to visiting time. He closes his eyes, weariness filling him, and drifts off into a semi-nap.

'Theo.'

His eyes spring open.

'The writing class take it out of you?' Don is smiling broadly.

'Not enough sleep recently.' Theo stands and offers his hand. 'Good to see you again.' They exchange a quick handshake.

'I'm having a session with Rose after visiting time.' He sits back down but Don remains standing. 'Is Rose friendly with Cathy Ross, do you know?'

'Cathy?' Don says. 'Yes, I think they do talk. Cathy had a problem with chronic tiredness a few months back. The prison GP was at a loss to know what the problem was. It was Rose who suggested she was checked for pernicious anaemia. A shot of vitamin B12 did the trick.' Don looks at Theo. 'Why?'

'I just wonder if she has opened up to Cathy.'

Don sits in the chair next to him. 'Emotionally, you mean? I wouldn't be surprised. Because of Cathy's...' he coughs, 'matter-of-factness, shall we say, Rose may well feel she can open up to her. No danger of being engulfed by empathy.'

'Not all that she seems, though, Cathy,' Theo says. Don is telling him too much again, and although he appreciates this flaw in the man's professionalism, he's decided he really doesn't like the way Don operates. Although thinking of the restaurant and Marion, he isn't one to pass judgement.

'I can't discuss Cathy.'

'No, of course.'

'How are you getting on with Rose?' Don says.

'Good. She's still got a fair amount of her story to go, though.'

'Perhaps when she gets to the end, that will be when you hit the seam.'

'Maybe.' Theo shrugs.

'There's something I'm not getting, and if she shares something with you, I'd like to know. To help her.'

Don can't help Rose. But Theo can. He remembers Cathy's words. He needs to see Miles again.

He looks at his watch and pushes himself out of the chair. 'Right, visiting time.'

'It surely is, Theo.'

–

Walking into the visits hall, Theo glances around quickly. Today Rose is inclined back in her chair and looking much more relaxed. Her hair is down, and even from the doorway he can see she's wearing some make-up. A sliver of lipstick, maybe even some blusher. He nods to the custody officer and makes his way over, the hovering expectancy inside his stomach increasing as he approaches. The whole situation with Rose has taken him unawares, and he thinks about the book advance. Greg emailed the finer details after their phone conversation. They want well-written, but reading in between the lines, they also want copious amounts of tasteful salaciousness.

He can't do it.

She's watching him walk towards her. Those eyes, dark and brindled. Eyes that take you in and keep you there, locking you inside so you can't get out. Although no man would want to leave. Theo certainly doesn't.

'You look pleased with yourself, Theo,' she says.

'Thanks for turning up.'

'Of course I turned up. Why wouldn't I?' She peers at him from underneath thick lashes, but today, despite her light mood, he's more aware of the lines crossing her forehead, the spidery crawl around her eyes, the greyness that fills in the fragile skin beneath. Underneath her facade, she looks unwell. 'As it happens,' she carries on, 'I didn't have much on today.' She wriggles in the chair. 'You already done your class?'

'I have.'

'Cathy loves them.'

'She does, I think. You two friends?'

'I like Cathy, she doesn't judge.'

'Do you judge her?'

'It's not my place to judge anyone in here. That's already been done.'

'True.'

'Her angst about having kids she didn't want is just as strong as mine about not having the kids I did want.'

He's sitting now, facing her, leaning forward. She has perfume on. He likes to think it's for him. Perhaps Miles brought it in for her. Guilt surges through him.

'How did Miles feel about you not being able to have children?' he asks.

'Sad.'

He takes an extended breath, as if finding more oxygen will help him say the right thing. 'Miles was at the hospital the day of Abe's death, on duty in the unit where Abe was recovering.'

'So was I. Abe's mother was there too.'

'Did it matter to you that you were put in here, Rose?'

178

She moves her head, and a curl drops in front of her left eye. 'Of course it did.'

'*Did* it?'

'Let me carry on with my story. That's why you're here, not to question whether I'm guilty or not. I am. I was found guilty at the hearing.'

'Because you admitted to doing it.'

'Because I *did* do it.'

'But now. Would you want to leave this place *now*?'

She avoids his gaze. 'Sometimes, Theo. Sometimes.'

'Okay, let's carry on.' He pulls out his notes. 'You've been to your mum's, and you're about to go to Spain.'

'Have you heard from my mother?' she asks him.

He can't lie, although he knows he should. 'She said she's been busy.' He spills about Sam, and the house in Majorca, the proposed holiday that isn't happening now. He doesn't mention Scandal, or the conclusions he drew from his meeting with Marion there. He won't mention Bella and Hugo yet either.

Rose pulls her hair into a bun and deftly ties it with a bobble from her wrist. 'Anything strike you about my mum, Theo?'

'I've found out some stuff from her that's made things clearer.'

'Like what?' she asks, suddenly alert, and suddenly too finding the quick of her nails.

'I think she was definitely aware of Abe's existence, a long time before your arrest. I believe she knew that Daniel Deane had a child – a son – after your split from him.'

Rose inclines her head, and then bends forward, holding her arms across her chest. 'I have no idea where her money is coming from.'

'You do, though, don't you?' he asks gently.

'You'll find out everything you can, won't you?'

'I will.' Splinters of icy pain shoot through Theo's veins. He shivers.

'Cold in here today, isn't it?' Rose rubs her hands together. It's surprisingly warm in the visits hall. 'Come on,' she says. 'Let me carry on. It's the finale.'

'Take your time.' Her arm is resting on the table and he reaches over and touches her.

'I will,' she replies. 'Off to Spain.' She pulls back her hair again. 'This is the longest part of my tale. Buckle up, Theo.'

37

Rose

3 July 1991

In the end, I persuaded myself that being in Spain with my placement revision notes and Daniel was much more appealing than sitting reading them in my damp-infested room. I was burying my head regarding the placement; something I rarely did, but doing so because orthopaedics was the area of medicine I was least interested in and therefore less good at. My placement hadn't started that well either, with the late submission of my pre-placement study. Mr Warner was one of the leading orthopaedic surgeons in the world. I'd met him once and disliked him, and I was soon going to be spending six weeks in his company. I hadn't told any of the faculty that I was pregnant. Daniel had suggested I shouldn't, and I knew he was right. *Leave it as long as possible*, he'd said. I certainly didn't want Mr Warner knowing. I'd be dead meat before I even started.

I'd packed a small suitcase, and a holdall stuffed with all my revision stuff. I didn't have a bikini, and couldn't remember the last time I'd got to wear one. Casey had lent me hers but she was tiny, and I convinced myself my boobs were already filling out; it would never fit. I'd packed it anyway. It lay at the bottom of my suitcase.

Our flight was at three. I checked the clock. Nearly midday already. I assumed we were flying from East Midlands. I'd forgotten to ask Daniel the night before on the phone; he'd just wanted to check I had my passport, but I was sure we should be there two hours before the flight.

The bell echoed through the dingy hall. I pulled on a jacket and opened the door. Daniel was standing there all calm and relaxed and looking as if he were on holiday already.

'All set? Got your revision stuff?'

'I have.' I picked up the holdall, which weighed a ton, and gave it to him. 'I bet you haven't as much luggage as me.'

He stuck his hands in both pockets and pulled out a pair of underpants from one, socks from the other. 'Nope.' He grinned.

'You do make me laugh.'

'I keep clothes at the villa.'

I checked the clock again. 'Aren't we cutting it fine to get to the airport?'

'Plenty of time. C'mon, the taxi's waiting.'

'I thought Ed'd be taking us?'

'Ed's coming with us.'

'To the airport?'

'No, to Spain.'

'You're joking?'

'I know he can be prickly. It's just the way he is. But he could do with a holiday too. It's my way of thanking him for all his help.'

'He doesn't like me, Daniel.'

'Ed likes very few people.'

'Who *does* he like, apart from you?'

'My sister, Abigail. She's already at the villa. She's really keen to meet you, Rose. I tried to put her off, but she was adamant. Sorry.'

'Why sorry? I'll love meeting her.'

He didn't look convinced. 'She's been having a tough time of it recently, so take her with a pinch of salt. Abigail can be blunt when things aren't going her way.'

'I'm sorry to hear things aren't good for her. Anything I should know?'

He shut the front door behind us. 'Problems with our dad, you know, family stuff. They tend to argue a lot. Don't see eye to eye.'

I felt I could understand this. 'I know what it can be like, navigating your way around parents.' I paused. I didn't really want to bring my mum into the conversation, but I did anyway. 'Heard anything about how it's going with my mother at Bluefields?'

'All good, so Ed tells me.'

'Ed?'

'She's had problems getting in for work occasionally, so he picked her up. It's what he does, sorts things, and he likes your mum.' He winked at me.

God, Ed and my mum. The thought made me feel queasier than I already did.

'Does Abigail know?' I patted my stomach.

'Course she does! She's my sister. I tell her everything.'

Once on our way, I took in Daniel's profile, his softened features. He grabbed my hand, squeezed it, and a current of desire ripped through me. I glanced at the driver, and at Ed in the front passenger seat, peering ahead at the road. The car pulled up sharply at a junction and he turned around, shook his head.

Almost imperceptible.

38

When we got out of the car at the airport, it was freezing. Daniel put his coat around my shoulders, and as he did so, I peered up at a plane skimming along in the sky above and pulled at his elbow.

'You okay?' he asked. 'Warm enough now? The weather in southern Spain is forecast to be great, so you won't be needing a jacket there.' He looked at me more closely, 'What's the matter, Rose?'

'I've never flown before. I'm scared.'

He laughed, then stopped abruptly. 'Seriously?'

'Yep. My heart's around a hundred and forty at this very moment.'

He swung around. 'Ed, do you have my beta blockers on you?'

'No, but I think I put some in my suitcase. Do you want me to find them?' Ed's tone had slid to one of concern. I couldn't imagine Daniel ever needing anything to calm him down.

'For Rose.'

'Ah.' His expression morphed into indifference.

'It's fine, Daniel, I can't take them anyway,' I said, again patting a non-existent bump.

'Of course you can't. You do look terrified.' He pulled me into his arms. 'Don't worry, I'll distract you.' But then he took a step backward and studied me. 'Shall we call it off? Stay home? It's not a problem.'

'No, don't be silly. I'll be fine. I'll sleep.'

'Good girl.'

184

Ed gave me a sideways glance that I ignored.

'What is it with Ed?' I asked once he was out of earshot, heading towards check-in.

'He's a bit jumpy. His mum's not well.' Daniel took me by the elbow. 'Let's get some disgusting coffee.' He smiled. 'Well, maybe you should have decaffeinated.'

—

Less than two hours later, I was on a plane for the first time in my life, and two hours after that, as I left imprints in the palm of Daniel's hand, we touched down in Malaga. After going through customs, Daniel and I made our way to the airport entrance. He had arranged a taxi to his dad's villa. Ed had volunteered to pick up the luggage.

We came into Nerja along the coastal road; the sea was a dark velvet blue in the distance, a lighter cerulean at the fringes near the beach. I opened the car window and gazed out. It was so different from the sea in Devon, Cornwall and the south coast of Wales. I couldn't believe I'd reached twenty-two and never been abroad.

I loved Spain immediately: its warmth, the smell of evaporating salt, of heated dust on the road, the sound of church bells resonating from the hills. Even sitting inside the car there was a distinct and pleasant scent of a flower that I didn't recognise but that faintly reminded me of a perfume from my youth.

'What's that smell?' I asked, my nose out the window.

'Either cinnamon, a smell that permeates through this part of Spain, or Spanish lavender. Probably the lavender you're picking up on. Gorgeous, isn't it? It's blossomed a little early this year; the season's a week or two ahead of schedule. Everything blooms in Spain.' Daniel hauled me over to him, playfully taking a handful of my hair. 'Like you, Rose. Blooming and fertile.'

'I can't wait to put Casey's bikini on, although it won't fit me properly. And get my notes out.'

'The notes can wait till tomorrow, eh? And I'll buy you a new bikini.'

I touched his knee. 'Yeah, tomorrow, and thanks.'

Ed said something in Spanish to the driver, who nodded and put his foot down. I swayed to one side as he took a curve in the road, surprised that Ed spoke Spanish.

Daniel laughed. 'Nearly there.'

We bypassed the town, heading up into the hills, making our way along a neatly tarmacked road, which came to an end at a gated entrance. Daniel got out and opened the gates, and in front of me sat an unostentatious whitewashed villa. A veranda ran across the frontage, blue and yellow flowers engulfing most of it. To the right was a small swimming pool with blue and yellow loungers dotted around, matching the flowers.

Ed leaned sideways, opened the car window and waved. He was smiling. A rare thing, I'd discovered. I looked closer. A woman was standing in the doorway, leaning against a thick beam and framed by the sun that poured in from the west. Abigail, I surmised. She was tall, same height as me, her hair, a light honey blonde, settled around her shoulders in corkscrew curls, and as I peered closer, I saw something of the carving in Daniel's bedroom, and something of me. She was smiling too, and her expression was inquisitive.

Ed had got out the car and was making his way towards her. I'd never seen him so animated. He *did* like someone other than Daniel. Daniel's sister.

'Abigail promised me she'd come over to make sure everything was ready.' Daniel said this not looking at me, but staring at his sister.

'I thought she'd be staying here?'

'No, she's staying in an apartment in Nerja town.'

'Ah.'

I opened the car door and the smell of lavender hit me. Ed was embracing Abigail. A thought crossed my mind then, that maybe something was going on between the two of them. The thought of Ed actually having a relationship with anyone made me cringe inside. They exchanged words I couldn't hear, and then Ed disappeared into the villa.

Daniel took my arm and we walked towards Abigail. She wore a white beach dress, and a white bandanna was wrapped stylishly around her head. I estimated her to be anything between early and mid thirties, but I knew she was older than Daniel, so she must be late thirties. She looked good for her age. Sheer freckled skin, no make-up. A slim smile hovered around her mouth and her line of vision moved towards Daniel's hand as it rested on my forearm.

'Rose.' She made her way down the two steps. 'I've heard so much about you.' She glanced at her brother. 'He's so taken.'

Daniel hugged her, then looked back at me. 'Taken with you, Rose, she means.' Abigail's tawny eyes settled on me, appraising; it was probably what sisters did. I felt the pressure of Daniel's fingers on my skin as well as the warmth of the Spanish late-afternoon sun. 'How are you, Abigail?' he asked her.

'Coping, little bro.' She turned her gaze on me. 'I've heard your wonderful news. Congratulations.'

'Thank you. A little unexpected, but—'

'But it's great.' Her eyes settled on my stomach.

'I won't show for a while yet,' I said.

A faint tinge of pink appeared on the apex of her cheekbones, and this sign of embarrassment surprised me. Abigail was very much like her brother, I'd decided immediately, self-assured and confident, but as I well knew, looks could be deceiving.

'No, I'm sure you won't.' She took a few steps nearer. 'What does it feel like?'

Before I could reply, Daniel had taken hold of my elbow. 'Let's go inside. Time you got out of the sun, Rose.'

I dug into his arm with a knuckle. 'You sound like a mother!'

'He sounds like an expectant father, Rose,' Abigail said quietly. 'He's looking after the mother of his child.' Her expression, though, was filled with amusement.

There was definitely a little bit of family conflict between brother and sister; subtle, but it was there. I wanted to let them talk but didn't want to go inside alone in case I ended up with Ed. Instead, I took in this microcosm of Spain. It was a lovely place and I had the greatest desire to jump in the pool and submerge myself in its cool water.

'I'll see you all later,' Ed said, emerging from the villa. 'I'm off to Abigail's flat. A leak in the bathroom. The landlord'll take forever to fix it, so I'll see what I can do.' He addressed all of this to Daniel and Abigail, ignoring me. 'There's a nice supper in the kitchen. Señora López has been busy.'

A woman appeared. Señora López, I assumed. She was very handsome and didn't look old enough to be married. *Stupid thought, Rose. You're old enough to be having a baby.* She walked towards Daniel.

'Good to see you, Señor Daniel.'

'You too. Always good to see you.' He winked, and Señora López blushed, then he turned back to Ed. 'It's okay if you stay at Abigail's. I know you prefer it nearer to the sea.'

Ed nodded. 'I may well do.'

And off he went. Thank God.

'Why don't you freshen up and go for a dip, Rose?' Abigail said to me.

'Thanks, I'd love that.'

She gave me a brilliant smile. 'I'll show you to your room.'

'You do that, Abigail. I need to make a few phone calls,' Daniel said, disappearing around the back of the villa.

I followed Abigail towards the main door. We walked through the open-plan entrance and into the building's cool interior. It was completely different to the house in Nottingham – hints of Spanish culture, but modern and slick in its cream and dark-wood decor.

'Has the family had this place very long?' I asked.

'Daniel bought it ten years ago.' She paused. 'I think. Terrible memory.'

I'd thought he'd told my mum the villa was their dad's. Maybe he was embarrassed that he owned another home, I reasoned. I decided not to question Abigail further, saying instead, 'If he were my brother, I think I'd be here all the time.'

'Yes, I do come pretty regularly.'

'You didn't have to stay somewhere else, you know.' By then we were in the kitchen, which seemed to be the only part of the villa that was traditionally decked out. All wood and pretty quaint fabrics.

'I know, but the truth is, I like it in town.' Abigail swept her arm towards the table laden with food. 'I hope you're hungry,' she carried on, her tone almost conspiratorial. 'Señora López does like to look after Daniel.'

'It looks amazing,' I replied, checking out the table.

'Daniel thinks Señora L is amazing.' She folded her arms.

Ignoring what I felt was her loaded comment about Señora López, I said, 'I appreciate it. Food often isn't the top of the agenda on our course.'

'I'm sure.' She paused. 'How are you going to manage your course and having a baby?'

'We'll work something out.'

'Do I hear wedding bells?'

I laughed. 'I'm really not sure.'

'Well, I think there should be.' She looked pointedly at my stomach.

I wanted to ask her what she did for a living. Maybe she didn't work. Maybe she didn't have to.

She broke into my thoughts and I realised she'd been analysing me. 'Come on, I bet you're knackered. I'll take you to your room so you can freshen up.'

The villa was on one level and Daniel's room was located at the rear of the property. Abigail pushed open the door with her foot but didn't step inside, waiting on the threshold.

'Just give me a shout if you need anything. Looks like Ed brought your luggage in.' She pointed to the bags sitting neatly on the queen-size bed. 'I'm off back to the flat. I've booked a table at Daniel's favourite restaurant in town tomorrow for lunch. Three o'clock. Hope that's okay with you?'

'Sounds great.'

'Make yourself at home. I'm glad you came, Rose.'

'Me too. It's so nice to meet you.' I'd had a terrible feeling we wouldn't get on, but Abigail seemed perfectly okay. I was thinking that her problem wasn't with me, but more her brother.

I turned to the bags on the bed. I'd bought her a small gift that I'd shoved in the holdall with my revision stuff, which I'd checked into the plane's hold. That probably hadn't been my best idea. I hadn't checked either when Ed had brought the luggage to the car at the airport. I stared at the bed.

'Is there a problem?' Abigail said, concern lacing through her voice.

'My holdall with my work in isn't here.'

'Don't worry. I'll get Ed to check. Maybe he left it in the taxi by mistake. It's no problem. We know the taxi company well.'

I sat on the bed. 'I hope so, because I need it.'

'Have a swim and relax, Rose. I'll sort out your bag.'

Trying to distract myself and not appear obsessive, I opened my suitcase and retrieved Casey's bikini. I held it up and looked at it, then smiled at Abigail. 'My mate's. It's far too small.'

'It does look it. Just put a T-shirt over the top,' she said with a grin, and in that moment, she really did look very like her brother. 'I'll see you tomorrow.'

'Sure.'

She turned, a vision of white, and disappeared, leaving that lingering aroma that seemed to permeate the entire villa. Cinnamon.

I put on the bikini and, as Abigail had suggested, pulled a long T-shirt over the top. I was so tired, my mind splintered. I glanced in the mirror that took up half of one wall, but all I could see was Abigail's image.

Trying to forget about my missing bag, I made my way back to the main living space and the doors that opened onto the pool area. Taking a deep breath, I dived in. The water, though, was warm, like heated liquid silk on my skin.

I'd been swimming for no more than fifteen minutes when I heard Daniel. 'Rose! C'mon. Let's eat!'

Ignoring the pool steps, I pulled myself out easily. Daniel handed me a towel.

'Thanks... Daniel, my holdall isn't here. Abigail says it might still be in the taxi. I'm panicking.'

'Relax. She'll sort it.' He gathered me to him. 'I sent Señora López home. We're alone.'

He'd changed into shorts and a T-shirt with *Big Boss* on the front. He looked different. Both the shorts and T-shirt were tatty and old, unlike the clothes he usually wore. He was at home within the villa's space, and I wondered about Morocco and the house his dad lived in. Then I thought of Abigail and her place in Herefordshire. A family so split. But then I forgot all those thoughts as Daniel led me towards the doors and inside, guiding me to a sofa.

'Not here,' I said, smiling, but something about seeing him so free, uninhibited and reckless tore into me.

He unclasped my bikini top and peeled down the bottoms. His fingers touching and probing, I felt him so near, and my hand moved down his back and inwards to where we were meeting. The orgasm rolled and twisted towards my stomach, down into my thighs, loading my entire body and finally merging into a breathless tightness inside my chest. I let out a cry, and then I heard Daniel's, and felt his palms holding my face.

He dropped a soft kiss onto my forehead, causing a fluttering inside my stomach, but then an image of white hovered as a ghost inside my mind, and for a beat the flutter increased in strength, moving towards my throat.

It took my breath away.

The room was silent, nothing but peace and solitude, until the sound of something, a clinking, came from the direction of the kitchen, and my body tensed.

'Someone's here,' I said.

'Hush, no one's here.'

I looked over his shoulder and thought I saw a hint of white, a suggestion of scent, of cinnamon, but then it was gone. I grabbed the towel, wrapping it tightly around me.

He pulled on his shorts. 'I'll get us a drink. Relax. We'll find your bag tomorrow, don't worry. That's what's worrying you, isn't it?'

It *was* worrying me, nearly as much as the image and the smell, but maybe I had overreacted. I was imagining things; smells and noises. 'A drink would be good.'

While Daniel was in the kitchen, I made my way across the room towards the window, noticing the uneven colour of the white paint on the far wall. Obviously he didn't take quite as much care with the decorating in the villa as he did with his house in Nottingham, his ruffled clothes compounding this Spanish trait.

I stared at the wall, waiting for Daniel to return with the drinks.

–

After making love again and eating Señora López's food in bed, we slept. When I woke up, the sun had disappeared. I checked my watch as Daniel snored quietly beside me. Eleven. A raging thirst encouraged me to reluctantly get up and make my way to the kitchen. I didn't bother putting on the T-shirt, and wore only knickers. Craving a Coke, I headed to the fridge, and then heard a clunk. I swivelled around, arms across my breasts, thinking it was Señora López or Abigail.

It wasn't either. Ed was staring at me.

'You scared me.' Frantically I looked for something to cover myself, but only found a tea towel, which I pressed against my chest. Ed didn't move, didn't flicker a reptilian eyelid. Had he been there earlier, when we were making love in the lounge? The thought made me want to vomit.

'Look, can you...' My eyes darted around the kitchen. 'Pass me that jumper on the back of the door.'

He moved over, retrieved it, threw it at me. I put it on. 'The taxi company can't find your bag. You must have forgotten it,' he said.

'I didn't forget it.'

He shrugged in the way only Ed could. 'How can you be so unseeing, Rose?'

'What's your problem with me?'

'None. Absolutely none.'

'I need my stuff,' I said.

'Ed, I've told you to buzz when you come in.' Daniel stood in the doorway, tousled with sleep and completely naked.

I threw a look at Ed. No reaction; or perhaps a little, as I watched his gaze move to Daniel's penis, which was half erect.

Daniel carried on, oblivious. 'Have you got Rose's bag?'

'Taxi company don't have it.'

He shook his head and left the kitchen, returning a few minutes later wearing a pale grey silk kaftan. He put his arm around me. 'Don't worry. I've some old notes here you can look at, and textbooks.'

Ed watched for my reaction. I didn't give him the satisfaction. I was pregnant and I was going to fail the placement. Tears stung my eyes.

'Ed, can you tell Abigail we can't make the lunch tomorrow. Tell her I'll call her.'

'Of course.' He left without saying another word.

–

The next few days passed without incident. I sunbathed, I swam, I read Daniel's old textbooks. He talked me through orthopaedic clinical practice. It was late in the afternoon, and I was lying on a sunbed when a shadow fell over me.

'Hey you. Enjoying yourself? Ed and I missed you at the restaurant.'

'Abigail, so nice to see you. I did want to come.'

I hadn't really wanted to, but that was only because I was certain Ed would be there. Daniel deciding not to go had surprised me a bit, but families were often a law unto themselves. And I knew that relationships between siblings could be particularly tricky. Mine with Sam hadn't been what it should have been these last few years. He was turning into someone I didn't know, becoming more and more like our mother – economical with the truth, and somehow missing the inherent moral compass most of us were born with – and this concerned me. He had already been in trouble with the police.

'It was a fabulous lunch,' Abigail carried on. 'Lovely group of people who it would have been nice for you to meet seeing as you're now part of the family.'

As she talked, I slipped my sunglasses down my nose and looked up at her. Today she wore a sky-blue maxi dress, white sandals, a glint of diamonds in her ears, though for all I knew they could have been fake. It wasn't these material accessories that caught my attention, though; more her facial expression, or lack of it. Or maybe I was imagining things again. Or maybe she *was* annoyed that Daniel and I hadn't gone for lunch with her. Maybe she was pissed off with me. I didn't want her to be pissed off with me. I wanted things to be smooth. Having the jagged relationship with Daniel's mate was enough.

'I'm hoping I'll come again. So next time?' I said with the biggest smile I could find.

She plonked herself down on a lounger. 'I'm sure you will.' I pushed my sunglasses back up my nose. 'I've bought you a present.' She gently thrust a bag into my lap.

'You shouldn't have done, honestly, but thanks.'

'You didn't have a decent bikini, so I chose one for you.' She made a point of staring at Casey's bikini top. Either it had shrunk in the last few days, or my boobs really had grown. I pulled the contents out of the bag. Bright red. Scarlet.

'Do you like it?' she asked.

'I do.'

'Put it on, let's see if it fits. Mind you, I'm guessing it'll be too small in a few months.'

'I'll go and get changed inside—'

'Rose, you don't strike me as the shy sort. We're all girls together. Slip it on here.' She paused a moment. 'There's only Daniel around, and me. You have nothing I haven't got, no? And certainly nothing he doesn't know about.'

A slow heat ran through my body with her words, even though I knew she was right. And I wasn't the shy sort, at all. Med school beat that out of you. 'Honestly, I'll go inside.'

'Suit yourself,' she said, lifting her shoulders a fraction and making me feel gauche, unworldly, and too young.

I was beginning to wish I'd questioned Daniel more about his sister so that I knew more about her, although I did know she didn't have children. I assumed she wasn't married, but she might well have been divorced. I took a look at her ring finger. A definite white mark. Maybe that was why she and her dad were at loggerheads. A recent divorce.

I went inside to put the bikini on. It fitted perfectly.

When I returned to the poolside, Daniel was sitting upright in my lounger next to his sister, his hand resting on her knee. Suddenly I was utterly self-conscious.

'Great fit,' he said.

I grabbed my T-shirt and quickly put it on.

'Excellent fit, yes,' Abigail said, looking pleased.

'You look amazing, Rose,' Daniel said.

'I'll be making a move and leave you two in peace.' Abigail got up. 'See you both back in England.' She bent forward and kissed her brother on the lips.

'Have a good trip,' I said.

Despite the hassle with my bag, which the taxi company finally found on the day we were due to go home, my body sighed with physical contentment on the flight back to England. It was good that I'd met Daniel's sister, but although I liked what I'd seen of her, I wasn't quite sure if I'd seen anything other than what she'd wanted me to see. My last impression of her was her kissing Daniel; it had left an imprint inside my mind that persisted for hours after her departure. But during our Spanish sojourn Daniel and I had talked a lot about the baby, and the plan of action regarding my course. My placement loomed, but I'd get through it. And we'd take everything from there.

39

I was sitting on the edge of the bed in the sterile nurses' accommodation bedroom at the Leeds Royal Infirmary where the esteemed orthopaedic consultant Mr Michael Warner worked. Daniel had dropped me off the day before, saying I'd have time to get organised before the start of the placement.

It was just before 6 p.m. and the evening sun was still gushing through the greasy window. My stomach grumbled, and although I was hungry, I couldn't face eating. The nausea had got a lot worse since Spain. I'd bought food and put it in the communal fridge, but I had no inclination to cook anything, and so I just sat there and mulled over my melancholy.

I was feeling vulnerable and insecure after failing my writtens, although I'd been sent a letter from Wilko himself informing me I could retake. Daniel had been great, supporting me a hundred per cent. On the journey to Leeds he'd concocted all sorts of plans about how I'd continue my studies, pass the re-sits and finish the course and still be able to be a mum to a new baby. But now, here, I realised the morning sickness wouldn't allow me to function at my best. Mr Warner would be an absolute devil to be a student under at the best of times. This wasn't quite how I'd planned this part of my life, but already I loved the baby with a driving passion. And I loved Daniel too.

The thoughts were still swirling round my head as I got into bed, but I was exhausted, and with the sun on my face and an empty stomach, I quickly fell asleep.

I woke up the next morning to tapping on my door. One of the other students on the same placement as me. Stella.

'Rose, some bloke's just delivered flowers.'

I looked at the clock. 6.30 a.m. I'd slept for hours. We had to be in the hospital's main reception to meet Mr Warner at 8.30 on the dot. I jumped out of bed, opened the door. 'Who?'

'I'm guessing the flower delivery company? But he didn't look like a delivery man.'

I moved quickly towards the greasy window that overlooked the car park and saw the MG. I peered closer. Ed in the driving seat. Daniel had sent him all that way to deliver flowers. Typical. Ed would have hated having to do it. My mood brightened. 'It's my boyfriend's mate, I think.'

'It's a huge box. They're in the kitchen. Someone loves you, Rose,' Stella said, grinning at me.

I liked Stella. She studied at Queen Mary in London. I'd been offered a place there, and for a moment I wished I'd taken it, because then I'd be on the same course as her. But if I had taken the place I wouldn't have been near my mum and Sam, and I wouldn't have met Daniel. And I wouldn't be pregnant and hanging by my teeth onto the course and career I'd always wanted.

I rushed down the two flights of stairs to the kitchen, Stella behind me.

The flowers were beautiful. I read the card.

With love, Daniel. Good luck, and keep our little family safe. X

'I'll put them in a vase for you while you get ready.' She surveyed my dishevelled appearance.

'Thanks, Stella. You're a peach.'

I was in my room when I heard screams coming from the kitchen. I ran back down the stairs.

Stella was standing there, the flowers on the table, an old tin hospital-issue vase ready to go. Her hands were covered in blood. 'Your boyfriend's a nutcase, Rose.'

'What is it?'

She moved to the sink and picked up a mass of I-didn't-know-what. I stared at it. Viscera. Wrapped in cling film. Nausea overcame me. I pulled at the thin plastic. It looked like a uterus; I'd seen a few during my surgical placements. I peered closer. Definitely a uterus, but not a human one. Probably a cow, a sheep, maybe. I looked around for a plastic bag, found one and put the thing inside. Cleared up the sink. Stella hadn't moved.

'Wash your hands,' I said. 'I'll deal with this. I don't want you to be late for the first meet with Mr Warner. Where was this?' I pointed to the mass inside the bag.

'In the bottom of the bouquet box. Bloody hell, Rose.'

I felt so sick; I had no idea how I'd cope with the first day at the hospital.

Stella left. I carried on clearing up. I put the flowers in the bin along with the bag holding the uterus. Then I went to the communal loo and threw up.

I didn't know what to think, but I couldn't think about anything, because I *had* to make the 8.30 start.

–

That first day was a nightmare. I couldn't remember anything about the human body, and Mr Warner clearly hated me. Stella kept me going and knew enough not to ask me anything. But she was aware I'd been throwing up most of the day.

It took Mr Warner and his cronies a week to put two and two together, and another week for them to recommend a termination of my placement. When they used that phrase, *termination*, I laughed uncontrollably. Then began to cry.

That was when Stella asked who she could call to come and pick me up. I gave her Daniel's number.

I hadn't mentioned the flowers or the uterus to Daniel in the calls we'd made to each over the past grim two weeks. I'd thought about it, but then the misery of the placement overtook my anger at Ed, and to some extent at Daniel for having a mate like him.

I waited for Daniel in the car park with a holdall on the ground either side of me.

'You can finish your training after the baby's born, defer a year,' he said, putting the bags in the boot. Then he opened the door and helped me in.

I stared out of the window at the rain, waiting for him to get into the driver's seat. 'Daniel, did you ask Ed to deliver flowers on my first day?'

'I did. You never mentioned you'd got them and I didn't want to press or hassle you. I wanted you to settle in.' He glanced at me. 'What's wrong?'

'Apart from me being kicked off the placement and undoubtedly kicked off the course?'

'They can't kick you off the course for being pregnant.'

'They'll find a way, and anyway, I'm quitting.' He didn't respond, and I carried on. 'Ed put something in the bottom of the flower box.'

'What?' He turned to look at me.

'A cow or sheep's uterus, I'm guessing. Does he know I'm pregnant?'

No response.

'Daniel?'

'Yes. Look, did Ed give you the box?'

'No, he gave it to Stella, another student. I was in my room.'

He burst out laughing. 'That old trick, eh? Your mates pulled a prank on you, Rose. Don't tell me you've been a med student for four years and no one has done anything like that before?'

They had. In my second year, I'd been told to take the vital signs of a geriatric on ICU. He had pancreatic cancer, final stages, and was intubated. I couldn't find a pulse. I pretended

I had, like students often did. I remembered saying it was 98. The man had died an hour before. My supervisor and a few of the other students were huddled at the other side of the unit, sniggering. Once I'd got over my mortification, we had a laugh about it. The humour amongst med students was juvenile as well as black.

I allowed myself a smile. 'It has happened before, yes.' I fell quiet. 'But Stella told me she'd put the flowers in a vase for me. Why would she do that if she intended me to find it? And her shock at finding the uterus was as genuine as mine.'

'Sounds as if Stella is a good actress as well as a budding doctor. I don't know, but honestly, that's what it was: a silly med student prank.' He picked up a pack of mints and popped one in his mouth. 'Those flowers cost me a fortune.'

He'd put it into perspective. Stella had been great, but she was a bit mischievous. Fun. Like I'd been once, though then I wondered if I ever had been any fun. 'I don't know what's wrong with me.'

'Hormones,' he replied.

I tutted at the male response. Briefly he touched my knee, his hand high up on my thigh, and for the first time since meeting him, there was no spark of sexual anticipation.

He carried on. 'It's all going to be okay. I'm taking you back to my house. I've spoken to Tom and Casey, and they're packing up some stuff you might need. Ed's going to pick it up.'

I swivelled around. 'I don't want Ed picking anything up.' I didn't want Ed anywhere near me, or my baby.

'You really are hormonal.'

I sighed, suddenly too tired to argue. Maybe the astute Stella had known I was pregnant as soon as she met me. I was that easy to read. And that was why she'd put a uterus in the flower box. Maybe I had it all wrong, and Daniel was right.

'I love you, Rose. Why don't we just enjoy ourselves until the baby's born?'

My dream of qualifying next year had been obliterated, but I was going to be a mum; I was with Daniel. It was enough, for now.

'It's a thought,' I said. 'And afterwards? We'll have fun afterwards too?' I tried to smile. It was difficult.

'I've made dinner already for tonight. You're too thin for a pregnant woman,' he replied, not answering my question.

'You made dinner? We could have gone to Mussels.'

'Not my scene any more.' He started the engine. 'Too many blacks and gays in there these days. Must be Noah's influence.'

'What the hell do you mean, Daniel?'

He glanced at me. 'Nothing. I mean nothing. I'm sorry. I'm just worried about you.'

I held my stomach, a rolling feeling lurching through me, like soldiers marching unrelentingly to their next battle.

40

24 *July 1991*

Daniel had gone to town with dinner – roast lamb, dauphinoise potatoes and four different veg – and as he prepared it, and I watched, he apologised again.

'We're half a generation apart,' he said as he made the mint sauce. 'I'm sorry, it was a crass comment.'

'It really was. And being older doesn't excuse it. At all. You really need to work on your prejudices.' I paused for effect. 'Work very hard.'

'I do.'

He served up the dinner, but my appetite was poor, and I pushed the food around my plate, silence hanging between us. The more objective Rose recognised he was doing the right thing by not talking. He was more than aware that communication was off the agenda and that nothing good could come from it anyway when I was so tired and fractious and still reeling from his car comment.

It was the doorbell that saved me. He got up from the table and touched my shoulder as he walked by. 'You eat as much as you can, and then go get some sleep.'

I nodded and looked at my watch. 'Late for visitors.' I got up too. 'I'm going to bed. Thanks for the food and I'm sorry your efforts were a waste of time.'

'It doesn't matter.' He held my chin, looked at me. 'My mum always fed me when I was sad.'

'Night, Daniel.'

As I made my way up the stairs, the bell went again, and by the time I heard Daniel open the front door, I was already brushing my teeth.

I lay in bed for half an hour, unable to sleep. I was thirsty, too. I got up, put on a jumper and made my way downstairs to get water. I heard voices coming from the kitchen, and assumed it would be Ed.

It wasn't Ed. I recognised the voice as Miles's. Despite them being colleagues and Miles working at Bluefields, he never came to Daniel's house. I got that, though: socializing and working together could be too much.

'I'm letting you go, Miles. It's time. I'll give you all the references you need.'

'Why now?' Miles replied. 'I wanted to leave years ago.'

'I want your desk cleared and you gone by the end of the week. Here.'

'I don't want money.'

'Suit yourself,' Daniel replied.

'And can I trust you'll say nothing in the future?' Miles said.

'You have my word.'

Then silence. I waited for more.

'Take care of Rose,' Miles replied. 'And tell her—'

Daniel interrupted. 'With all due respect, Rose is none of your business, and never was.'

One of them or both were moving towards the slightly ajar kitchen door. I turned on my heel and almost ran back upstairs. When I got to the bedroom, I rushed to the loo and threw up.

I heard Miles's car start up outside. I waited a few minutes, then made my way downstairs again and found Daniel washing up. He turned when he heard me.

'That was Miles. I've asked for his resignation. I didn't want to say anything to you before.' He wiped his hands with a towel. 'It's time Miles did what he really wants to do, which is work within the NHS. He's been wanting a job in intensive care for years.' He paused and took a short breath. 'It's time I stopped coddling him.'

'Coddling?'

'Miles has, or did have, a little bit of a drug habit. But I think he's on the straight and narrow now. I feel happy to let him go, and back into NHS medicine.'

'Are you sure that's okay?' I leant against the wall. 'I mean, is he... you know, all right? You have a duty, Daniel... safe-guarding patients.'

'It's fine. Miles is safe. I've been monitoring him.'

I hated the thought of secrets between us. 'I did hear; I came down for water. What did Miles mean, that you should take care of me, and tell me what?'

'Tell you about his problem.'

'That has nothing to do with me.'

He shrugged. 'No, but Miles is a pretty straight bloke really. Maybe he just wanted you to know.'

'Did you offer him money?'

'I just want to help him out. Make the transition easier.'

I turned the kitchen tap and filled a glass with water. 'I sensed something sad about Miles. A few students on our course have dabbled with drugs. Amphetamines to keep them awake to cram, and for the long shifts when on placement.' I paused. 'Did he start taking them at med school?'

Daniel nodded.

'And you've been protecting him?' I took a sip of water.

'I've tried, and I have helped him, but it's time for us to part ways.'

I kicked at the edge of the kitchen mat. 'I'm going up. I'm so tired.'

'You do that. I'll sleep in the spare room. I don't want to disturb you.'

When finally Daniel came upstairs, he did go to the spare room. In the middle of the night, I got up and made my way there, finding him fast asleep. I climbed into bed and moulded myself to his back, looping my arms round him. He didn't move; just took my hand and kissed it.

'I love you, Rose, and I'm sorry for what I said about Noah.'

41

25 July 1991

The next morning, I called my mum, who was just about to start an early shift at Bluefields. She told me she'd be back at three o'clock.

I took the bus and was there at two, but didn't let myself in and instead sat outside on the step waiting for her. It was a lovely day – warm but not too humid – and I was reminded of my childhood, when I'd often forgotten my key. Despite my mum's general benevolent neglect, I did remember that after quite a few times of me forgetting, she began leaving one in a welly by the back door.

She wasn't all bad, and today I needed to talk to her.

Half an hour later, she was making me a cup of tea in a tidy kitchen.

'How's the new job going?' I asked.

'Fine.' She glanced at me as she put milk in the mugs. 'What's wrong, Rose?'

'Apart from quitting my course—'

'Oh love, what's happened?'

'It doesn't matter, and it's not that that's bothering me. It was always on the cards.'

She took a step closer and I thought she was going to give me a hug. I waited. It didn't happen. 'You can go back to your training after the baby's born,' she said instead.

'It's not just that.'

'You having second thoughts?'

'About what?'

'An abortion.'

'No! Definitely not. I'm having second thoughts about Daniel.' I fidgeted. 'I can't let it go.'

She sighed. 'I thought you had a lovely time in Spain.'

'I did, it's just—'

'What? He loves you. You love him, don't you? He'll be good for you, good for our family.'

I knew my mum liked him. 'I do love him… but he said something the other night and it's really bothering me.'

'What did he say?'

'Basically, a racist and homophobic comment.'

'Why are you always on a mission to be so correct and proper? Daniel's a different generation to you.' She paused, smiled a little. 'He's only five or six years younger than me.'

'That's true.' It was exactly what Daniel had said that morning.

'He's in a position to look after you.'

'I'm not like you.'

'No, you're not. Never were.' She sighed again. 'You don't have to struggle like I did with you. Daniel adores you, Rose. Give him a break. So he made one comment you don't agree with, so what?'

I took her in as if seeing her clearly for the first time. I'd never asked her in any detail about her own childhood and upbringing in Ireland, sensing she didn't want to talk about it. I knew though that it had been tough, and maybe one of the reasons she was the way she was. I should have asked more, delved deeper, and then I might have understood her better. Maybe I was, as she sometimes said, selfish and self-indulgent, but then she really hadn't set the best of examples.

'Was your childhood very bad?' I asked.

'It wasn't good.' She bent down to get the biscuit tin out and without facing me said, 'I'm sorry I haven't been the best mum. But now's the time to break the cycle, eh, love?'

I nodded. It was the frankest and most real conversation I'd had with her, ever.

As she arranged biscuits on a plate, I made my way through to the sitting room and was greeted by a large, immaculately upholstered and brand-new suite.

'Very nice settee!' I shouted.

She came in, plate in hand. 'It is, isn't it? Daniel gave me a bonus in last month's pay cheque.'

I tried to smile and somehow could not, although by the time I got back to Daniel's house, I'd decided all my angst was out of proportion. I was having Daniel's baby; he was looking after my mum. I loved him, and my mum had said he adored me. And regardless of her issues and our chipped relationship, I believed her.

I put his comments about race and sexual orientation down to his age and his privileged upbringing, and there was also the fact that his own mixed heritage probably meant he felt he could get away with the race comment. I chose to believe him when he said he'd work on his prejudices. After everything he'd already done for me, it seemed possible.

42

I was sitting in the kitchen relaxing and sipping herbal tea; Daniel had just left to take my mum home. I took in the well-equipped space, accepting that the house really was beginning to feel like home.

I'd moved in with Daniel soon after the conversation with my mum, making the decision when he'd asked Ed to move out. Spain had shown Daniel that Ed and I together did not make for a good environment, so he'd asked him if he minded staying with Abigail, to help out at her place. It turned out Ed didn't have a home of his own; it had been repossessed after he'd lost his job. Daniel had shown me pictures of his sister's house, and I'd been a little surprised at its size. When I mentioned this, he finally told me about her divorce two years before.

Over the past months, as I came to terms with crashing off my course, I'd carried on working at Mussels for a short period, and had only given the job up a few weeks before. Tom and Casey had been to see me, although Tom's iciness with Daniel did annoy me a bit. Casey, though, really liked him, and unlike Tom, she wasn't fazed about my situation, admitting that despite her strong feminist view of the world, what had happened to me was the most natural thing. *You've got Daniel. He adores you. What's an extra year or two? You can finish your training. No problem.*

But it was the visits from my mum that had been the greatest surprise. We hadn't argued once and she'd even managed to give me the odd hug. The previous weekend, she'd stayed the night, keeping me company when Daniel went to visit Abigail. She'd regaled me with stories about her two births, and assured me that being so young, I wouldn't find it a problem going back to pick up my studies after I had the baby. *Youthful energy is a godsend with a new-born. A lot to be said for having them young.* She'd even offered babysitting duties.

She was enjoying working at Bluefields and really did seem to be in control, and taking her meds. Today we'd even looked through baby catalogues together, and ordered a fair amount too. I'd pointed out to her the huge number at the bottom of the bill. She'd just shrugged. *Daniel'll pay, won't he?* I'd thought she was footing the bill and so judicially deleted most of the items.

I told Daniel this later on as we lay in bed.

'She's your mum. Give her a chance,' he said, amusement in his voice.

I snuggled closer. He kissed my nose and then moved his head beneath the covers. His lips skimmed over my stomach, finding my wetness. It was as if I had no control over my body, or my mind, or how I felt about this man whose tongue delved into my core. I arched my hips, waiting for the roll of ecstasy I knew was imminent; my body was more responsive than ever before. We had a baby forming inside me, and this thought gave the orgasm that sat on the very tip of an abyss an intensity that shocked me.

'Jesus, Rose, I had no idea you'd do this to me.'

He looked away, at the pillow, and I heard a moan: of ecstasy, of relief? But as I drifted into sleep, his murmur became a sound of grief.

The next day we were both up at the crack of dawn. I was booked in for my twenty-week scan and I'd been given the first morning slot. Daniel was awake, showered and dressed before I'd even finished my tea, which he'd brought me in bed.

'You don't have to come,' I said.

'I want to come.' He fiddled with the duvet cover, folding the top neatly over my stomach, punching up my pillow, which was wedged against a thick wooden curl.

–

The hospital was teeming with people when we arrived. The receptionist nodded to Daniel and smiled at me. It was common knowledge by then that I was Daniel's girlfriend, and that, I had to admit, did sit uneasily with me. It wasn't the first time I'd thought it might have been better to go to the NHS hospital, but I already knew so many people at the maternity unit. I liked Cam, my midwife, although my internal jury was still out on Mark Stephens. He was okay, but not my favourite person.

Daniel whisked me off to Mark's room, where he was ready and waiting.

'Take a seat, Rose.' He glanced at Daniel. 'You too.' He looked at me, his lips in the shape of a smile but his features telling me another story. 'One day in the future, after your baby's born, I'm absolutely confident you'll go back to your training and become the doctor you deserve to be.'

I cast a glance at Daniel, lifted my shoulders in question. How did Mark Stephens know I was stressing over my course? I'd said nothing to him during our appointments.

'Mark, could you give us five?' Daniel said.

Mark coughed. 'I've a fifteen-hour labour to check on, so no problem.' He left the room quickly.

'Why are you discussing me with Mark when I'm not there?' I asked.

'He was a little concerned about your state of mind… I think your mum mentioned something to him.'

'Jesus…'

Daniel shuffled in his chair. 'C'mon.'

'I don't want people knowing things about me and me not knowing they know. Especially not my doctor.'

He pulled his chair closer to mine, placed his hand on my belly. 'Mark's a good man.' He paused. 'He has a daughter your age. She's blind and both mentally and physically disabled. A consequence of measles when she was three.'

'That's terrible.' I peered at him. 'But I'm still pissed off you discussed me with him.'

'Your mother discussed you.'

'Whatever.'

The door opened and Mark returned.

'You going to pop on the bed, Rose?' he said, his voice a little too loud.

I hauled myself up while Mark pulled the ultrasound machine nearer. He waited as I pushed the thin pillow beneath my head, then said, 'Off we go, then.'

Daniel was standing next to me, his hand resting on my right shoulder. 'Do you want to know the baby's sex?' he asked.

I'd thought about this, coming to the conclusion that I did want to know. I nodded.

Mark grinned. 'Let's get this show on the road then!'

Daniel moved away so as he could see the screen. Mark pressed buttons and concentrated, and I lay back, waiting.

'Do you want to have a look?' he asked.

I lifted my head as Daniel pulled the machine closer. Mark had taken away the ultrasound's head from my belly. The image of my baby on the screen, captured.

'I can see,' I said in wonder. 'A girl.' Anxiety darted through me, of the responsibility and commitment, but then love. Immediate love.

Mark later told me my baby girl was due to come into the world on 11th January 1992. I was a scientist by nature but knew two things immediately: she would be both a Capricorn and a monkey. My photographic memory relayed the characteristic traits of our unborn daughter: intelligent, eloquent, adaptable, flexible. Brilliant, smart, agile. Disciplined. I liked this description, and wondered whimsically if one day she would want to be a doctor too.

Mark went on to tell me that her organs, bones and brain were all completely normal, and although I hadn't fretted overly about the health of my growing child, I was hugely relieved that she was forming normally. I couldn't help thinking about what Daniel had told me about Mark's daughter.

In the end, I left the hospital elated, and at peace. I was content. All I'd ever wanted was to qualify and be a doctor, a paediatrician, because I loved kids and medicine, but I was young and had come to accept that I could be a mother, in love, and eventually have the career of my dreams too. Why not? The world awaited. I'd only just begun.

After the scan, Daniel took me into the city centre and we mooched around the shops looking for baby clothes and furry toys. Despite my secret guilty pleasure of knowing too much about the zodiac and Chinese horoscopes, I wasn't superstitious, and it was fun browsing for and buying baby stuff. We spent hours in John Lewis looking at cribs, and Daniel surprised me when, after carefully examining the craftsmanship of the mass-produced products, he declared he'd make one himself at home. I did like that he was a practical sort of bloke.

After lunch at Pizza Express, we went home, and because I could, I went upstairs for a power nap before starting on the dinner. Tom and Casey were coming over later and I was making risotto, a new recipe and a new me. I didn't cook.

I'd fallen asleep almost immediately, and it was the doorbell chiming that woke me. I waited for Daniel to answer, but the chime went on and on, and then I remembered he'd told me he was going to the garden shed to start on the crib. I smiled to myself. I really couldn't imagine him making a crib, although I liked the thought of him attempting it.

I got off the bed and made my way downstairs, and still slightly blurry-eyed opened the door. A man stood in front of me. I didn't recognise him, and as his huge grin and startlingly scarlet complexion filled the space between us, my immediate reaction was to close the door slightly and take a step back. The man lifted his arm, placing his hand on the door. It was then that I registered the tattooed snakes slithering down his fingers, and it was then that I recognised him. The man from that long ago day in Mussels; the day I met Daniel for the first time. I'd spilt dregs of wine on his shirt.

'Nice to see you again.' He licked his lips, peered at my stomach. 'Dan around?'

'And you are?'

'It doesn't matter who I am, love. I just need to talk to Dan.'

'He's in the garden.'

'Ah, well if you don't mind, I'll go down there and find him.'

Nausea staggered through me. 'The gate to the garden is locked. You'll need the code.'

He grinned. 'Have it.' He looked me up and down, then turned and made his way round the side of the house.

Giving up on my nap, I walked to the kitchen, opened the recipe book and began to prepare dinner, disquiet folding through me. Half an hour later, Daniel made his way through the back door.

'Smells good! You want me to go pick up Tom and Casey?'

I shrugged. 'Up to you.'

'What's wrong?'

'The man—'

'Ah, thanks for sending him down.'

'He was in Mussels the day we met. The one who grabbed my arse.'

'I don't remember that. He's a builder, has done some work on the house.' Daniel walked up behind me, placing his hand on my bottom.

I pushed him away. 'Don't.'

'What is it?'

'You told me you didn't know him. And it turns out he works for you.'

'I didn't say that, did I? Jesus, Rose, I probably didn't even clock who he was that day.'

He sat down, rubbed his hands through his hair. 'Do you want me to go and pick Tom and Casey up or not?'

'Not. I'm going over there to see them. Alone.' I threw down the kitchen utensil I was holding. 'You can make your own dinner.'

–

Later, at my old digs, Casey brimmed with explanations for Daniel, and even Tom stuck up for him, which did make me think I'd overreacted. Casey ended up making the dinner they were supposed to be having at ours. We ate scrambled eggs on toast and Tom huffed a lot. After we'd finished eating, he got himself a bowl of corn flakes to top up. He really did have hollow legs.

Casey took hold of my hand. 'It's been a tough time for you. Hang on in there, and go back home to Daniel. Sounds to me like something you shouldn't be worrying about.'

Tom was standing behind her. 'You know I'm not that keen on the father of your baby, Rose, but I do think on this one you're going over the top... a bit.'

They gave me the money for a taxi and I went home, where Daniel was waiting for me in the driveway – Casey must have called him. When I plonked myself down on the sofa in the sitting room, he went over to his desk and picked up a large sheet of paper, which he placed on my lap. With petulant reluctance I took a look. A crib design.

'Do you like it?' he asked.

'I do.'

'I honestly can't remember the incident in Mussels.' He sat down next to me and pulled me towards him. 'I was too busy trying to figure out a way to impress you.'

'He's a vile man.'

'Good at his job, though.' He paused. 'I'll find someone else.'

'That's a very good idea.'

43

8 December 1991

The kitchen smelt heavily of pine, mixed with the divine aroma of percolated coffee. Moments before, Daniel had hauled the huge Christmas tree through the kitchen to the lounge, where we planned to decorate it the following day. The coffee was for Daniel, although I was dying to slug down a mugful. I was doing all the things a pregnant woman should do, and mostly it hadn't been a problem, but coffee was the thing I was missing the most. Daniel, though, encouraged me all the time to be good. He was obsessed with my pregnancy, and my body; I felt like a goddess or something, and since our disagreement concerning his comments about Noah, whom he had invited around for early drinks on Christmas Eve, and the man with the snake tattoos, our life had been serene. Only occasionally did I feel a little smothered by his attentiveness.

I looked longingly at the coffee machine again. When the craving bit, all I had to do was hold my stomach, feel the movement, and the feeling disappeared. It was what I was doing now, perched on the kitchen stool.

I was just about to grab my coat, shoes and overnight bag when Daniel, with beads of sweat covering his brow – it was a huge tree – poked his head through the door.

'I'll take you to Tom and Casey's.'

'I'll get the bus. I need a walk, some fresh air.'

'Rose, you're huge. Let me take you. You have the bag to carry.' He pointed to my holdall.

He was right, I was huge. Everyone I met told me so: strangers in the street, on the bus, in the park. At first I found it amusing that people I'd never met before, and would probably never meet again, felt they could make such personal comments about the shape of my body, as well as my baby's sex. All up front meant a boy, apparently.

'Honestly, it's not that far, and my bag's tiny.'

'Okay.' He handed me an umbrella. 'You might be needing this.'

I grinned, pecked him on the cheek. Tonight had been planned for weeks. The student who'd taken my place in the house was away, and I had her bed. 'See you in the morning. You okay picking me up first thing?'

'Course. No probs at all.'

I made my way through the estate, luckily all downhill, although it still took me a good half an hour to get to the exit. It wasn't until I'd been standing at the bus stop for fifteen minutes, the slicing December wind whipping up my hair, that I realised I'd forgotten the presents.

'Bollocks,' I said out loud. The couple who'd been waiting with me looked at my stomach, mouths agape. The bus had just turned up too. 'Don't worry, *she* can't hear me.' I smiled at them as they got on the bus, then sighed and began to walk slowly back up the hill. I'd pick up the presents then get Daniel to drop me at Tom and Casey's.

When finally I arrived at the house, exhausted, sweating and still cursing myself, I saw a car in the driveway I didn't recognise. I opened the front door; the house was quiet and Daniel's study door was closed. I walked towards it and was about to knock when I heard a familiar voice.

Slowly — I really did just want to sit down — I moved closer.

'God, you're so in love with her, aren't you? She has you wrapped round her little finger.'

A hand on my shoulder. I jumped, thinking I was going to go into labour there and then.

'Hello, Rose. Been a while.' Ed appraised my bump, while at the same time looking at the closed door and rubbing his concave left cheek. 'You're big.'

'What's going on, Ed?' I said dropping my bag on to the floor.

'A sister can visit her brother, can't she?' He took hold of my arm.

'Do *not* touch me.' I shoved him away.

At that moment, Daniel's study door opened and I found myself face to face with Abigail.

'Rose! Daniel said you were out for the night. I'm so glad you're back; I was pissed off I'd missed you,' she said.

'I forgot something.' She was dressed in a white trouser suit, a sapphire necklace resting on her chest. She looked as if she was on her way out for dinner or something. 'I didn't think you were coming until next weekend.'

'I wanted to see my little brother... and you.' Her eyes dropped to my stomach. 'Wow.' Before I could reply, she'd turned to Ed. 'Can you get the bags from the car?'

'I can,' Ed said. 'You planning on staying?' he asked her.

Abigail smiled but didn't look at me. 'I think it's a good idea.'

Daniel emerged from his study, his lips tense and twitching slightly. 'Rose, you okay?'

He'd moved towards me. I stepped back. 'Forgot the presents.'

'I'll run you to Tom and Casey's. It's no problem.'

'I'll meet you outside,' I replied, not looking at him and turning to Abigail. 'There's two rooms ready to go.'

'I know. I checked.'

'C'mon, Rose,' Daniel said, taking hold of my arm.

I shook him off, picked up my bag together with the forgotten presents I'd left by the front door and followed him outside to the car.

I opened the door and manoeuvred myself down into the seat. I hadn't said a word.

'You okay?' he asked.

'Not really.'

'I'd no idea they were turning up tonight.'

'Give me some credit, please. I might be pregnant, but I'm not stupid.'

'I didn't know, Rose. Ed said he'd tried to call us to let us know, but we didn't pick up.'

The landline *had* been ringing out a lot that day. Sometimes the mobile signal here was non-existent, but Abigail and Ed turning up unannounced was not my problem. 'Why is your sister so surprised that you're in love with me? What's going on?'

'You were listening at the keyhole?'

'Christ's sake, no, I wasn't listening at the keyhole. Stop the car and let me out.'

'Hey, calm down, babe.'

'Do not call me babe either.'

He'd stopped the car. 'My sister has some mental health issues... it's the problem our dad has with her. He wants her to have treatment and she refuses. It's causing a rift between them.'

'What are you trying to tell me?'

'Abigail's complex.'

'What, Daniel? Just spit it out.'

'She has problems... with the women in my life. She had a problem with my relationship with Ed's sister too.'

'Are you saying what I think you're saying?'

He nodded and started the engine. We didn't speak again until we got to Tom and Casey's.

'I'm not coming home until Abigail and Ed have left,' I said.

'I'll pick you up in the morning. They'll be gone by then.'

I attempted to lumber out of the car, but all my energy had dissipated. Daniel was by my door within seconds. 'Leave me alone, I can get out myself.'

'I can ask them to leave tonight.'

'No, you can't. But I want them gone in the morning. Your sister and Ed, they both freak me out.' He tried to kiss me. I turned away, not wanting to even think about what he'd just told me. 'When our daughter arrives, I really don't want Abigail anywhere near her when I'm not around.'

He placed his hand on my arm. 'I'm sorry...'

'It's weird, Daniel. *She's* weird, and so is Ed.' I paused. 'We need to talk about this tomorrow. It's time.'

He moved his hand onto my belly. I didn't push it away. In reality, Daniel was caught in a deep, dark place. I could see that, and maybe it was what I'd seen when I'd first met him. Broken water. When the time was right, perhaps I could talk to Abigail and suggest she get help.

It was only Casey I told about Daniel's sister. She laughed and asked if she could use it in her dissertation. *Christ, Rose, if Abigail having an unrequited sexual thing for her brother is the only skeleton hanging in Daniel's family's cupboard, you'll be doing okay. She sounds like a needy, attention-seeking little witch.*

I loved it when Casey got like this, which wasn't often. She was the kindest person I'd ever met and as a rule never had a bad word to say about anyone.

But that night I couldn't sleep, and my hands rested on my stomach until the fingers of dark winter light told me I could finally get up.

44

3 January 1992

Daniel had returned from his mercy mission to Herefordshire only an hour before, having left at short notice mid afternoon on New Year's Day, and after a distraught call from Abigail. I'd been remarkably chilled about him going and put it down to the euphoria of the coming birth. I was so excited.

Abigail was in a bad way, he told me as he sat in the kitchen drinking tea whilst I lay on the floor, spread-eagled, attempting to take the burden away from my back. Lying supine with a pillow shoved under my neck, I shrugged and huffed. I really didn't want to think about Abigail having an unhealthy thing for her brother.

'She needs to grow up and get her life together,' I said, lifting my head to look at him. 'And sort out her stuff… with you.'

'You're right, she does. And she is. I think it got worse after her divorce.' He leaned down and grabbed hold of my foot, giving it a quick massage. It felt good.

I'd lost all sympathy for Abigail, although I was looking forward to meeting Zakaria in Morocco once the baby was born. The old man had written to Daniel (he refused to use the phone, and didn't even have one), and two of the letters included sections he'd written for me to read.

Daniel got up. 'Right, I've got paperwork to do for Blue-fields. Off to the study for an hour.'

I remained on the floor, thinking. We'd had a good Christmas and had spent the day itself with my mum and Sam.

The only other person at the dinner table had been Mrs Finsbury, who still came to clean the house once a week (I always looked forward to Thursdays); she'd come at Christmas without her son, who was, despite Daniel's help with a decent solicitor, spending Christmas inside. I'd felt sorry for the unknown non-law-abiding Rob. Being inside a prison would kill me.

Finally I managed to get up from the floor. I walked into the hallway and through to the big lounge, where I sat down clumsily on the lime-coloured sofa. God, I was so uncomfortable. I'd be glad when the baby came. Patting my stomach, I sank further into the plump cushions. *It's all going to be good, little one.* I loved my baby more than I despised myself for not being in the final year of my training, but September wasn't that far away, and that was when we'd decided I'd pick up my studies again. Daniel had suggested a nanny, which I'd told him I didn't want. *We'll figure it out,* he'd said. I knew, though, that a September restart was just a dream on my part, and his, but neither of us said that out loud.

Hauling myself up very slowly, I made my way upstairs to our baby's room. On entering, I checked the Winnie-the-Pooh clock ticking placidly on the rose-pink wall. Just after eleven. Closing the door, I went to sit in the rocker, admiring the crib Daniel had made. He'd spent hours in his workshop, and I smiled thinking about it.

I was meeting Casey later in the afternoon at the local pool for our weekly swim. She said she looked forward to our meets just to see my huge stomach. My due date was still three days away, but I was so big I couldn't see myself lasting that long. Mark had said he suspected an earlier birthday for my child.

I heard the nursery door open. Daniel.

'You okay?'

'I'm good.'

'Do you need a lift to the swimming baths later?'

'It's fine I'll get the bus.'

'Rose, you can hardly walk ten metres.'

I grinned. 'I know.' I looked down at my belly. All up front, as the strangers liked to tell me.

He crouched down, putting his hands on the top of the mound, and nuzzled my ear. 'How's Samira?'

'Waiting for her swim.' We'd already agreed on a name. Moroccan in origin and Daniel's idea, but I did really like it. In Zakaria's last letter, he'd told me he loved the name – it was his great-grandmother's apparently. I'd tried to work out old Samira's relationship to our Samira, and thought it was three 'greats'. 'Doing lots of swimming inside Mum, I'd imagine,' I carried on.

His hand slipped over my bump and downwards, easily finding its way into the top of my elasticated trousers, his fingers rubbing softly at my pubic bone. 'Rose, you're beautiful. I love you like this. Big and pregnant.'

I let out a sigh. During the past few weeks my libido had been sky-high, or was it just Daniel who did that to me? Despite our disagreements about Abigail, Ed and the man from Mussels, and the grief about my course, I was in love, and still in lust. I was having a baby, I had Daniel, and even my relationship with my mother had improved.

He pulled his hand away and rested his head on my shoulder. 'I didn't know it would be like this.'

I turned. 'Like what?'

'The way I feel.'

I placed my hand on his hardness. 'Like this?'

'You've bewitched me,' he groaned.

He helped me up and we lay down on the floor. Clumsily I turned on my side on the long, soft fibres of the rug, feeling the warmth from the torrent of winter sun that cascaded in through the window and onto my face. He pulled at the elastic of my maternity trousers. I heard him taking off his own, and he moved behind me, pushing forwards a little. Then, warmth in between my legs.

I wouldn't be going swimming with Casey later. My waters had broken. Samira would soon be welcomed into her new world, and I was so happy. So very happy.

'My baby is ready,' Daniel whispered.

'Our baby.'

He turned his head away and got up. 'I meant you're ready, Rose.'

I didn't move as the first wave of pain began to ricochet through my body. Daniel had already left the room, to call all the relevant people.

He never called me baby. Babe occasionally, but never baby.

45

It felt as if Daniel was gone for hours. From Samira's room I could hear his barked instructions, although I couldn't make out the words, and when another contraction overtook me, I stopped trying to do so.

Finally he returned, and with him holding me upright we made our way downstairs and into the car. A stab of pain, and he started the engine, driving too quickly out of the entrance. There was a sickening crunch of metal as he caught the side of the MG on the brick pillar.

Mark was waiting outside when we got to Bluefields, flanked by Cam. He smiled broadly, as if the event should be savoured, and I supposed it would be afterwards. I'd seen how new mothers, even the ones who'd been through the most horrendous pregnancies and births, forgot most of it by the end of their first day in the job – that was of course if the baby was well and healthy. If not… well that was another story. Another contraction came, stronger, and I nearly fell out of the car.

Daniel rushed around the other side to help me, saying to Cam, 'Could you make some calls?'

I'd assumed he'd already done that at home. But then a skewering pain rammed at me from inside and I broke out into a sweat. I was finding it hard to breathe, and for the first time since going into labour, I was scared.

Mark had hold of my left arm and Daniel the other, but before we started to move, Mark gently pulled up the sleeve of my jumper and I thought I felt the prick of a needle. Then the three of us staggered towards the hospital's entrance.

Catching my breath, I turned to Daniel. 'Something isn't right.'

'Everything's fine,' he said soothingly. 'Mark's the best. Let's get you inside so he can look you over. Don't fret. Everything's under control.'

I looked up and thought I saw someone standing close by. Was it my mum? I was so glad she was there. But then she was gone, before I could call to her. Was I imagining things? She *could* be there, it might be her shift, but my sight was hazy and I was unable to focus. She couldn't be there, not unless Daniel had gone to pick her up. And he was here with me, not picking up my mum. Then I remembered my thought of only moments before. She might be at work today.

'Come on, Rose,' Cam was saying. 'Everything is good. You're panicking.'

'I'm not panicking.'

I felt Daniel's arm around my waist as we entered the main atrium of the hospital. 'Everyone is here and ready for you.' His tone sounded more relaxed, and that calmed me.

'She needs oxygen,' I heard Cam say, although I couldn't see her. She was behind me, attempting to hold me upright.

I managed to glance at Mark. His face was blurred, but I could see that his huge annoying smile had dropped to the ground somewhere between the outside of the hospital and here.

'Get a trolley,' Daniel said quietly. Thank God he was there. I felt the reassuring pressure of his hand on my arm.

Cam was beside me on one side, Mark on the other. I managed to lodge my bottom on the trolley. 'Give me a minute,' I said. I leant forward a little, my palms resting on my thighs, my eyes resting on the reception area's sea-blue carpet. I felt everyone around me waiting. 'Just a minute... please.' Finally I looked up and my vision was clearer.

'Rose, please, we need to get you to the delivery room.' Mark's voice. Then he and Daniel were lifting my legs.

I laid my head on the pillow, felt Daniel's hand on my forehead. 'Try and relax, let everyone do their work,' he was saying.

The trolley was being rammed through the delivery room doors. I hadn't had another contraction since arriving. Mark was lifting my blouse, his stethoscope on my belly, then his hands. Lying down wasn't what I was supposed to be doing. I wanted to be in the birthing pool, but knew I wasn't going anywhere near the water, and a fleeting image of Casey flashed through my brain. I wished I'd seen her today. Would I ever see her again? I was going to die, my baby was going to die. Why was I thinking that?

'She's okay, Rose. Samira is okay,' Mark told me. 'These are normal labour pains.' His face seemed enlarged, engorged. Distorted.

'I can't do this.'

'You're fine.' It was Daniel, whispering into my ear. 'Mark has you covered. Of course you can do this.' He took hold of my hand. But then he let go, and I couldn't see very much.

'Do you love me?' I asked.

'I do love you.'

'Is my mum here?'

'No, not yet. But she's on her way.'

'I thought I saw her.' I lifted my head.

'Rose, you need to concentrate on giving birth to Samira.'

He said he loved me, but he'd moved away. Everyone around me was reshaping into people I didn't know, or people I was imagining. And there was a hardness in Daniel's voice that pierced me.

His lips were close to my face again. 'I do love you, Rose... I did from the beginning.'

'My contractions have stopped.'

'Hush.'

I couldn't feel his touch any more.

Only an hour before, we'd been about to make love. Of course he loved me. The drug was swallowing me; what had Mark given me? I tried to be objective; hadn't I seen the hysteria of so many women during labour? I was being dramatic. I was probably hallucinogenic. I had to calm down for Samira.

Tomorrow we would be in her nursery, together.

But the tears were saturating my face, and there was no touch from Daniel.

'Let's get everything ready,' I heard Mark say. His voice was so different. Different altogether from the one I'd been listening to for months. Or was it? Cam was putting a cannula in my arm, and at that moment I felt the oxygen mask being clamped over my face. What were they doing? The contractions had stopped. Terror flooded through me.

'What time is it?' I asked.

'It's just after midday, Rose,' Cam replied softly. 'Wednesday.'

'Be quiet,' I heard Mark say.

I wanted to feel Daniel's hand on my skin, but there was a vacancy. I put my own on my stomach, trying to touch my baby.

'She's on her way.' Mark was speaking loudly. Was he talking about Samira? She wasn't on her way. Everything had stalled.

But *I* was on the way now. The blackness behind my eyelids was becoming grey, then white, and Samira's image played like a film inside my mind. A baby who hadn't been born yet but whose life I already saw. A toddler, a young child, a teenager, a woman. I would not ever meet her.

Daniel was already a distant memory.

A mistake. All of this was the universe's revenge. My body had become enslaved to Daniel and now it was kicking back.

I saw a figure standing in the delivery room doorway, but I couldn't make out who it was, not until they spoke. A voice that sounded familiar. A scent that smelt familiar.

Don't you dare do this, Daniel.

Despite the situation, I was still Rose, the med student and scientist, and I knew I was most likely hallucinating. And this knowledge calmed me as I lost consciousness.

46

I opened my eyes, but a long strip light flickered above and I quickly squeezed them shut. I waited, then tentatively tried again, squinting into the laser-like glare. It took seconds for me to remember where I was, who I was, and about Samira. I tried to move but could not; only my eye muscles seemed to be functioning. There was a man in the doorway. He turned away quickly, but I recognised him. He looked agitated and anxious. Was I imagining Ed as I'd imagined my mother? Why was he there? Where was my baby?

Cam was standing next to me. She must have been there all the time.

'Where's the man gone?' I said.

'What man?' Cam replied, her voice tense. 'It's all right, Rose. Try not to move.'

'My baby, where is she? I want to see her.'

'She hasn't been born yet, Rose. You've been asleep for a while.'

I was just about to answer when a tornado of pain shot through me. 'The contractions—'

'Mark's examined you and Samira will be here soon.'

'How long have I been asleep?'

How could I have fallen asleep?

She didn't answer immediately. 'A while.'

'How long?'

'It's very late in the evening, Rose. Shush, Daniel'll be here soon.'

231

'I don't want Daniel. I want to have my baby. What the fuck is going on?' But before she could answer, Mark appeared.

'Contractions are regular,' Cam said to him, as if I were not there.

But then a searing pain.

Mark was standing at the bottom of the bed, and I tilted my head. My legs were elevated. 'Full dilation.' And as he said it, another contraction, tearing my body in two.

It seemed to go on like that for hours. I heard Cam and Mark talking about getting SCBU ready. 'What the hell is happening?' I shouted, although I knew my voice was only a whisper. Where was Daniel?

A horrendous pain.

'Push, Rose, push,' Cam was saying.

Mark at my feet, holding forceps.

'What's wrong?' I tried to ask, unsure if the words had fallen from my numb lips. But then the pain subsided, and along with it, so did I. I tried to lift my head and saw my baby, the cord, saw the problem Samira had been having, and despite everything, I sighed with relief. She was out. I waited for her to cry, but Cam was cutting the cord and my head had flopped down again in exhaustion; then Daniel was standing next to me, holding my baby, wrapped in white.

I tried to sit up, but couldn't move. The carotid artery in my neck was pulsating at a rate I knew was too rapid. I closed my eyes and counted. One hundred and twenty. I became acutely aware of the blood pounding through my body. And I felt hot. So very hot.

'You haemorrhaged badly, Rose, but it's under control,' Daniel said.

I managed to focus on Daniel, and my baby.

'They did everything they could—'

'Let me see her,' I croaked.

'I'm so sorry.' He pulled away the blanket's whiteness and placed my daughter gently on my chest.

I gazed at her face, so unwrinkled. She didn't move. I held her tight and the tears burned my cheeks. 'What did you do?'

'The team did everything they could. Samira's cord prolapsed; your contractions caused too much pressure, stopping the blood flow to her—'

'You killed my baby.'

'Don't do this.' He stepped forward, leaned closer. 'You need to rest.'

My daughter was dead. I was dead. My relationship with him was dead.

He placed his hand on my arm, touched the blanket near to my daughter's beautiful face. 'It was never meant to be like this,' he whispered.

No, it was never meant to be like this.

It was never meant to be.

I held Samira so close, somehow hoping that by doing so I could return her life to me. Daniel bent forward again. 'Leave me,' I tried to shout, but it came out as a trail of condensed air on a winter's morning. 'Leave me with my baby.'

'I've lost a child too.'

'It's over. Everything is over.' I meant it, and I would never change my mind. I wasn't sure what I expected him to say. I just wanted him to go and leave me with Samira. But then the old Rose reappeared. 'I want to see the surgical notes.'

'Don't be ridiculous. You need to get some sleep. We'll talk later.'

He thought I didn't mean what I said. Hysteria rose and filled me from the inside out. 'You killed my baby.'

'Stop it, Rose.' His voice was quiet. 'Your mum's in the waiting room.'

'Leave me alone, Daniel.'

He flinched but didn't move.

'Is Abigail here?' I asked.

'Of course Abigail isn't here.'

'I saw her... smelt her.'

'Rose, she's in Herefordshire.' He took hold of my hand, and its coldness jerked at me. I was so, so hot.

'Ed was here too.'

'Of course Ed wasn't here, just as my sister isn't.' He touched my forehead again. 'Try to sleep.'

He left without another word, and then Mark came into the room with Cam.

'We need to get you to your room, Rose,' he said. 'Get you comfortable.' He touched my arm, which still had the cannula inserted.

'You killed my baby.'

Cam was standing on the other side of the bed, trying to get the syringe tip into the cannula. I wanted none of it. I wanted to be awake and lucid.

'Get *off* me,' I said, still holding Samira.

Mark snatched the syringe from her and adeptly managed to do what Cam could not. Apathy approached.

And they took her away. Samira. My child.

47

When I woke up, Cam told me it was the next day and that Daniel was waiting to visit me. I refused to see him. They were all expecting me to change my mind. I did not. And Daniel did not come.

It was a full forty-eight hours after my baby had died that my mother finally came to my room. She entered holding a huge bouquet of flowers, placing them on my bedside table and not saying a word. I thought she was waiting for me to mention her belated appearance, but I was past that. I was past everything.

At last she spoke. 'Daniel asked me to give them to you.' She sat down.

I didn't reply.

'How are you feeling, love?' she carried on.

'I don't feel anything.'

'I mean, are you in any pain?'

I looked at her then. 'Of course I'm in pain.'

'Then tell Mark. He can give you painkillers.'

'It's not my body that hurts.'

She leaned closer. 'You look terrible.' She wasn't hearing what I was saying. 'You should stop being so silly, Rose, and let Daniel see you. He's beside himself.'

'There's nothing stopping him walking through the door.'

'He won't if you keep saying you don't want to see him.'

'It's over between us.'

'You'll change your mind.'

I peered at my mother. 'He hasn't killed himself coming to see me. Maybe he's glad this has happened.'

'That's a ridiculous thing to say.' She carried on. 'Mark says you're stable and can be discharged tomorrow.'

I was just about to answer when an excruciating pain shot through my abdomen, one I'd been feeling since Samira's death and hadn't mentioned to Mark or Cam. Maybe the pain would get worse. Maybe I'd die. I felt so empty that dying wasn't such a bad thought. I waited for it to abate, and waited for my mum to mention the death of my child. She did not.

'Were you here when Daniel brought me in?' I said, finally finding the strength to carry on talking.

'Daniel said you thought you'd seen me. No, I wasn't here, Rose. I'd been out all day sorting something out for Sam. I didn't know you'd been brought in until the next morning.'

She explained all of this while rearranging the flowers, the scent of which, together with the pain in my stomach, was making me feel sick. I didn't bother asking her why it had taken her so long to turn up at my bedside. The mother-and-daughter healing of the past seven months had been forgotten.

My mother went on, 'What's happened is tragic and unfortunate, but it does happen. You know that, love.' She paused. 'I have to go, my shift starts in ten minutes and I've got to get changed. I'm meeting...'

'Who?'

'No one. I mean, I'm meeting the receptionist I report to. I've sorted out your old room at home. Sam's staying with his girlfriend at the moment, so the house has plenty of space.' She touched the bed, but not me. 'It's best you stay with me,' she finished with weary acceptance. 'Daniel's got Ed to move your stuff. He's dropping it,' she looked at her watch, 'around now, I'd imagine.'

'Ed has a key to your house?'

'He does.'

I had no fight left in me to ask more about Ed Madden. I didn't care any more, although I did ask about Abigail. Had I seen her the day I was brought in or had I imagined her? 'Have you seen Daniel's sister?'

'No, I haven't. She lives in Herefordshire, you told me. What would she be doing here?' She didn't wait for me to answer. 'I have to go, Rose,' she said. 'I'll pop in after my shift's finished.'

She didn't return that day, or before I left the hospital.

It was Tom who came to see me that evening, and it was Tom who looked over the notes that sat near my bed and pointed out my elevated temperature. I told him I didn't feel anything, and it was true, I didn't. Nothing. I didn't feel ill. I was totally and utterly empty. The sporadic and terrible pain living within me was a physical hallucination. That was what I told myself.

Tom disappeared for a while, I suspected to go and talk to Mark, because later, Mark came to examine me.

Nothing untoward, he said. *Only a slightly elevated temperature. Nothing to worry about. Your young student friend is overreacting.*

And I did think then that the pain was completely psychosomatic. Mental pain transferring to my physical body.

48

5 January 1992

The next day, I left Bluefields in a taxi that took me to my mother's. I'd done a complete circle, back to where I'd started, but maybe being at my old home would be the best thing, for a while, until after Samira's funeral anyway. Tom had thought me mad going back and suggested I stay with him and Casey. I couldn't do that to my friends.

Neither Mark nor Cam mentioned Daniel as they helped me into the car. And that suited me fine.

We were over.

–

That night, lying in my childhood bed, I woke up lathered in sweat and entrenched in pain. Real pain. It was only when I finally made it to the tiny bathroom across the hallway that I saw it wasn't sweat. Blood covered the floor like a vermilion liquid blanket.

I sat on the toilet, in shock as well as agony. Was I going to die? Oddly, this thought composed me. The blood was still gushing, all over both the bathroom floor and me. With difficulty I got up from the toilet and lay on the floor, legs outstretched, waiting, the pain coming in more frequent waves. I don't know how long I'd been there when my mum came in, took one look at me and called Bluefields. I heard her on the phone.

'Mark says you'll be okay until the morning. He says that a little bit of blood goes a long way. It's no emergency,' she said, mopping up the blood with a towel.

By then, and despite my loss of reason, I knew that if I wanted to live, I had to go to A&E. 'Mum, call 999.'

She sat beside me. 'No need for that. We'll do as Mark says.' She touched my forehead and I wanted to feel her love. 'Shall I call Daniel?'

'No! Don't you dare.' I was disconnecting then, and it was a not unpleasant sensation.

She didn't call an ambulance, but helped me back to bed.

I only found myself being rushed into theatre at the NHS hospital because Tom had an early shift on his placement at a GP surgery nearby and had popped by very early to see me. He ignored my mother, who was trying to call Bluefields again, and dialled 999.

I woke in the recovery room encased in a silver heat blanket; it was as if I were in a spaceship. I felt no pain, but I was shaking so much I could hear the trolley on which I lay rattling and banging as if I were on a fairground ride.

Part of Samira's placenta had been left inside me and I'd haemorrhaged badly.

To save me, the surgeon had taken away my womb.

49

Theo

26 April 2016

As Rose comes to the end of her story a long, heavy breath escapes from Theo's throat.

The way Rose was treated was shocking, appalling and callous in equal measure. Why didn't she disclose details regarding her relationship with Daniel, and about Samira, to her hearing judge? To her barrister, or her husband?

Theo takes hold of her hand. Her eyes filled as she came to the day she woke up in the recovery room of an NHS hospital. Theo can now decipher her motivation for her crime. In a moment of injudicious madness, she committed murder in Queen's Hospital high dependency unit.

'So you see, Theo. You see now? I was Abe's nurse, something I never wanted to be on so many levels. Ed had been sabotaging my attempts to pass my degree out of spite. Daniel abandoned me the moment I stepped into that hospital. Before then, even. They took away my career and they took away my ability to have more children.'

Theo squeezes her soft hand in his. There's a profound pain in her eyes, but something else lies in the depths of them too. Something she's not telling him. 'There's more to the story, isn't there, Rose?'

She nods; her words seemed to be trapped deep inside her.

'How did you know Abe was Daniel's son?'

She gasps, withdraws her hand from Theo's. Her face is resolute as she steels herself for what she is about to say. 'Because on the day Abe died, his mother came to see him in the hospital. I met her.'

'And you recognised her?'

She nods once. 'It was Abigail.'

Something electric fizzes through Theo. Something not unlike rage. 'Daniel's sister?' He remembers the scrap of paper that Rose found in Daniel's bedroom all those years ago with *A's birthday* scribbled on it. The pink envelope on the passenger seat of the MG.

Ed wasn't going to see his mother. He was going to see Abigail.

'The woman who was introduced to me as Daniel's sister, yes. When I saw her at Abe's bedside, my breath left my body. My life disappeared in an instant, became nothing in a moment. Abigail was Abe's mother.' She holds her stomach. 'She was not Daniel's sister, but his wife.'

His wildest theory, the one that only passed through his mind fleetingly, and a speculation he disregarded as being too ludicrous, too fantastical, turns out to have been born out of tragic fact. 'Rose—'

'After seeing the woman who had pretended to be the sister of *my* baby's father, the hatred inside me overflowed. Abigail Deane was the mother of this young man, while I could never have children.'

Theo studies Rose's face, which is corrugated with grief. But none of this is an excuse for such a terrible and premeditated revenge on an innocent man.

Every thread of his body is still telling him that Rose is not a murderer.

'I fell for the wrong man, Theo. I saw the man I wanted to see. It wasn't until Samira, and afterwards, that I saw clearly.' She looks at him. 'Maybe before, maybe I saw before, but I was pregnant. Perhaps I didn't want to see.'

'I'm so sorry, Rose.' He rakes his hand through his hair. And he is sorry, but then he thinks of Natasha, of Mia, of Abe, and the conflict living inside him writhes. He wants to share with Rose his schism, but instead he says, 'The mistake with the placenta… the operation afterwards?'

'Mark resigned. I didn't pursue it further. Tom wanted me to, but it was pointless. I'd lost my child, and my womb, and nothing… nothing would bring either of them back.' She falters, 'Mark Stephens emigrated to Australia soon after he resigned.'

'Yes, and was killed in a car accident in the Outback less than a year later. I've already looked into him, after you mentioned him in our earlier meetings. There were questions at the time from the Australian police regarding the cause of the collision. As far as I know, the case is still open.'

Rose shakes her head. 'I regret what I did, Theo. I want you to know that. I regret it every day. Every moment.'

'You should have made that clearer. Why didn't you, Rose? Why?'

'I was guilty. I'm here.'

He nods, and for moments silence encases them.

Theo rests his elbows on the table. 'Why did you cool off towards Daniel? You were in love.' He coughs. 'The whole thing was terrible, losing Samira, the loss of future children, but why? You didn't know about Abigail then.'

'Our relationship was so wrong.'

'Why didn't you tell your barrister about Daniel and Abigail deliberately misleading you?'

Her eyes fill with desolation. 'Abe was dead. I couldn't undo it.' She pulls at the sleeves of her jumper and then wrenches at the skin around her nail, drawing blood. She wipes away the tear that stands proud on the smooth skin of her face, leaving a faint trace of blood from her finger. 'I was embarrassed,' she continues. 'I was so unseeing, like Ed had said. I couldn't share it with the world. I didn't *want* to share it with the world.'

'Oh Rose.' He wants to leap over the table and hold her, take care of her, in a way she believed Daniel Deane would look after her all those years ago, but catching the eye of the custody officer, who's watching them more intently than usual, he checks himself.

Rose glances up at the officer too, shuffles forwards in her chair, pushes the fingertips of both hands through her hair. 'After Samira died, it was as if I could really see Daniel. I didn't love him, I never had. It all became clear when my daughter was put into my arms. It was as if I saw everything that I hadn't seen before.' She pauses. 'That I didn't want to see before.'

'What happened after you were discharged from the NHS hospital?' he asks gently.

'I left my mum's house. I couldn't bear to be near her. She should have called an ambulance, and she didn't. I stayed with Tom and Casey, and that's when Miles contacted me. He came to see me and then came to Samira's funeral. He kept in touch in the months afterwards.'

'Did Daniel go to Samira's funeral?'

'No. I didn't want him there. My mum didn't go either. Just Casey, Tom and Miles.' She flicks a glance towards him. 'My mother carried on working at Bluefields, for God's sake. She thought I was mad to drop Daniel.'

'Did Daniel try and reconcile with you?'

'He called once in the weeks after Samira's death, but I wouldn't take his call. He never tried again. And that suited me fine.'

Her eyes dart around the brightly lit visits hall. 'When I saw Abigail at the hospital all those years later, visiting Abe, and realised when Abe had been born, the stark reality of Daniel Deane struck me so hard. He'd had no intentions at all towards me, and would have dumped me if Samira had lived.' She pauses. 'Abigail must have fallen pregnant with Abe very near to my due date for Samira. Maybe even near the time of my daughter's funeral.' She lays out her clenched hand on the table as if clawing at the plastic.

'I did see the notes,' she carries on. 'Maybe they did do everything they could. The haemorrhaging I experienced isn't uncommon. It doesn't happen often, but it does happen.'

She waits for him to answer, but he only shakes his head.

She ploughs on, releasing the floodgates that have been tightly closed for too long. 'When Abe was brought in and I saw Abigail, I recognised the fact that deep inside I'd always known something was very amiss during my affair with Daniel. The carvings on his bed. Abigail *looked* like me.'

There's still something she's not telling him. *Patience, Theo. Patience.*

'Do you think Daniel asked for Miles's resignation because Miles knew something more about him?' he probes gently.

'No, it was Daniel who had a hold over Miles and his career, as you know after listening to my story. Miles had wanted to leave Bluefields years before.' She looks at him. 'I don't know why, suddenly, Daniel allowed him to go. Miles doesn't know either.' She holds the edge of the table, her knuckles white.

'Is there more I should know about Miles?' he asks.

'Don't you think that's enough?'

'A lot of doctors fight addictions,' he says.

'Miles would never have got a decent position in the NHS – anywhere – if this had come to light.' She leans towards him. 'When he was a medical student, he began swapping a drug – morphine – that was meant to be used on his patient, giving the patient a placebo trial drug instead. Miles was a morphine user; he was addicted. When a savvy ward sister got wind of it – realizing her patient wasn't responding to the drug – she started to ask questions and worked out that Miles was on shift whenever this occurred. Daniel stepped in. He and Miles worked on the same general medicine wards. After the nurse had taken the incident a step further, reporting it to the med school's head of faculty, Miles was invited to take a voluntary blood test. Daniel took the rap for him, saying it was his mistake; he claimed he was the one who'd administered the wrong drug to the patient, inadvertently. Miles was in his debt then. Forever.'

'They kept Daniel on the course after that?'

'Yes, because he took the blood test and he was clean. Daniel was never a drug taker.'

'Unbelievable.'

'Miles loves his job… loved his job, it was what he lived for. He's been clean for years. He's paid for his mistake.'

'And you'd have done anything to protect him, because you felt you owed him? You'd have done anything so he could carry on practising?'

'I wanted him to continue working, yes.' She goes to bite her nail but instead jams her hand in her jean pockets. 'Tell me more about Elliot.'

And Theo does, because he doesn't think Rose will tell him anything more about her husband. He talks about Elliot, and about the sort of man he knows he is. An ex-hack, a man who disregarded his wife, a father who ignored his son at a time when Elliot needed him the most. A writer who hates failure so much that he has contemplated sensationalizing her story.

She listens intently, her eyes boring into his own.

He's fallen for Rose. But the story he's hearing from her is not yet complete. It's time for her to be totally truthful with him. What neither of them has anticipated is the current of energy flowing between them. But Rose is married, and she loves Miles, and he certainly knows Miles loves her. It is this that lies at the root of her confession and conviction: their shared love and loyalty.

What is Rose still not sharing with *him*?

Has she taken the blame for Miles because she felt she owed that much to him?

Or did she kill Abe in revenge for what Abe's parents did to her? Was that her motivation? If it was… If it was, it doesn't bear thinking about, because it makes Rose a psychopath. Theo studies her. She is not a psychopath, he knows that.

The warning bell for the end of visit time fills the hall.

'I'm seeing Ed Madden's partner,' he says, quickly shaking off his previous thoughts. 'There's something I think he can tell me about Daniel Deane.' He pauses. 'And I've met Bella Bliss.'

'Has she told you anything? I've written to her, but she hasn't replied. I've told no one about what she said.'

'Ed's partner, Hugo, is Bella's brother. I'm hoping to find out from him what Bella didn't tell you. Abe knew something too, I'm sure of it. I need to discover what it was.' He extends his back into his chair. 'Do you really think you saw your mum, Ed and Abigail at Bluefields the day you went into labour?'

'It's all so hazy, but I'm certain my mum was there, and Ed. Abigail, I'm not so sure.'

Ignoring the warning stare of the guard, he leans over the table and kisses her on the cheek. She turns her head and briefly his lips touch hers.

'Don't beat yourself up about your son, Theo. You're a good man.'

He lifts his shoulders in reply, smiles sadly and turns to leave.

Darkness fills him as he makes his way to the prison exit. In his car, he flips on his mobile and a stream of texts appears. The one that snatches at his gut is from Natasha, sent three hours before.

> I've found an email from Abe, sent the morning of the day he was taken into hospital. It was in my spam. He did go to see Ed Madden, who told him he wasn't Abigail's son. Abe thought he could find out who his real mother was. Maybe Daniel wasn't his father either?? Call me, Theo.

Ed Madden could have been lying to Abe out of spite, but something tells Theo he wasn't. It all fits. Abigail's treatment of Abe as he was growing up, the argument between her and Zakaria... yes, it all makes sense. And as for whether Daniel Deane is Abe's real father... it could be true and would explain why there was no love lost between father and son, because Theo has seen no evidence of Daniel's love for Abe. He didn't even go to see him in hospital. Maybe Abe had been adopted by the couple, which would explain Abe's feeling of isolation as a child and teenager, always feeling as if he didn't belong. But then why had they adopted him if they didn't want him? If they'd adopted a baby, Abe's EDS wouldn't have yet been diagnosed and the couple would have been unaware of Abe's imperfection.

He calls Natasha, and then Bella to check that Hugo is still coming to his flat. He also needs to make a surprise visit to Marion soon.

He starts the car and thinks of Rose, and cannot stop thinking about her for the whole journey home.

50

Rose

Theo's been gone for two hours, and I'm in Don's room waiting to be interviewed by DI Alison Greenwood again. She's due at 3 p.m. I've been in here for half an hour already. Restless, I stand and take the few steps towards the other side of the small room and stare at the digital clock on the wall. It shows 2.59 p.m. and as it flips to the hour, the door clicks open. As I already know, Alison Greenwood is efficient. I liked her when I met her before and I've no reason to believe I won't still like her on a second meeting, although I'm intrigued to know what's instigated it.

She smiles at me, and then at the custody officer who has accompanied her. He closes the door and she turns. 'Rose, it's good to meet you again.'

'You too,' I say, walking back to the chair and sitting down. I do still like her, and she still has an honest face.

'There is something you should know, Rose, and I wanted to tell you myself.'

An ominous feeling pervades the pit of my stomach.

She carries on. 'Daniel Deane and his wife have disappeared.'

'Disappeared?'

'Yes.'

'That's not a crime.'

'No, it isn't, but his criminal involvement at the Mount Clinic is. Several months ago, a woman came forward with serious allegations against the clinic and Daniel Deane. I didn't tell you about this on our first meeting for various reasons, one being that it's an ongoing investigation. However, during these investigations, Daniel and Abigail Deane have absconded.' She pauses. 'And since their disappearance, we've had several other women contact us.' She looks at me. 'We're keen to find him and his wife.'

I study her well-structured features. 'I don't think there's anything I can tell you. I really don't. I wasn't lying to you before; I had no knowledge of the Mount Clinic.'

'I believe that to be true,' Alison Greenwood says.

I nod. 'I hope you find the Deanes.'

'We will.' She hasn't moved position. 'Rose...'

'Yes?'

'The prison's director tells me you are talking with the writer Theo Hazel.'

'I am.'

'Do you think that's a wise move?'

'I think it's a very wise move,' I reply.

She buttons up her raincoat. 'I'll be in contact soon.' She lays the palm of her hand on my arm and looks me in the eye. I smile, but I know it's a desolate attempt.

The detective turns and leaves me alone in the room.

51

I look across at Cathy. We are sitting at a table in the canteen that only accommodates two people. I am playing with my spag bol. I can't eat it. Alison Greenwood's visit a few days before is still bothering me. Where is all this leading?

'Do you feel any guilt at all about what you did?' I've never asked Cathy this direct question before.

'Yes, I do,' she says, her voice low and barely audible.

'Is that really true?'

'No.' She watches me. 'But I know *you* feel guilt, and you shouldn't. You shouldn't be in here. You've been dealt the worst of hands, Rose.'

Only Cathy has known the truth since the beginning. The real truth about Abigail, Spain, my pain, my distress, and what happened that day on the unit.

'But you loved your children?' I ask.

'When I was with them I did. When I wasn't, I forgot about them. As if they didn't exist. Or existed somewhere else.'

'I don't really understand,' I reply.

'I know you don't, and neither do I.' She pauses. 'What's going to happen with you and Theo?'

'I think about him all the time.' And I do. I'm glad I have someone I can tell about my feelings for Theo, because it's the first time in years I've felt something other than chronic desolation.

She takes my hand. 'You think you've helped Miles, but you're destroying him.' She scoops up a mouthful of paella. 'It's time you let him do what he wanted to do.'

I stroke the palm of her hand. 'It can't get any worse, can it, Cathy?' I hear the hoarseness of my voice.

She looks me in the eye, so unusual for Cathy. 'You won't die, Rose. You *will* get better with treatment... but there *is* something more.'

I wasn't asking Cathy about my mortality, and there is the chance that it's already too late to worry about that. Cathy, though, does seem to have an intuition about the future. The missing part of her has been filled by something other, or maybe she just has a crystal-like understanding of the world in which she cannot participate and she's not a seer at all. I've never questioned this aspect of her, only accepted it. It's why she accepts me; why she understands so much about me, even the things I don't.

'What is the "something more", Cathy?' I know, though. Deep down, I know. And so does she, I believe. Alison Greenwood's visit and her news has confirmed it for me. About Abe and the feeling I experienced so vividly the day he died.

Cathy looks at the plate of dehydrated vegetarian paella sitting in front of her. She cannot eat dead animals. 'You need to talk to Miles.'

For the rest of the meal she does not look at me and she does not speak.

52

Theo

27 April 2016

Theo has woken up with the insidious beginnings of a head-ache; his temples are throbbing and he's feeling very slightly sick. He swallows, and then lifts his head to look at the bedside clock and squints. Christ, it won't be many years before he'll need glasses. 7 a.m. He turns over and buries his head beneath the pillow, trying not to think but thinking anyway – of Rose, and what really happened in the hospital in Chesterfield.

The pillow isn't working and the morning noise is finding its way through the tiny window of his room. And then he hears the abrasive sound of his intercom.

He gets up, pulls on trousers and a T-shirt and makes his way down the communal stairs. He can see through the glass of the front door that it's a woman and a man. For a moment he thinks about ignoring them and returning to his flat, back to bed. This early it has to be someone selling something, or religious types, but then the man takes out his ID.

Wishing he'd combed his hair, because he knows it'll be looking like a bush, Theo opens the door. The woman smiles at him. Her face and features are as dazzling as the laser-like morning sun. Theo grimaces into the brightness.

'Good morning, sir. Mr Hazel?'

He nods.

'DI Alison Greenwood, and my sergeant. May we have a very quick word with you?'

'Of course, come in. I'm on the third floor.' He turns, and as he does, he pulls the free weekly newspaper from his delivery box. Gives it a quick glance. Does a double-take and forgets about the police in his foyer.

Deanes Disappear As Allegations Against the Mount Clinic Escalate.

Front page.

'I take it you haven't read the papers yet this morning?' DI Alison Greenwood says, but as she does, a mobile phone calls out and the sergeant pulls his device from his jacket pocket.

'Other case we're on, guv,' he says.

'Go take it in the car.'

The sergeant disappears outside and Alison Greenwood follows Theo upstairs to his flat. In the kitchen, he asks her if she wants coffee and is glad when she says no. He's out of milk, and when he looks inside the coffee jar to make himself one, he's out of caffeine too.

'What can I do for you, DI Greenwood?' he asks, attempting to smooth down his hair while at the same time trying to read the front-page story in the newspaper now lying on his counter. Nothing like being on top of things; he now knows why he's getting a police visit.

'I visited Rose Marlowe yesterday, Mr Hazel.' She nods towards the newspaper. 'I'm investigating the Deanes' disappearance. I was hoping Rose might be able to throw some light on the allegation. Actually, make that plural. Allegations. We received the first one a few months ago. Unfortunately, just when we'd gathered enough evidence to question Daniel Deane concerning illegal activities at the Mount Clinic, he and his wife did a bunk.'

'I knew nothing about this… not until just now.'

'I gather.' She glances at the paper and leans against the kitchen wall. 'The prison director and Rose's therapist tell me you have a friendly relationship with her... You're about to make a killing with this story, I'd guess, Mr Hazel.'

Heat envelops him. He'll never write Rose's story. Never. Women like Alison Greenwood would hate him. But that's not the reason. The reason is much more profound. He's fallen in love with Rose Marlowe.

Finally he replies. 'From the beginning, it was my gut feeling that everything was not as it appeared.'

'And it seems you were correct. Is there anything Rose has divulged to you that might help us locate the Deanes? Anything she's told you that will help our enquiries at all?'

'I'm afraid not,' he says.

She sighs. 'Are you aware of her relationship with Daniel Deane, Abe Duncan's father, in the early nineties?'

'I am. Now. I wasn't before she spoke with me.'

'It seems that no one was aware at the time of her hearing. Has Rose talked to you about the baby girl she gave birth to in 1992, and the child's subsequent death at Bluefields Hospital? And then soon afterwards Rose's emergency surgery?'

'She has.' He can't share the information about Abigail Deane. That is up to Rose.

'Is there anything more you can tell me about Rose, Mr Hazel?'

'I don't believe she is guilty of murder,' he says.

'How close are you to Rose Marlowe, Mr Hazel?'

He doesn't answer, but neither does he avert his eyes from her gaze.

'Mr Hazel, it really would be in Rose's best interests that we find the Deanes.' She hands him a card. 'Get in touch when there's something you'd like to share with me. I'll make my own way out.'

Before he hears the click of his flat's door, he's already devouring the day's breaking news. The investigations into Daniel Deane are explosive. The press are all over it, he discovers as he googles the story on his mobile. It's everywhere,

Deane's alleged involvement in illegal abortions at the Mount Clinic in Nottingham during the nineties, and whilst he was the manager at Bluefields. The connection to Rose Marlowe – her arrest and imprisonment for the murder of Daniel Deane's son – is peppered throughout the reporting. The Deanes' disappearance has thrown open the floodgates, encouraging women who were patients at the Mount Clinic to come forward. The current management at Bluefields are denying any knowledge of Deane's activities, and any ongoing connection with him.

Theo folds the paper and clicks off his phone. Takes a deep breath, stretches his arms upward and makes his way to the bathroom to brush his teeth. Later he'll venture out to stock up on caffeine.

53

Theo is dragged from a tattered sleep by the sound of his mobile pinging. He went to bed late the night before, his mind on fire with theories and facts about Rose. As he's brought to wakefulness in the frigid light of morning, Rose's story is dropping into place. He should have told DI Alison Greenwood what he knows, but he wanted to put it off until after his meeting with Hugo Bliss.

He reaches for his mobile. 7 a.m. And a message from Sophie.

He'd forgotten about the manic voicemail he left for her in the middle of the night – he wasn't even drunk, only high on adrenaline. He has no one to share news of his new project with, only Sophie, and she's the only one he wants to talk to. He rambled on, telling her that he doesn't believe Rose is guilty of murder.

> That was a long message! I'm around if you want
> to talk. Nick's away on business. I have time S x

Waking up properly, he smiles into the dawn light of the room. Despite everything, Sophie's still here for him. He really has to work on that. He thinks of Rose, the only other woman for whom he's felt anything. Sophie was his first love at university, although he made up for his lack of promiscuity during his youth in the years following Elliot's death, and his divorce from Sophie.

He is just about to reply to her text when his intercom rings out. He hauls himself from the bed and peers out of the lounge window, but can't see anyone at the entrance door to the block. Returning to the bedroom, he pulls on a sweatshirt and joggers and goes downstairs to investigate. He sees an envelope that has been shoved underneath the door rather than put in the communal letter box, his name scrawled on the front. His heart misses several beats and he bends down to pick it up.

A piece of A4 paper has been folded neatly into a third of its size to fit in the envelope. He opens it quickly.

> *Stay out of affairs that are none of your business. Stay away from Rose Marlowe. Stop visiting her.*
>
> *If you don't take this advice there's a chance that something very bad will happen to your ex-wife and her new daughters. And I'm sure you don't want that – for Sophie to lose another child, and for the blame to lie with you, again.*
>
> *Stay away from Rose.*

Theo doesn't move, as if his feet are glued to the concrete floor. It's not until the woman who lives in the flat above nudges gently at his arm that his muscles switch back on.

'Theo, do you mind moving, I need to get out...'

He peels his eyes away from the typed words. 'I'm so sorry...' He steps to one side and she pushes her double-width buggy past. Two pairs of eyes stare at him, full of curiosity.

'The twins are looking very cute today,' he says, feeling guilty that he didn't see her struggling down the stairs. He'd normally help her.

She tosses her head. 'They haven't been sounding very cute all morning.' She manages a tight smile. 'Got to go, Theo.'

He opens the door for her and she humps the buggy over the threshold.

Theo sprints back upstairs and finds his mobile in the kitchen. He calls Sophie immediately.

'Theo, so glad you've called, but this is a bad time—'

'Soph, I need to be quick. Have you taken the girls to school yet?'

'No... just about to leave. Theo, what's wrong? You sound demented. You were obviously up half the night, given the time you left the voicemail. Are you all right?'

'I'm fine, but can you not take the girls to school this morning? Not yet. I'm sorry, I don't want to scare you, but I've received a... a threatening letter.'

'About what?'

'It's linked to my investigations into Rose Marlowe. Someone's trying to scare me off.' He takes a breath. 'Whoever sent the letter is threatening you and the girls.'

'Do you think it's authentic? I mean... I mean...' He hears the increase in the pitch of her voice. 'Theo, you really do attract bad luck, don't you?'

'Sophie, I'm sorry. I need to go. I'm calling the police. Stay home with the girls. I'll call you back. Is Nick home?'

'He's out of the country on business. I told you.' The line crackles. 'I'm scared, Theo. I love the girls.'

'I know you do. Sit tight, and I'll be in touch soon.'

He ends the call and feels cold sweat trickling between his shoulder blades. Making his way into the study, he slumps onto his chair, gives himself a minute and then calls DI Alison Greenwood's direct number. He should have done this yesterday.

'DI Greenwood speaking.'

'Hi, it's Theo Hazel.'

'Ah, Mr Hazel. What can I do for you?'

'I'm calling you because I've just received a typewritten letter hand-delivered to my building, warning me that if I don't lay off the Rose thing, something will happen to my ex-wife and her two young stepdaughters.'

'You really should have cooperated earlier, Mr Hazel.' Her voice has slipped into a monotone. Theo guesses it's her annoyed voice. She carries on. 'Give me your ex–wife's number. I'm calling her now.'

He gives her Sophie's details. 'Please keep me informed.'

'I will, Mr Hazel. I believe in sharing information for the greater good.'

Her tone is still absolutely flat. He really should share the information from Natasha's text about Abe's parentage. *After seeing Hugo.* He has to give her something, though. 'It's Ed Madden you need to be talking to about the letter, DI Greenwood.'

'Ed Madden? I know about his connection with the Deanes.' She clears her throat. 'I'll be in touch. We will need to interview you, Mr Hazel. Ideally we should be talking in person now, but distance is an issue.' DI Greenwood is based in Herefordshire. 'Ensure you're available to answer my calls.'

Ten minutes later, Sophie calls him.

'A DI Alison Greenwood is sending the local police to the house,' she says. She sounds more together. 'I'm absolutely furious with you.'

'Soph—'

'Don't call me that.'

'Sophie—'

She's already disconnected.

The only person apart from Rose who knows he's been asking questions is Marion. He can't envisage Marion making it to Manchester to slide the letter under his door. Which only leaves two options: Daniel Deane or Ed Madden. Deane has disappeared, and Theo doesn't think he'd risk it. That leaves Ed.

He attempts to clear his mind so he can focus on Hugo's visit. The interior designer isn't due until 1 p.m., but Theo needs to go to Asda to stock up on Desperados.

He contemplates calling Alison Greenwood back and telling her about Natasha's message, but he knows he needs as many facts as he can gather before speaking to her again. And tomorrow he'll confront Marion about Daniel Deane.

54

Hugo is bang on time, and Theo makes his way to the communal entrance to let him in.

'Bit of a bastard to find, I have to say,' are Hugo's opening words.

'Great to see you. Thanks for coming. How's Bella?'

'She's good. I kipped on her floor last night. It's healthy to go back to basics sometimes. She dropped me off here, wanted to come in but has lectures.' He pauses. 'She wanted me to have some time alone with you too...'

'I think your sister wants the best for you, Hugo.'

'She does.' He rearranges the collar of his shirt. 'She says hi.' He searches Theo's face. 'You all right, mate? Look a tad distracted.'

'I'm okay. Just had some news.'

'Not good, I take it?' Hugo asks.

'A solvable problem. C'mon in.'

Hugo scans the foyer of the flat complex. 'Nice development.'

'I'm sure this isn't your usual gig.'

'I get all sorts.' He holds out his hands in an expression of acceptance.

Theo can't help but smile. He's sure Hugo doesn't get that many two-bedroom flats in Chorlton to do up.

'Third floor.' He gesticulates towards the lift, which Hugo declines.

Theo follows him up the stairs, which he's taking two at a time; Hugo brims with unexpended energy, and Theo laments the passing of his thirties. He likes Hugo and doesn't like what he himself is about to do, although both Bella and Hugo to a certain extent have intimated that Hugo is here to unburden himself.

DI Greenwood will be contacting Ed Madden soon, but clearly she hasn't yet – or if she has, then Hugo is unaware of it. He wouldn't be here if he knew.

Inside the flat, the young designer paces and Theo watches. 'It's small, but good light. You said the lounge and kitchen?' Hugo questions.

Theo nods. They're now standing in the kitchen. 'Beer?'

'Shouldn't really, at work and all that, but Bella said she'd pick me up and take me to the station. I don't drive. I'd have liked to stay with her tonight too, but Ed wants me home.' Theo hands him a Desperado. 'Cheers, mate. Our favourite. Mine and Ed's.' He takes a swig and quickly goes on to finish the bottle.

Theo's limit is three of the tequila-infused beers. He hands Hugo another from the fridge.

Hugo loosens up pleasingly quickly. 'The kitchen's bigger than I'd thought in a two-bed flat. There's a lot we can do in here.' He scribbles down notes on a leather-bound clipboard, but already he isn't as deft with a pen as he was in the shop. He finishes bottle number two. 'The lounge,' he continues, 'is… compact, but it's got good light coming in from the balcony doors. Nice feature. I'm sure I can do something with that. Shall we go through some ideas?'

'Sure. Let's go sit on the balcony.' Theo gets out more beers and takes them outside. It's a cool day, but he long ago invested in a small outdoor heater. Hugo sits down on the narrow terrace and crosses his legs. He looks at home there. Theo plonks another Desperado in front of him, and flicks on the heater to its highest setting.

'I like it here,' Hugo says. 'Good vibes.'

Theo begins. 'So how long have you been with Ed?'

Hugo begins to fidget. 'Five years. He comes across as a bit crabby, but I love the old sod.' His green eyes glitter in the bright but cool sun.

'He must have come with a bit of baggage?' Theo delves.

Hugo eyes him. 'Don't we all? You attached?'

'Divorced, hence the small flat.'

'Ah!'

'Another beer?' Theo asks.

'Don't mind if I do.'

He gets up and returns with two more, cracking them open, handing both to Hugo.

'Ta, mate.' Hugo uncrosses his legs and allows his knees to splay wide as he slouches into the chair. 'Ed *does* have a lot of baggage. Bella doesn't like him. Wants me to finish it. Thinks he's bad news.' He sighs, gulps down more beer. 'He's certainly not perfect...' He pauses. 'Bella says I should talk to you.'

'It might help,' Theo replies softly.

'Daniel Deane and Abigail, Ed's sister, *were* bad news—'

'Abigail Deane is Ed's *sister*?'

'Yep.' Hugo peers at the bottle in his hand. 'These little devils are strong.'

'Wow.' Theo waits. 'That's not a known fact, is it? In the public arena, I mean. It wasn't mentioned at the time of Rose's hearing?'

'It wasn't. Why would it be? Abigail managed to drop off the grid after meeting Daniel, although she'd changed her name before she'd even married him. She'd wanted to reinvent herself, apparently. Determined to shake herself free of her working-class heritage, according to Ed.' He pauses. 'And now... they've both dropped off the grid, it seems.'

'Yes. Big news.'

'It is.' Hugo sinks the beer.

'Have you met Abigail?'

'Nah. But I think she's a nasty piece of work.'

'What makes you say that?'

'Gets everything she wants... although there was one thing she couldn't get. And that's what led to all this. Rose Marlowe, everything. The outcome for Abigail wasn't exactly what she'd bargained on.'

'What outcome? What couldn't she get?'

'I can't say. I can't do it... A child. Abigail couldn't have her own child.'

'Ah. I see.' And Theo *is* beginning to see. 'What do you know, Hugo?'

'Jesus Christ, I can't tell you. I'll get banged up. Ed definitely will. But it's been playing on my mind since he told me. And even more now that the Deanes have done a bunk.'

'These are people's *lives*.' Theo takes a glug of his own beer. 'Rose's life.'

Hugo wipes his forehead with the back of his hand – the outdoor heater is a bit too effective. He is clearly dying to get things off his chest. Bella understood this about her brother. And the Deanes' disappearance will be pushing him.

'Bloody tragic, Rose Marlowe,' he says. 'Her baby...' He stops and checks himself. 'Then, at the hospital, her finding out that Abigail was Daniel's wife, and about Abe's existence. But Christ, going on to murder Abe...' He drinks more beer and peers at Theo. 'What's Rose like?'

'She's... very sad.' Theo exhales.

'Abe wasn't Abigail's son. That's the thing.' Theo is getting closer. 'I've only been able to talk to Bella about it all. She told me to go to the police.' Hugo slumps into the chair; his arm drops downward, the beer bottle dangles from two fingers. 'But the thing is, the thing is...'

'What, Hugo?'

'I'm calling Bella to pick me up.' He stands up and stumbles. The empty bottle clanks to the ground.

'Is Ed in touch with his sister and Daniel Deane?' Theo ploughs on.

An expression of despair takes hold of Hugo's handsome, symmetrical features, and a bead of sweat makes its way down one neatly sculpted dark sideburn, nestling on the apex of his cheekbone. 'What sort of partner am I? I'm a traitor, a Judas. But I can't stop thinking about Rose Marlowe.'

Theo sees real conflict, real distress, and he is beginning to piece together the collage. He tells himself that keeping all this inside was torturing the young designer, and that he's doing Hugo, and Bella, a favour.

Hugo continues. 'The worst thing is that Ed knew. Knew all along. How can I love a man like that? That's what Bella says.'

'*What* does Ed know?'

Hugo holds his head in his hands, and then, like a Catholic parishioner in the confessional, he finally tells him.

55

Bella has arrived to pick up Hugo. They've put him in her Corsa and she and Theo are standing next to the car.

'Tell him to send his bill and I look forward to seeing his ideas,' Theo says.

'Hugs told me he talked.'

'He has.' Theo shifts his weight from one foot to the other.

'I'm glad. Although I'm guessing it's all going to come out soon anyway.' She bends down, checks on her older brother, who is now lying in the back seat snoring gently.

'I'll have to share this with the police, Bella. I'm sorry,' Theo says.

She straightens up, closes the car door. 'I know. My lovely big brother.'

'I'm so sorry.'

She lifts her slim shoulders a fraction. 'I'll look after him.' She gets in the driver's seat. 'We'll deal with the consequences. It's time.'

Theo watches her drive off and then makes his way back to his flat. Thinking of Rose, he pulls a Desperado from the fridge. He'll have to tell Alison Greenwood that Hugo is his source. He doesn't want to but there's no alternative. As he takes a swig of the beer, his mobile rings out. He's had it on loud since Sophie's call.

Alison Greenwood.

'Mr Hazel.' Her voice is deep, her tone no-nonsense. 'Sophie and her stepchildren are safe. A DS Mulholland is leading this investigation up in Manchester. I need to ask you some questions. We need to know if Rose Marlowe has revealed information to you she has not shared with the police. Considering what has now happened with your ex-wife, I need to know what you know, or what Rose knows. I expect you to tell me.'

'Have you picked up Ed Madden?'

'What do you know, Mr Hazel?'

'Rose Marlowe did not kill Abe Duncan. DI Greenwood, are you aware that Ed Madden is Abigail Deane's brother?'

Silence.

'I am now.'

'Like, *just* now?'

'Recently.' Her voice is louder, her mouth, he guesses, closer to the receiver. 'And why do you think Rose admitted to murder, Mr Hazel?'

'That, I'm really not sure about, DI Greenwood.'

'What *are* you sure about?'

'It's come to my attention that events in 1992 at Bluefields Hospital in Nottingham, more specifically...' he pauses, bites his lip and tastes the iron, 'what happened to Rose Marlowe in Bluefields, are *very* pertinent to this case.'

He has to tell her about Hugo's revelation. He has to tell her about Abe going to see Madden in the spring of 2015 when he came to England, and what he believes Madden told Abe during that visit.

He weighs up what he knows. He needs time to think. 'Sorry, DI Greenwood, someone at my intercom. Give me a minute.'

He presses mute and lays down the phone. He has to gather his thoughts. Hugo was telling the truth, he's certain.

Why didn't Rose tell DI Greenwood about the fiasco in Spain, and afterwards? *Has* she taken the rap for her husband? Why would she do that? Rose wanted to be put in prison – this is how much she values her life and how incredibly broken she really is. She sacrificed her own freedom for Miles. Christ, is Marion aware of what Daniel Deane and Abigail orchestrated?

Alison Greenwood is still on mute, and Theo is still mulling. It's time for the police to know everything. The letter delivered to his flat has moved the goalposts. A chill gathers around him in his overheated study, and it's not only connected to Abigail and Daniel Deane, but also to Ed Madden. Madden was behind the letter, and he's sure the act was carried out at Daniel Deane's request.

Theo should have alerted Alison Greenwood to Natasha's retrieved email. A bone-biting guilt spreads through him.

When the truth about Abe Duncan is revealed, Rose will disintegrate, shatter, and the only thing that might save her is the existence of a little girl in San Francisco. Natasha and Abe's daughter. Despising himself, Theo quickly writes this line down on a notepad, and then finally presses un-mute.

'Hi, DI Greenwood, sorry. Big delivery, signed-for only.'

'I'm waiting.'

He gives her the facts as he knows them, including Hugo's revelation. Silence follows, and it's Theo's turn to wait.

Finally Greenwood replies. 'I see. I was planning on coming to Manchester in the morning to liaise with DS Mulholland, but I need to come as soon as possible. I will be there late this evening, when you can give me a formal statement in person.'

Theo looks at his watch. 'You won't get here until ten at the earliest.'

'Is that a problem?'

'No, but I really think you should be taking me seriously and finding Ed Madden.'

'Units were dispatched to Edward Madden's property soon after your earlier call, Mr Hazel. And forensics are, as of a few minutes ago, checking DNA.' He hears her shout an instruction and imagines her sitting in a busy office. 'I'm a woman. I multitask. I'll be in Manchester sometime after eight tonight.'

56

DI Alison Greenwood and her sergeant arrived just after 9 p.m. last night and stayed for two hours. Theo gave a formal statement, although he'd made a conscious decision not to mention Marion in any context. Rose wanted him to find out the extent of Marion's involvement, and despite the fractured relationship between them, Marion *is* Rose's mother, and Rose loves her regardless of her suspicions. He suspects this is why she asked him to investigate, rather than going directly to the police; he's understood this from early on in his visits. Whatever Marion has been up to, it's something that Rose has no desire to share with the police.

Theo contemplates whether the tables might be in opposite alignment for Marion compared to the blackmail Daniel Deane used with Miles. Is Marion blackmailing Daniel? Or is there an agreement between them that's been in place from the beginning, going back to the day Rose went into labour? Why, though, he wonders, did Marion agree to speak to him? So that she, and therefore Daniel Deane, could gauge the progress of what he was discovering?

He leans against the kitchen counter sipping a cold coffee and eating a Mars bar. His mobile vibrates on the unit and he answers.

'Just to let you know, we're acting on your information, Mr Hazel,' DI Greenwood says.

'Ed Madden?'

'I can't discuss anything with you. But I can put your mind at rest and tell you that we are now aware of the letter sender's identity.'

'And the Deanes?'

'I can see what you've been doing, but it's time to leave it with us. I don't want you speaking to Rose Marlowe until we've followed this through. I mean it.'

'Okay.'

'Have a good day, Mr Hazel.'

Theo puts the Mars wrapper in the bin and then calls Sophie. 'You all okay?' he asks.

'We're fine. I'm sorry I barked at you.'

'Have you told Nick?'

'Yes, he'll be home tomorrow night,' she replies. 'Theo… Rose Marlowe?'

'She's not guilty of murder, Soph.'

'You still going to write the book?'

Theo sees the money pass him by. He doesn't answer.

'You're in love.' Although he can't see her face, he sees her smile. 'What about the money? The advance? What are you going to do?'

'Probably move out of the flat. Rent a room somewhere. I don't know, Soph, but I can't write about Rose.'

'Nick said we can lend you money, with no time frame on paying us back.'

'Aw, you didn't tell Nick, did you?' He doesn't know what's worse, Sophie knowing he's a failure and skint, or her husband knowing.

'We don't have secrets between us, Theo. He knows I've been worried about you.'

'It's okay. I don't need your money. Or Nick's.'

'Offer's always open.'

'I know. Speak soon.' He disconnects.

Within ten minutes he's in his car and trying not to like Nick. But it's impossible. He does, and always has. He glances at the dash clock: 7.32 a.m. He could be at Marion's by late morning. He needs to discover if she knows the whole story. If she does, it's easy, he'll inform Alison Greenwood. If she doesn't, he'll say nothing. Perhaps he – and Rose – has it all wrong about Marion. But if not, what then?

He slumps into the car seat. He does not know.

–

On the M1 leg of his journey, he succumbs to an attack of conscience and pulls in at the services to call Marion and let her know he'll be dropping by. No answer on the landline, so he tries her mobile. Maybe she's away visiting Sam. Maybe he has it all wrong and Sam's father-in-law really is helping him buy the villa.

Maybe he shouldn't be doing this.

Her mobile rings for minutes. Finally an agitated Marion answers. 'I can't speak, Theo. I have the police with me.' She rings off.

Suddenly needing air, he gets out of the car. Marion didn't sound confrontational towards him; whatever has encouraged Alison Greenwood to visit her is not connected with what he told the policewoman, therefore it must be associated with what Ed Madden revealed during questioning.

Or maybe Greenwood is just a good detective.

As the wind whips up in the service station's exposed car park, Theo buttons up his jacket and gets back in the car. He returns to the motorway and at the next junction does a U-turn, travelling back the way he came.

He makes his way to Chesterfield and Old Whittington, hoping Miles will be at home. He doesn't bother to call. What will be will be, although he does wonder if the police have beaten him to it.

–

Theo is sitting in Miles's kitchen. Miles has cleared up since his last visit. He's put his house in order, as if he were going on holiday.

They sidestepped any pleasantries. Miles puts on percolated coffee and pulls out a bag of croissants, and the smell wafting over tells Theo they were bought fresh that morning. Today Miles is shaved and appears less forlorn than he did on Theo's previous visit.

'Good timing,' he says as he places two croissants on separate plates. 'Best croissants in Old Whittington.'

'Have the police been in contact with you?'

'No, not yet, but I'm sure they will be soon. I've already spoken to a barrister, and Rose's solicitor.'

'Was it you, Miles?'

Miles sits down on the chaise longue, the plate holding his croissant balanced precariously on his lap. He picks up the pastry and takes a bite, chews laboriously and puts it back on the plate, setting it down next to him. He doesn't answer.

Theo continues. 'I had a wild theory that it could have been Abigail Deane who killed Abe and that you and Rose have been protecting each other, thinking the other did it.' He contemplates his croissant. 'But I'm wrong, aren't I?'

'For Christ's sake, I don't think even Abigail Deane is capable of murdering her own son, and why would she? No, it was me. A doctor, a saver of lives.'

Miles doesn't know that Abigail is not Abe's biological mother, and he certainly doesn't know who is. Why then is he confessing to Abe's murder; what is motivating him to tell the truth now?

'Why did you allow Rose to take the blame? You love her.'

'It's what she wanted,' Miles replies.

'*Why* did she want it?'

'That's for Rose to tell you.'

'It might need explaining in court.'

'Rose has already served some time in prison,' Miles says. 'The prosecution won't pursue her for the perversion of justice.'

'Is that what your barrister said?'

'No, it's what Rose's solicitor said.'

Although he was starving in the car, Theo leaves the croissant untouched. 'I want to share something with you, Mr Marlowe.'

'I'm waiting.'

Time stands still and Miles's expression doesn't change as Theo drops the Armageddon bomb.

That Abe Duncan was Rose's child.

At last Miles turns away. His shoulders begin to move, small waves, but then after seconds they jolt, and his sobs echo through his tidy kitchen. A fresh wind circles in through the open window, caressing the upright hairs on Theo's arms.

Finally Miles faces him. 'There is no reason to tell Rose,' he says. 'What's done is done, and cannot be undone.'

'I think you are forgetting…' Theo's own throat is full, Elliot so clear in his mind, as is the fact that he and Sophie had their son for fifteen years. 'About Abe's daughter. Rose has a grandchild.'

'Yes, you are right.' Miles moves closer to him. 'You have feelings for Rose?'

'I…'

'I killed Abe. Not Rose. Never Rose. She thought I had much more to lose than she did. She went to prison for me so I could carry on working. But I couldn't work. I let her down in so many ways. Her sacrifice was for nothing. It's imperative she leaves prison. More so than ever because, as you say, she has a granddaughter.'

'I'll do everything I can to help,' Theo says.

'She'll need all the help she can get,' Miles replies quietly. 'There's one last thing you need to know. But that really is for Rose to tell you.'

Theo stands up and puts his plate on the countertop. 'I'll make my own way out.' He turns to go, but then stops and swings around. 'How could you let an innocent woman, your wife, go to prison for a crime she didn't commit?'

'I am weak. And this has always been so.'

Theo walks from the kitchen and towards the front door.

—

Back in Manchester, he decides he needs to clear his mind. He makes a quick stop-off at his flat to pick up his swimming stuff, then heads to the local public pool, unable to go to his health club because he cancelled the hefty subscription a month before.

There's nothing more for him to do except wait for news from the police, if indeed they decide to share anything with him, which is highly unlikely.

The ending to this story is too tragic and harrowing, too darkly ironic to comprehend.

57

10 May 2016

Eleven days later, Daniel and Abigail Deane are breaking news again.

Theo is reading page 5 in *The Times*: *Deanes Arrested in Morocco As New Evidence Comes to Light in 2015 Abe Duncan Murder Case: Rose Marlowe Granted Bail*. He folds up the newspaper, and as he does so, a call from Alison Greenwood pops onto his phone.

'Hello, DI Greenwood.'

'Good morning, Mr Hazel. Just to let you know that you are now free to go and visit Rose Marlowe. Although as I'm sure you're aware, she will not be in prison for much longer.'

'It would seem so. Miles Marlowe came forward?'

'I think you know that, Mr Hazel. He did, and he has been arrested. He's in custody. I am sure Rose will fill you in when you see her.'

'How is Rose?'

'I saw her this morning. She is devastated.'

'What have the Deanes said?'

'I can't discuss that with you. I'm only calling you now out of courtesy.' Silence. 'I appreciate your information.'

And with that, DI Alison Greenwood disconnects.

58

Rose

10 May 2016

It's Cathy I seek out after Alison Greenwood's visit. My head throbs and hammers and focus in both eyes is affected as I make my way to her cell, and I wonder if it's the result of Alison's news, or my illness, or a toxic composition of both.

A son. I had a son.

Alison's words, although confirming my darkest suspicion, have nevertheless still eviscerated me. My insides have been ripped apart and laid out in separate mental and physical spaces. I didn't think things could get any worse, because deep down I hoped beyond hope that my intuition on the day Abe died was wrong. I remember my question to Cathy. Did she know that things could get worse? Did she somehow know that Abe was my son? My mind revisits that day at Queen's Hospital, but I can't stay there long. I knew. Afterwards. After Abe died.

Alison sat on my bed as I vomited into the small sink in my cell. She handed me a handkerchief from her handbag and did not avert her eyes from mine. I admired that. I admire Alison Greenwood. She did her job, asking me why I'd lied and admitted to a murder I had not committed. She is patient but also astute. There was nothing she could say to me, and she didn't even try, telling me what she had to and only mentioning Theo's ex-wife and stepchildren to encourage me to talk. I couldn't talk, though; I don't want too many questions, too many obstacles. I don't want to muddy the waters.

That day in the unit is so fragmented within my mind now, I'm unsure what really happened. I could not tell the detective the entire truth because I'm not sure of that truth.

Ed Madden. Daniel Deane. His wife's name I cannot say, even inside my head.

I'm nearly at Cathy's cell door. It's free association time, although I know that even if it hadn't been, the custody officers would still have let me visit Cathy in her cell. They are giving me a lot of latitude. The other prisoners are too. The grapevine in here is breath-taking. God knows how any of them know, but I can see by their dipped looks and their lack of eye contact that they do.

I am broken, and my devastation is so visceral it is impossible to comfort me. So no one tries, as if they have taken their cue from Alison. My horror and isolation will surround me forever. But despite the blackness, because of Mia and, I admit, Theo too, I must now seek treatment. If it's not too late. I must give Theo the key, but despite what I feel about him, I am unsure. Can I tell him?

I nudge open Cathy's door.

She's sitting on her bed, her expression as it always is. Until she looks up and sees me, and then, for the first time since knowing her, I see what I decipher as seamless sympathy etched onto her extraordinarily pretty face. She lies down and pats the bed. I lie down too, my feet at her head, her feet at mine. Top-and-tailing.

'I'm so sorry, Rose.'

I don't answer. I find her foot and stroke the smooth skin around her ankle.

And then she tells me that she loves her children still, and loved the daughter who died.

'I can't explain, Rose,' she says, 'but I hope just a little bit of you can understand some of me.'

I think I can. She's never spoken so lucidly, and I know it's just this one time. But it's enough yarn for me to weave a more three-dimensional picture of Cathy on my mental loom, and I know I can ask her.

I tell her what I need. 'Will you do this for me? Will you write a story for Theo?'

She nods.

We lie in silence. My friend is a detached entity, and for a short time on the high dependency unit, alone with Abe, I was a separate entity too. Cathy's moral compass is absent, although her self-awareness is honed enough to at least recognise this fact. And I question whether I am more like Cathy than I want to admit.

After free association, I'm booked in to see Don. I don't want to see him, but the director insisted, plus my barrister suggested it was a good thing to do. I am to leave this place soon. It's Miles who will be putting up my bail.

Don is Don, delving but knowing he'll get nowhere. It's a short session. I wonder if he will be speaking to Miles; if he works in other prison institutions. I've never asked him what he does the two days he's not here. Miles will not talk to someone like Don.

My husband was allowed to see me directly after Alison Greenwood's visit; I think they planned it that way. We didn't have to meet in the visits hall and were allowed to speak in my cell. He held me and I sensed he was trying not to cry. He never wanted me to be in here. I foresee that this is the part of the story that will be hardest for Theo to grapple with: Miles's easy acquiescence to my plan, and the reason for that acquiescence.

After Miles left, I cried. The first time I'd cried so hard since Samira's funeral.

Samira: another poor woman's dead child.

What Daniel and Abigail did to me and to that woman and her baby is unforgivable. Vile.

But I ask myself: are they any worse than the baser part of me?

59

Theo

20 May 2016

Theo is looking forward to finally seeing Rose again because although Alison Greenwood had given him the green light to visit, Rose had not, saying she needed more time. The past ten days have been excruciating. As he makes his way through prison security it hits him that this is the last time he'll be sitting on the uncomfortable visits hall chairs, although he'll be carrying on with the writing classes that are running until July.

He had a call from Don Whiting the previous day. Theo said he'd pop into Don's office before seeing Rose. Now he knocks on the door, but there's no answer.

A custody officer he recognises walks by. 'Don's off sick today, Mr Hazel,' he says.

'Ah.' Over the officer's shoulder he catches a glimpse of Cathy. He doesn't think she's seen him, as her head is bent forward and she's looking at the floor, but she's making her way in his direction.

'Cathy, don't you have somewhere you should be?' the officer says as she approaches.

Cathy's vacant but pretty face looks at neither Theo nor the officer as she speaks. 'It's still free association.'

The officer glances at his watch. 'Indeed, but you shouldn't be loitering in the corridors.'

'I have something I want to give Mr Hazel.'

'You know that's not going to happen, Cathy,' the officer says.

'It's my homework, my story. C'mon, I spent ages writing it, and he missed our last class.'

Indeed he did. Theo smiles at her.

'I'd like to read it,' he says to the officer.

'One day, Cathy, you'll be the cause of my disciplinary hearing.'

She gives her work to Theo.

'Thanks, Cathy,' he says. 'I look forward to reading it, but it could have waited until our next class.'

She shrugs, turns and lopes down the corridor. Theo puts the A4 sheets into his rucksack.

'Strange 'un,' the officer says.

'Good writer, though.'

The officer laughs, his large protruding belly moving in unison with the waves of sound.

Theo makes his way to the visits hall, and to Rose.

–

Theo has been dreading this moment since Hugo's inebriated revelation, although he questions whether Hugo was as pissed as he thought at the time. There is so much about this situation that is tragic, and made more so by Marion's involvement. Marion didn't question too deeply the events at Bluefields on the day her daughter was taken there to have her baby, and neither did she question activities at the Mount Clinic, where she carried out cash-in-hand cleaning for Daniel Deane.

Marion – Rose's own mother – as guilty as the Deanes.

He takes a deep breath and swallows. In the most immeasurable parts of his imagination, he can't conceive Rose's state of mind. But he knows how he felt on discovering the body of his only son.

Shock, guilt, horror, distress, anguish. Grief. Insufferable and never-ending grief.

He got it all so wrong with Elliot, only realizing his neglect when he untied the camping rope and Sophie's scarf from the bedroom door handle and laid his dead son on the floor. He cannot get it wrong again with Rose. And he will not.

Rose watches every step he takes as he walks towards the table. The visitor room is strangely empty today, just him and Rose, and another pair on the other side of the room. He wonders if the director has had a hand in this. If he has, Theo is grateful. As Rose stands and takes a few steps towards him, he tries to ignore the warm sweat glazing his face. The officer on duty turns his head away, scrutinizing the other prisoner.

Rose is already a free woman.

She lifts her right hand. He takes hold of it. So soft, so warm, so yielding, but the fine vibrations of her muscles translate to his. He pulls her closer and holds her for a moment. They sit down.

'I have no words.'

'It's okay to say nothing, Theo.'

'You wanted me to find out about Marion.' Somehow this feels like safer ground. Rose's suspicion about her mother was the only reason she agreed to talk with him.

'My mother's been a shadow, a ghost on the edge of my dreams.' She speaks so quietly he can hardly hear.

'I'm so sorry you turned out to be right about her.'

She lifts her shoulders and tucks that beautiful hair behind her ears. 'My mother was there the day at Bluefields when I went into labour. She knew something was amiss.' Fatigue outlines every syllable. 'But surely she couldn't have known that Abe was my son… her grandchild?'

Theo's suspicion is that Marion *did* know about Abe. She must have put it all together. Rose is still protecting her mother.

She carries on. 'I buried someone else's dead child, Theo. That poor woman. That poor baby. Alison Greenwood told me what happened. An immigrant woman from the Mount Clinic was waiting to go into labour with her already dead baby girl. Daniel paid her to be induced, so that he and Abigail could take my live baby boy and give me her dead child in his place. They gave me the opposite drug, a tocolytic, to delay my labour.'

As Rose speaks, there are no tears in her eyes. Like Theo with Elliot, she's used them all up. 'I should have known,' she continues. 'Alison told the woman what happened to her daughter. She's been to Samira's grave to pay her respects. I've arranged to meet her next week and we'll go to the grave together. I called her. They let me call her.'

'That's good, Rose. A wonderful idea.'

She's looking at him, searching his face. 'A mother who has carried her child for nearly nine months should know whether a baby is hers.' She tilts her head, finding his eyes.

'Don't do this to yourself, Rose.'

She plunges on. 'If it hadn't been for you, Theo, I'd never have found out.' Pulling the sleeves of her sweater over her hands, she twists the fabric in between her fingers and bites hard at her thumbnail. A thin sliver of blood.

Theo can't look at her and instead finds the eyes of the custody officer, who shakes his head imperceptibly.

'All Miles ever wanted was a child,' she continues. 'All I ever wanted was a child.'

'I want to look after you, Rose,' Theo says.

She takes his hand again, leans over the table and places it on her cheek. 'What is Natasha like?'

'She's lovely.'

'And... Mia?' she asks softly.

'I've only seen a photograph.'

He spoke to Natasha yesterday and told her everything. He asked her if she had a photo of Mia he could show to Rose. She sent one straight away. A clear image of Abe's daughter.

Rose's granddaughter.

'Would you like to see it?' he continues.

'I would.'

He pulls it from his coat pocket, together with a photo of Natasha, and gives them to her. She takes them gently, as if she is touching something sacred, and studies the images. 'Mia has my hair, only darker.'

'She does, doesn't she?' He pauses. 'Rose, why did you take the blame for Miles?'

She shrugs.

'Tell me.'

'I need to go, Theo. I need some time alone.' She gets up from the chair, but then hesitates. 'What will happen to your book?'

'Gone. History. I've many other ideas.'

'I'll see you on the other side, then?'

'I hope so, Rose.'

60

Rose

Because I'm leaving, and probably because he feels sorry for me, the prison's director has allowed me to call Natasha from his office. Theo has put her number on the back of the photo.

After Theo left, I went to the prison library, where I googled Natasha and found a photo of her and Abe from 2014. I think it was from an old Facebook page. Looking at the image, my stomach pitched, just as it did when Alison Greenwood told me the horrifying truth. My son's face staring back at me, a face that was so familiar from the many times I washed his skin on the unit and tended to the growth on his chin.

At the hospital that day, afterwards, the punch of a mother's grief landed inside my stomach; low and aching and located where my womb was not. Why did the kernel of realization and the warmth of Abe show itself to me only then?

I stare at the image on the internet. God, how I hate that information can never be eradicated. Stains everywhere. Immovable, as mine will be.

The director has already left his office, so I can make the call in private; he only asked that I don't stay on the phone for hours. *We don't have funding for calls to America, Rose*, he said.

I punch in the number.

'Hi, Natasha speaking.'

'Natasha, it's Rose.' Silence. I carry on. 'Theo thought—'

'I told him you could call me, Rose. It's okay.'

Natasha has an American accent, but it's not strong. Her voice is soft and lilting. I could tell her now. 'I don't know what to say.'

'I'm coming to London at the beginning of September, for work.' I hear the sound of a child's cry. 'I'm bringing Mia,' she says. 'Would you like to meet her, Rose?'

'I really would, and I'd like to meet you too, Natasha.'

I hear her inhaling. 'Abe knew, Rose. God knows why Ed told him then, after so many years.' She takes a breath. 'He would have found you.'

The tears are now falling down my cheeks and onto the director's leather-framed blotting pad. I've only just noticed the old-fashioned nuances of his office. A green banker's lamp, the blotting pad, a Montblanc fountain pen. It reminds me of my old lecturer's office. I'm sure Wilko will be long dead.

'Natasha, I'm so sorry.' I pause. 'How can you forgive me?'

'This is not your fault. You've gone through enough.' Again Natasha inhales deeply. 'Mia looks very like Abe. Like you.'

Daniel would hate the colour of Mia's skin. I think about meeting Abigail all those years ago, and my own skin crawls. She wanted to meet me – the woman who was sleeping with her husband, with her permission. It's only now that I see the perversity of their marriage. All this time later, the images of Señora López and the maître d' at the Riverside Restaurant, even my midwife, Cam, make my stomach ripple with self-loathing.

'Was Abe happy?' I ask.

She moves the position of her phone. 'He was really happy with me.'

He was taken from a contentment he'd only just found, but I need to connect with this life I have unearthed. One of my last remaining loves emerging from my only hate. I might not have that long. But the terrible pain that began with Alison Greenwood's visit and which has stripped the lining of my stomach, as well as the integrity of my heart, is transmuting into something other – into a resoluteness of purpose. There is only one objective. There can only be one objective.

Mia.

Otherwise there will be nothing, even with Theo.

I cannot allow myself to think of Abe. But I can let myself think of Mia, and how perhaps I have so little time left for her.

Natasha carries on. 'So, we'll see you in London in September. Theo wants to be there. That okay?'

'That's good. I have to go. I can't stay on the line long. I'm still in prison. Out tomorrow.'

'See you soon, Rose.'

On cue, the director returns. 'Time for you to start packing, Rose.'

61

Theo

The story surrounding Abe's identity broke earlier this morning with footage of Rose leaving the prison with her solicitor and Alison Greenwood, together with two uniformed police officers. It's all over the morning news.

It is to her marital home that Rose returns, and to Miles, who is on bail awaiting his hearing.

Theo is on edge and can't settle. He spent all of yesterday in his study, and last night too, plucking up the courage to make the dreaded call to Bella — a call he still hasn't made. Now, at last, he picks up his mobile and taps in her name. After a few seconds, she answers.

'I've been waiting for you to call.'

'I thought you'd be angry with me,' he says.

'I knew the score, and Hugs did too.'

'Are the police charging Hugo?' he asks.

'No. Ed didn't implicate him — he told the police Hugs didn't know anything. Seems that Ed really does love my brother.'

'Look after Hugo. And work your ass off for that first, which I know you'll get.'

Standing in the kitchen once they have said goodbye, he debates with himself about what to do. His eyes flick around. There is no way he's going to be able to hang on to this flat; he'll have to sell, and then rent. He takes in the faded decor.

He's done nothing with the place, could never afford to. *Never liked the place anyway.* But he will not take the advance, he will not sign the contract.

He will not publish Rose and Abe's story.

He returns to the study and opens a filing cabinet, takes out a manuscript. A book he wrote after Elliot's death. It's never seen the light of day. Not his usual genre. A love story. He packs it into a large Jiffy bag, seals it up and writes his editor's name and address on the package. He'll post it later, and then call Greg to tell him the bad news about Rose's book.

He takes Elliot's photo from the same drawer and places the framed image of his son on his desk, where it will stay.

Then he sits back in his chair, eyes roaming the room. They settle on the rucksack he took to the prison the last time he saw Rose.

Cathy's story. He'd forgotten all about it. He gets up and retrieves the bag, opens it and pulls out the loose crumpled sheets. He reads the title out loud. *Unsaid Things.*

He begins to read.

After finishing the last paragraph, he starts again at the beginning. Rose watching Abigail visiting Abe in the hospital. Abigail's lacerating words that pierced Rose's heart like a spear. But Rose didn't know then that Abe was her son, and neither did Miles. *Oh Rose. We are all fallible.*

Cathy's story shows Rose's hidden festering anger towards Daniel and Abigail Deane, which exploded on listening to Abigail's heartless tirade that fateful day in the hospital. And it reveals something else about Rose. Why has she kept this to herself? His heart reaches out to her as he thinks of everything she has had to endure alone. Even the cruel diagnosis of cancer.

He reads the words again, but this time a wave of comprehension rips through him as he registers the invisible lines, the ones Cathy did not write.

He could be wrong, but he thinks he is not. Cathy would do anything for Rose.

A tear falls and he watches as the salty liquid is absorbed into the paper. He waits, and eventually the wetness dries.

As if the tear had never been there.

62

7 September 2016

Both Daniel and Abigail Deane admitted to all the charges brought against them and so their case did not go to trial. They were given their sentences the previous week. Miles's hearing finished six weeks ago and he is now residing at Her Majesty's pleasure. Rose is an exonerated woman. In Theo's telephone conversations with her – they haven't seen each other since his prison visit – he's mentioned nothing about reading Cathy's story. He's hoping she will talk tonight, and if she doesn't, then he will.

His own interpretation will remain hidden within him, no matter what his visit to see Miles in prison unearths.

His train is late getting into Euston, and so by the time he walks into the Premier Inn's bar area, navigating his way through a throng of people, Natasha, Rose and Mia are already there. Natasha is sitting on a leather sofa by a huge piano, while Rose is perched on the piano stool with the child sitting precariously on her lap.

Mia is pretending to play the piano, her chubby fingers unperturbed at the barrier of the substantial maple lid that covers the keys. Theo smiles. She appears very calm and a long way yet from the toddlerhood he still remembers as being quite hellish.

The child is a very dark blonde, with wiry curls, and when he gets closer, he can see her huge caramel-coloured eyes, her skin the colour of the piano's dark wood. She has inherited her grandmother's hair and eyes, but her father's facial plan. She has, though, her mother's physique, he notes as Rose swivels around on the stool; Mia is long and narrow, like Natasha.

His gaze falls on Rose and her luminescent smile. Is the smile due to her release from prison, or the fact that she is here with her granddaughter? But now he knows the truth regarding her cancer, he notices the dark circles below her eyes, and feeling her inner distress, his heart is lead inside his brittle chest.

He takes a breath and picks up his step. Rose is wearing a grass-green dress, her hair held in a loose ponytail, straggles of curls hanging down each temple.

She holds up her hand and waves, but it is Natasha who shouts. 'Theo! Come on over!'

He glances at Rose; she smiles even more widely at him but at the same time mouths something to Mia, who then grins at the woman she only met hours before. Rose shrugs in pretend nonchalance.

Rose stays at the piano with Mia, leaving Theo to talk with Natasha. The cacophony of bar noise ensures that she won't hear their conversation.

'This is so good of you,' he says. 'How's it going?'

'Good. I like her,' Natasha replies. 'Abe would have done too.' She throws an indulgent glance towards her daughter, who is utterly engrossed with the piano and with Rose.

'Has she talked?' he asks.

'She has. We're both staying here, same floor. I chatted with her alone in her room while Mia slept earlier. She's told me everything. Her mother, Marion—'

'Marion says she didn't know about the swap, although she admitted to seeing Ed outside Bluefields later that evening with a baby. The baby from the Mount Clinic.'

'This is why Daniel Deane's been giving Marion money all these years? To ensure her silence?'

'Yep. But the money began to dry up after Rose went to prison. Daniel probably felt he could get away with it. Hence why Sam was unable to buy the villa – it was Marion who'd have been footing the bill, not Sam.'

Natasha shakes her head. 'Do you know how Marion feels now?'

'She called me after the police released her. She asked me to beg Rose's forgiveness on her behalf.'

'Why did Rose become suspicious of her mother all these years later?'

'Bella Bliss's visit. But Bella stopped short of telling her the entire truth – that Ed was giving money to Marion on Daniel Deane's instruction, to keep quiet about Rose's baby. Ed assumed because of the money that Marion knew about the swap. But Marion didn't know Abe was her grandson. So she says.'

Natasha checks on Mia, whose attention is still focused on Rose and the piano. She turns back to Theo. 'Why did Daniel do this to Rose?'

'He wanted to please his dad. Zakaria was desperate for grandchildren, and more desperate when Daniel's older sister – his real sister – died during childbirth in 1978. Abigail was unable to have children. They'd been through lots of IVF and Daniel had no wish to adopt someone else's baby, as easy as that would've been for him, knowing what we know about the Mount Clinic and his involvement. He wanted his DNA in his child, and didn't want the mother to be some faceless, desperate girl. He never for a moment contemplated that Rose wouldn't fall for him. Daniel was a serial philanderer; Abigail knew that and accepted it. All she wanted was a baby. Daniel made sure that any contraception he and Rose used would be as ineffective as possible, going so far as to ensure that the morning-after pill she took was a placebo.'

Again Natasha shakes her head, small silver earrings glinting in the subdued lighting of the bar. 'But Rose would have had a scan. Surely she'd have seen—'

'The baby she saw on her ultrasound scan was a static image. One saved by Mark Stephens of another female baby. There was no radiographer present. Only Mark Stephens, the midwife and Daniel.'

'This truly is a Greek tragedy.'

'It really is,' he says. 'Daniel didn't want his father to know what he and Abigail had done. Zakaria was utterly in the dark about Abe's true parentage, until Abigail let something slip on one of her visits to Morocco with Abe. I believe the argument Abe heard at his grandfather's house in Morocco, between Abigail and Zakaria, was connected to his true identity. He buried what he heard. Buried it deep.'

Natasha's eyes have moistened. Maybe explaining tonight isn't his best move. 'Do you want me to carry on?' He flicks a look towards Rose and Mia, but both are totally oblivious to what is going on around them.

'I want to know.' She wipes her eyes and sits up taller. 'So it is Rose who carries the EDS gene.'

'Yes, but she never found out.'

'Because she couldn't have more children.'

He nods.

'It's the meticulous planning that creeps me out.' Her voice is a whisper and he leans closer.

'Daniel and Abigail lied to Zakaria about Abe's date of birth too, making his birthday later, September instead of January. Daniel even went so far as to compose fake letters to Rose, supposedly written by Zakaria.'

Suddenly Natasha turns to look towards the piano. Rose and Mia are not there. She half stands, and her eyes sweep the crowded room, seeking out her daughter. Rose is ordering a drink at the bar, Mia held securely in her arms.

'Mia's safe with Rose, don't worry,' Theo says.

'I know. I can't help it, though.'

'Parenthood. Never off duty.'

'So true,' she says.

He shuffles in his seat. 'I was going to call you before you met Rose today. Something I wanted to tell you…'

Rose and Mia have made their way back from the bar and he doesn't finish his sentence.

'Hi, Theo,' Rose says quietly. 'It's so good to see you. Thought I'd let you two chat while I got to know Mia better.'

Theo jumps up, and in this environment so different from the prison visits hall, a feeling of awkwardness overtakes him.

Rose takes in his body language. 'This is strange, isn't it?'

'It is a bit. So good to see you... outside.' He grins.

Natasha pulls herself up from the sofa. 'I'm taking Mia to the loo. It's nappy change time.' She scoops her daughter into her arms. 'And then I think I'll turn in, if it's okay with you two?'

'That's fine,' Theo says. 'Sleep well, Natasha.'

Rose leans towards Mia. 'You sleep well too, little one.'

Mother and daughter leave.

Theo turns back to Rose. 'You look good.' And she does. Maybe Cathy is wrong about her illness. Maybe her story is fiction. All of it.

Rose sits in Natasha's vacant space. 'Something's bothering you, Theo.'

Suddenly the air seems overly air-conditioned. 'There's a roof terrace. Fancy going up there for a pretend cigarette?' he says.

Her face lights up and only a trace of the underlying sadness shadowing her features remains. 'Of course.'

He pulls her up from the sofa. 'C'mon.'

They walk to the lift, and inside the enclosed space a hint of her scent hits him. He turns his head and studies her profile, his heart drumming against his ribcage and every muscle in his body tensing. She turns towards him and takes hold of his hand, kisses his cheek, and as she does, he moves his head and their lips meet.

It's Rose who pulls away. She presses the button for the sixth floor, and the lift stops.

'We'll go to the roof later. My room's this way.'

He follows her and does not say a word as he watches her unlock the door. She steps in, but he waits on the threshold.

'Please, come in.' She sits on the bed, her shoulders straight, her legs uncrossed, her hands lying in her lap, and Theo notices her ringless left finger.

He closes the door, strides across the deep-pile carpet and sits down next to her.

Slowly Rose peels off her dress and takes off her underwear, then she pushes him down gently. Theo closes his eyes. She kisses him and the tension in his neck, shoulders, groin is exquisitely overwhelming. He moves away a fraction and removes his own trousers and shirt.

There is no clumsiness and no embarrassment as Theo becomes a part of Rose. All their meetings, all their talk, and this is the beginning, a new beginning. He tries not to think of the end. He feels her quiet release and the bite of her teeth on his chest, and allows himself to join her. He will never leave her.

Lying widthways across the hotel bed, she turns to him. 'It was as I knew it would be.'

'Ditto.' He smiles, but it quickly fades. 'I saw Cathy at the prison. She gave me a piece of creative writing. A story. Your story.' He watches for her response. She's not surprised, but the expression he saw so often in prison hovers around her features. Fear? Sadness? Guilt? Relief? He isn't sure, just as he was never sure during his prison visits.

'You could have told me, Rose.'

'It was easier to let Cathy tell you.' Her head is buried in the crook of his neck, and he strokes the silken skin on her back, lifts the weight of her hair. 'I'm as guilty as Miles,' she says.

He rests his cheek on her spine. 'Stop, Rose. Stop.'

In Cathy's story, Rose and Abigail argued at Abe's bedside, Rose absolutely distraught at Abigail's sheer callousness towards her. When finally Abigail left, Rose *did* think of taking Abe's life, in a moment of madness. She left the unit to calm herself. On her return, she saw with horror what Miles had done.

'It was Miles's crime. Not yours,' Theo says. She turns away and he holds her tighter. 'Look at me, Rose.' He cups her face so he can see her eyes. 'And this is why you admitted to Abe's murder, isn't it? Because you felt it was your fault; and because you'd been diagnosed with cancer, you thought it was better that you took the blame.' He falters. 'Tell me what happened when you found out.'

And Rose tells him.

The appointment to see the oncologist to get the results of her biopsy was an evening slot, after her shift finished. It was at the end of that shift that she saw – for the first time – Abigail visiting her son, Abe. Rose's patient.

Half an hour later – after Rose's world had combusted when she realised Daniel Deane's sister was actually his wife – the oncologist informed her that she had low-grade breast cancer. She made it clear to the doctor that she would not seek treatment and told no one about her diagnosis. She wanted peace from her desperate depression and believed that by accepting the repercussions of refusing treatment, she would find that peace.

'I took the blame for Miles because what he did was precipitated by me.'

Theo says nothing. He moves her warm body to the side of him and sits up. 'You need to see the oncologist.'

'I will.'

–

Theo and Rose have dressed and taken the lift to the roof terrace. They walk to the perimeter of the building and cast their gaze over a darkened London skyline.

He gathers her to him. 'You didn't go through with it, Rose. You left to calm down, and when you returned to the unit, you found Miles there?'

'Yes, he was standing next to Abe's bed. I checked Abe's vital signs. There were none.' He feels her shoulders shaking, and the depth of her tears. 'When I turned, Miles had gone. I pressed the emergency alarm to alert the other staff, and then went to find him. I knew where he'd be: at the hospital's side entrance. It was where he went to think. Where I'd always find him when we'd lost a patient, someone we couldn't save.'

She unpeels herself from his chest and leans over the railings, taking in the city. 'Miles did what he did for me. He'd heard the terrible conversation between me and Abigail. He'd watched me after Abigail had left. He understood what I was contemplating. That was what compelled him to do such a terrible thing.' Still looking ahead at London's vista, she continues, 'I told him I was the one who should go to prison, not him. I told him I didn't want to live – and I didn't, Theo. Not until you, and then... knowing about Abe. And Mia.'

'And he agreed?'

'He did.' She holds her cupped hands to her face and blows with vigour.

'I can never forgive him,' he replies quietly, holding her, looking at the intense lights of the city.

She rubs her palms along the steel and shivers. 'Thank you for bringing me together with Natasha and Mia. You have no idea what this means to me. But I have to tell her about my insane thoughts that day.'

'I think... for you, you do.'

'The situation could easily have been the other way round,' she says quietly, as if to herself.

He's standing behind her, holding her, his face nestled in her hair, his arms loosely around her shoulders. He cannot see her expression. 'But it wasn't?'

He feels her chin moving on his forearms, which are holding her tight.

He interprets the movement as a no.

–

Two hours later, he's on the train heading back to Manchester. The smell from the burger that the man in the seat next to him is eating is too strong, and his stomach turns over. He swivels around and looks out of the window. Before he left Rose, he implored her to make an appointment with the oncologist. She promised she would. She promised him she'd be okay.

If Rose is okay, then he will be too, and the vaulted compartment of his mind that holds both the memory of the day he found his dead son and Rose's response on the roof terrace will remain locked forever.

63

Rose

I'm sitting on the train from Chesterfield to Peterborough. As I flick through the newspapers that I picked up at the station kiosk, my heart batters inside my ribcage. I really shouldn't be reading this garbage, and neither should the journalists be writing it. The inside pages are still heaving with my story. Somehow the news about my illness has been leaked.

I slouch into the seat – luckily there's no one else in my carriage – and try to think of the good things; try to put the Deanes behind me, although it's something I will never be able to do. But the cancer has not progressed and I've begun taking the medication. I've had a narrow escape, the oncologist said, though he didn't ask why I failed to seek treatment while in prison. I noticed his discomfort at my situation; he didn't want to get involved in anything other than my physical body. He's a good doctor, efficient, thorough and kind. All the attributes I once aspired to. I so desperately wanted to qualify, and eventually become a paediatrician. I wanted the dream: a stellar medical career, a home, a husband, a plethora of my own children. I did not want to be a nurse, but it was all I could be after Samira. After Abe.

I look through the train window, at fields and farmhouses, the horizon, and the vastness of life, and the futility of that life overwhelms me.

Soon, though, I will see Theo again.

–

'Can't keep away?' the security officer says to me, but with a kind smile.

'I miss some of it.'

'You'd be surprised how many say that.' He pauses, rubs his chin. I always liked this officer. 'I'm so sorry, Rose, about everything.'

I nod at him. My mother's involvement, despite her having been released, has been documented in most of the nationals. It was Ed who implicated her, by disclosing that she'd been receiving huge amounts of money from Daniel over many years. Ed Madden has been a bastard until the very end. But my mother didn't know about the swap, or that Abe was my son. I want to believe that. I can't face seeing her. Not yet. Maybe never.

I drop all my stuff into the box. It's strange being the visitor here. Cathy is sitting where I used to sit when Theo came. I wave at her but she doesn't wave back; she just leans over the table and pulls out a chair for me.

I sit down. 'How's it going?' I ask.

'Same. Nothing changes.'

'It's your day to see Don, isn't it?' Cathy sees Don every Wednesday.

'He's left. Well, they say he's taking unpaid leave, but he's left.'

'Ah.'

She looks at me. 'How's Theo?'

'He's good. I love him, Cathy.' I drum my finger on the table. 'Thank you for writing the story.'

She nods.

I can't come here to visit Cathy again. My mind revisits Abigail's words the day of Abe's death. *A good lay, but—* If I hadn't interrupted her, I might have known about Abe before. *If...*

'You know,' I say, 'I'm more like you than you think I am.' This is another reason I cannot stay in contact with Cathy.

She shakes her head. 'No you're not. Don't ever say that.'

'I hate myself, but I love my grandchild more than that hate.'

'Don't hate yourself, Rose.'

'And you?'

'I want to change. I've asked the director for help.'

'That's good.' I know Cathy won't change, but I also know she wants to get out of here.

'Try and be happy, Rose.'

I get up. 'I'll visit again soon.'

'Don't. Leave it be.'

I dip my head. We both understand.

I make my way to the exit.

64

Theo

17 September 2016

Theo's waiting for the taxi that will be taking him to Manchester airport, where he's meeting Rose. Her oncologist has given her the go-ahead for the trip. Her prognosis is good.

He's killing time reading the newspapers, which are still running stories on the Deanes and Rose. He reads various headlines, hoping that Rose has not.

Baby Swap Tragedy

Rose Marlowe's Husband – the Real Killer

Rose Marlowe Recovering From Cancer

Rose and Miles Marlowe to Divorce

Writer Turns Down Seven-Figure Advance for Rose Marlowe's Biography

The Mount Clinic – More Victims Coming Forward

He throws the papers to one side and opens his laptop to check his emails.

One from his editor.

Hi Theo,

Love the new novel. Who would have thought you had a love story in you? I plan to take it to next month's acquisition meeting.

This is good news, as since the Deanes' arrest and hearing, the advance on the Marlowe non-fiction has been increased by 50 per cent. I know you will say no, but I thought I'd let you know.

Best,
Greg

Theo wings back a reply:

Apologies, but it's still a no.

Best,
Theo

He clicks off his laptop and puts it in his carry-on, then folds up the newspapers, placing them in his carry-on too. He puts the bag over his shoulder, picks up his suitcase and makes his way downstairs to wait outside in the warmth. It's turning out to be an Indian summer.

In less than twenty-four hours he and Rose will be in San Francisco, staying at a hotel only a quarter of a mile from her granddaughter's home.

–

Inside the airport, he weaves his way through passengers checking in for holidays or business travel. The kids are back at school but the space is still teeming with kids, with mothers, with grandmothers. He sees what Rose will be seeing. He loves Rose, utterly and unconditionally. More than success, more than money. More than his own life. He would have given his own life for Elliot's. He would give it for Rose. He would give anything for Rose.

They meet in the departure area's Costa Coffee. Rose is wearing stone-washed jeans and a navy blue off-the-shoulder top, layered with a sea-green T-shirt. She still looks drained.

On spotting him, she moves towards him, but then stops abruptly. He strides quickly in her direction and without a word gathers her into his arms.

'So good to see you,' she says.

'You too.'

'We've got ages to wait for the flight. It's delayed.'

'Better to be here in plenty of time, though.'

'You're an early type of person, aren't you?' she says, pulling back to look at him.

'I am. Like everything in its place.'

'Shall we go and check in?' she suggests.

Theo nods and gets up, but as he does, someone brushes past, knocking his bag off his shoulder.

'Sorry,' the young man says.

Theo takes him in: long hair tied in a ponytail, American. The traveller crouches down, laying the book he's carrying on the floor so he can pick up the bag, which he hands to Theo. Then he scoops up the huge tome and places it under his right arm. *Gray's Anatomy*.

Unquestionably a med student.

'No problem.' Theo hitches his bag back onto his shoulder and glances at Rose. She's put on her sunglasses and is holding his hand in a vice-like grip. He pulls her nearer but says nothing, and they walk.

'So if you're not writing about me, what will you write?' she asks finally, but her voice is cracked; it's the same tone he hears in Sophie's voice when talking about Elliot.

They are approaching the check-in desk. 'My editor says that every big acquisition reported in *The Bookseller* at the moment is an epic love story,' he says. 'What do you think?'

'True-life crime isn't cutting it?'

'Not this week, fortunately.' He grins.

'You'd write a beautiful love story.'

'I've already written one. My editor's read it. He says he likes it. I like to think it's cushioned the blow about your... about my other project.'

'That's good news, Theo,' she says, but there is innate sadness carved into her features, and Theo isn't sure he'll ever be able to eradicate it.

Simultaneously they place their passports on the desk.

'Both travelling to San Francisco?' the assistant asks.

It's Theo who answers. 'Both of us, yes. Together.'

As they walk towards Customs, he stops suddenly, opens his bag, pulls out the newspapers and puts them in the nearest bin.

Rose takes hold of his arm. 'Theo, there's something I have to tell you. Cathy's story—'

He turns. 'There isn't anything to tell me, Rose.' He gathers her to him and an image of Miles burns. Rose isn't aware of his visit to see her ex-husband in prison two days before. And she will never know.

He tried to make Miles change his mind. But Miles was adamant, explaining that this was his apology to Rose for never telling her about Abigail, and for not intervening the day Abe died. *I want her to know her granddaughter, Theo. Look after her.*

65

Rose

Abigail is visiting late today. We don't keep to formal visiting times on the high dependency unit. I turn my head to check the clock on the back wall of the nurses' station: 9 p.m. My colleagues have just left for their coffee break; we're not busy tonight. I turn back around and watch Abigail holding her son's hand. They do look alike, and it bothers me that I look like Abigail; perhaps more so now than twenty-five years before. And because I look like Abigail, Abe looks like me. He could be my son. But he is not my son. I don't have a son. Or a daughter.

Since my cancer diagnosis, my encounters with Abigail are more punishing, and seeing Daniel's son every day I'm on duty is killing me just as slowly as the breast cancer might well do. How did I not know in Spain? I keep asking myself. Or the Christmas before Samira's birth? All the signs were there for me to see but a twenty-two-year-old Rose chose not to identify them.

My deep and unrelenting grief and anger is eating me; it has been slow and insidious but nevertheless constant since recognizing Abigail – the same day I discovered that the cancer of Abigail and Daniel Deane was slowly growing inside me.

My wrath towards the Deanes has been building.

I am not the Rose I was. I am not the doctor I wanted to be, the mother I craved to be. Abigail has everything. I want to take something away from her, as she and Daniel have taken so many things away from me. I hate them both. Daniel's duplicity and his wooden bed of lies. *Their* bed of lies. An image of the carvings on their bed mocks me. The compulsion to snatch something away from them is so strong, as if it sits outside me, outside the hatred. A detached entity.

I've attempted to treat Abe like any other patient, but he is not just another patient.

Finally I walk towards the bed, and Abigail turns around. She's uncomfortable, and I know this discomfort is because of me, although occasionally I've sensed she's uneasy in her son's presence too. A week before, when Abe was still in the intensive care unit, still comatose and intubated, and the unit's staff didn't think he'd make it, I saw Abigail speaking to him as if she were telling him a story. I've often thought in my career as a nurse that some part of the brain's frontal lobe is still active during coma. The day Abigail told her muffled story to her son, his heart rate went from 78 to 150, causing the monitor to bleep a warning. There were other times when I saw her at his bedside and she didn't speak to him at all. But that day she was intent, her lips close to his face, almost touching his cheek.

She looks up. 'His father will be coming in the next few days to visit him.'

'Daniel?'

'Yes, Nurse Marlowe, Daniel.' She takes her Louis Vuitton handbag from the back of the chair she's been sitting in and rearranges her snug-fitting silk blouse. 'Can we talk somewhere private?'

I indicate that we move beyond the half-wall partition, away from Abe's bed.

Leaning on the painted plasterboard, I take a deep breath. 'Why did you do it?' She's standing right in front of me. Brazen and cold. 'You and Daniel. Spain. Afterwards. Why? It was a game, you pretending to be his sister. Then when I was in hospital... with Samira, you were there, weren't you? You're both sick. And Abe was born not long afterwards.'

'Eight months afterwards, Rose. Daniel would never have stayed with you, even if your little bastard had survived. He soon saw sense.' She pauses. 'He thought he loved you. But after you had your womb taken away... well, you became like me. A beautiful empty shell. He lost interest then. He always did lose interest after a while, with all his diversions.'

I hate her. I hate Daniel. I hate their son. But more than anything, I hate myself. I've hated myself since Bluefields, since not being able to save my daughter. Abigail taps into every insecurity, and it is destroying me. Why is she doing this? A blackness fills me. I do not feel like myself. The vitriol bubbles, and like milk boiling in an unwatched pan, it spews viciously over the side.

'Why did you do it?' I ask again. I need to know. There must be a reason.

She looks at me, and I try to decipher what I see in her expression. I think it is envy. Why does she envy me?

'You thought you were special, with your body, your intellect, but you saw nothing,' she says. 'Gullible and stupid. Just like all the rest of them that Daniel fucked.' Her smile is thin, pinched. 'He's good in bed, isn't he, Daniel? Do you remember the maître d' at the restaurant, with the shiny blonde hair? Diana, I think her name is. Do you remember Señora López? And your midwife, Cam? They all thought he was good in bed too. He slept with anything; I mean, he fucked you. He truly fucked you, Rose.' She pauses to gather breath, then carries on relentless. It's too much. 'My husband was a good lay, but—'

'Why? *Why* did you do it?' I ask, because although reason is leaving me, the pragmatic, logical part of me knows there is a purpose. Cause and effect. Or are the Deanes warped beyond comprehension?

She begins to move away. 'Daniel will be here tomorrow to see our son. You might want to take a day off.'

Walking back to Abe's bed, she touches his bare arm, which rests on top of the white sheet that I've recently changed, then makes her way from the unit. She doesn't kiss him before she leaves.

She will regret that.

I check Abe's central line and then wheel the saline drip stand closer to his bed. His eyelids flicker like high-summer butterflies, and I prepare to do what I have to do. I don't feel like Rose, but then again, I haven't felt like Rose for a long time.

I go to the clinical store room and find everything I need and take it back to Abe's bedside. I make sure the emergency alarm is muted but then disconnect the monitor completely. I leave nothing to chance. I don't want to alert my colleagues to a problem. The air embolism might take longer to have an effect than I anticipate. I'm not going anywhere. This won't be a mystery. Being in prison will be a release.

I place the syringe containing more than two hundred milli-litres of air into his IV saline tube and slowly push down the plastic plunger. So much, and introduced so quickly, will be lethal. 'I'm so sorry.'

I wait. I give it time. Half an hour will be enough. I stand as if frozen, but I'm not looking at Abe; I've turned away. Eventually, I check my watch. More than half an hour. The unit is still empty. It's been a long coffee break. I'd known it would be, as it's our junior doctor's birthday.

I turn back around and finally put my fingers on Abe's wrist. I find no pulse. Nothing. I touch his cheek. I've touched him so many times – changed his catheter, cleaned underneath his arms, shaved him – but despite the fact that he's ceased breathing, I've never before felt his warmth like this. It emanates from him as a strong vibration, beginning in my fingers but rapidly travelling up my arm and into the very core of me, into the lower part of my stomach, where the space inside is so empty.

I stagger backwards.

What have I done? I've gone mad. Insane. I remember Abigail's words, and a strange clarity overwhelms me, filters through like an awakening as I register what should have been so obvious. *A good lay, but…* But what? What was she about to say?

A bitter ball of dread sinks deep inside my stomach.

But he couldn't get me pregnant.

And that is when I see Miles, his tortured expression taking in the scene before him. He moves to Abe's bed, finds his hand, lifts it, checks his pulse, and as he does so, I remember the terrible practical joke of years before when I was a medical student.

'How long have you been here, Miles?'

'The whole time. I heard your conversation with Abigail, all of it.' He shakes his head. 'Abe is dead.' He touches the young man's hair, smooths back the corkscrew curls from his forehead. In death, Abe looks so very like me.

'Go home, Rose,' Miles says. 'I'll tell the staff you've got a migraine.' He pauses. Coughs. Wheezes, as if he can't find breath. 'I'll finish up here.'

I glance at Abe's body. *What have I done?* Then I find my husband's eyes and my heart fissures even more.

'I heard *everything* Abigail said,' he carries on. 'I never knew. I didn't know Deane introduced her to you as his sister. You didn't tell me. All these weeks Abigail's been visiting, and you didn't tell me.'

He was here throughout my confrontation with Abigail, and while I was muting Abe's monitor and tampering with his central line. He didn't stop me.

My stomach twists even more as I stare at him, and my mind propels itself back to that long-ago day at Bluefields Hospital. My first appointment with Mark Stephens, and seeing Miles just before, sitting with him in his office.

'That day at Bluefields,' I say, 'when I told you Daniel had gone to see his sister. Did you know, Miles? Did you know that Daniel didn't have a sister?'

'His sister died years before.' He moves closer to me. 'I'm sorry.'

'In all these years, you could have told me.' *If you'd told me, I might have guessed.*

He nods. 'I'm a weak man, Rose. Go home. I'll finish up here.'

'There's something I have to tell you.' I need to tell him about Abe's warmth. *What is done cannot be undone.*

'Later, tell me at home later.' He touches my tear-laden cheek.

I will not be at home later.

Miles's stubble is dark with the dampness of his own tears. 'I could have stopped you,' he says. 'Go home, Rose.'

It's then that I tell him about my diagnosis.

'Rose—'

I look into my husband's eyes. What have I become? What has *he* become? We are both empty. '*You* go, Miles. Please. I don't want you involved. You need to keep working.' I look around the unit. 'This is your life.'

I turn away, and when finally I look back, Miles has gone. I kiss Abe's forehead, and the desolate cavity inside my stomach engulfs me. I am gone too. Never to return.

Pulling the emergency cord, I wait for my colleagues to pour into the unit.

A Letter from J. A. Corrigan

Thank you so much for reading *The Nurse*. I hope you enjoyed it as much as I enjoyed writing it! If you have the time to leave me a short, honest review on Amazon, Goodreads, or wherever you purchased the book, I'd very much appreciate it. I love hearing what you think, and your reviews help me to reach new readers – which allows me to bring you more books! If you know of friends or family who would enjoy my book, I'd appreciate your assistance there too. Help spread the word!

If you'd like to keep up to date with any of my new releases, please visit jacorrigan.com/mailing-list to sign up for my newsletter. Your email will never be shared, and I'll only contact you when I have news about a new release.

You can connect with me via my website, Facebook, Goodreads, Instagram and Twitter. I'd love to hear from you.

I began writing this novel with fire in my fingertips – Rose came alive inside my head immediately, as did Theo. The themes and nuances of the story, though, did take somewhat longer to gel. As someone somewhere once said, 'Writing is about rewriting.' Never has a truism been so... well... true.

I loved writing Rose and being able to draw on my own experiences from the medical world. I enjoyed creating Theo too, and although I took a gamble in making him a writer, a novelist, as he came to life in his first point-of-view paragraph I felt I'd got an angle on him instantly. With my two main characters created, the story, the premise, fell into place.

Readers often ask me how I can write such fundamentally dark stories. I think the answer is that as a writer of suspense fiction, I always ask 'what if?'. It is this question that drives my novels. It also helps that in my everyday non-fiction-writing life, although I have an active and fertile imagination, I'm grounded, stable and happy! Often I take a protagonist and give them an absolutely normal life, but then something extraordinary happens to them. How will they react? What will they do? How will they feel? These questions move the narrative on, and the characters are never the same at the end of the story as they were at the beginning. The trick is to ensure their journey is interesting and intriguing. I really hope that I have managed to do this for you, my readers.

JA
XXXXXXXXXX

PS Thank you again, so very much, for your support of my books. It really means the world to me.

Website: jacorrigan.com

Facebook: @jacorrigan

Twitter: @juliannwriter

Instagram: @corriganjulieann

Goodreads: JA Corrigan

Acknowledgements

I begin my acknowledgements with a huge thank you to my talented editor, Leodora Darlington, who picked up my manuscript with enthusiasm and verve and hit the ground running with it. A massive thank you too to my eagle-eyed copyeditor, Jane Selley, my proof-reader, sales and marketing and other members of the brilliant Canelo team. A special thank you to cover designer, Aaron Munday, who has absolutely aced the artwork. My experience has been joyous, and my publisher will have my everlasting gratitude for this.

I also extend my gratitude to my agent, Camilla Shestopal, who championed my work so readily. The publishing world is a tough business and so it's been a revelation, and a relief, to find an agent so easy to work alongside. This business demands a fair amount of compatibility and trust between agent and author, and this is something for which I am also grateful.

As always, many thanks to my trusty readers, both the early ones and the more recent – respect to all: Emma Haughton, Michelle Flood, Katerina Diamond, David Evans, Jan Beresford, Sarah Ward, Daniel Culver, and Laura Wilkinson.

I'd also like to say thank you to Arzu Tahsin, who very early on gave me advice regarding this story that really did shape how it was formed.

I owe huge thanks regarding research to Paul Bacon, mental health tribunal judge and solicitor, who was, as always, so generous with his advice and input. Thanks also to Judy Evans, a long-serving midwife; Dr Sue Chorley, a friend and GP; and the wonderful Essie Fox – all of whom have been so giving of their time when I asked (sometimes silly) questions. All faults in the novel lie at my door.

Love and gratitude to all of my mates, a small circle but perfectly formed: Tracey Dolan, Tigger Wilson, Andrew Johnson, Nicola Corrigan, Kam Chahal, Sarah Connelly, Farida Soto, Claudia Cruttwell, Shell – aka Michelle Flood – and Sarah Fox.

And to my mum and dad.

My thanks to the nursing and medical students I met during my training as a physiotherapist, my old lecturers, and to the wonderful intensive care staff I worked alongside in the early years of my career – all for giving me such exquisite material with which to weave my story.

As ever, and always, my biggest thanks go to my husband and daughter, whom I love to the moon and back, and for an eternity.